The Darien Chronicles:

Objects for Reflection,
A Journey into Love

PART ONE - IN THE BEGINNING

Steven Howard

BALBOA.
PRESS
A DIVISION OF HAY HOUSE

Balboa Press books may be ordered through booksellers or by contacting:

Balboa Press
A Division of Hay House
1663 Liberty Drive
Bloomington, IN 47403
www.balboapress.com
1 (877) 407-4847

Because of the dynamic nature of the Internet, any web addresses or links contained in this book may have changed since publication and may no longer be valid. The views expressed in this work are solely those of the author and do not necessarily reflect the views of the publisher, and the publisher hereby disclaims any responsibility for them.

The author of this book does not dispense medical advice or prescribe the use of any technique as a form of treatment for physical, emotional, or medical problems without the advice of a physician, either directly or indirectly. The intent of the author is only to offer information of a general nature to help you in your quest for emotional and spiritual well-being. In the event you use any of the information in this book for yourself, which is your constitutional right, the author and the publisher assume no responsibility for your actions.

Any people depicted in stock imagery provided by Thinkstock are models, and such images are being used for illustrative purposes only. Certain stock imagery © Thinkstock.

Print information available on the last page.

ISBN: 978-1-5043-5635-0 (sc)
ISBN: 978-1-5043-5644-2 (hc)
ISBN: 978-1-5043-5643-5 (e)

Library of Congress Control Number: 2016906579

Balboa Press rev. date: 06/08/2016

Preface

The seed for this book, and the two that are to follow to complete this trilogy, was truly a gift from Spirit, given to me in 2002 while I was in the midst of an aerobic workout on a treadmill at a local fitness center in South Florida.

The gift came in the form of a sudden vision that interrupted my mindless workout and sent an electric charge throughout my body. With this very brief vision of a young boy and, for lack of a better term, a wizard, I heard these three lines of dialogue between the two as the boy stood on a pathway looking at a pile of obstacles barring his journey.

Wizard: "What do you see?"

The boy: "Just these things blocking my way!"

Wizard: "Look deeper."

And with all of this came a book title: *Objects for Reflection, A Journey into Love.*

That was all I saw or heard, but I knew almost immediately that it was a seed for a story I was being given to tell. I quickly got off the treadmill, went to the service area in the center of the gym, and asked for a pencil and a piece of paper. My mind was beginning to receive a rush of thoughts that were fleshing out a synopsis of what the book was to be about.

Now, thirteen years later, that seed has become realized as a trilogy titled *The Darien Chronicles: Objects for Reflection, A*

Journey into Love. This particular book, which is subtitled *Part One – In the Beginning*, introduces you to the main character, a little boy called Darien, and to Sundeep, a Spirit guide, angel, or the friendly voice of God, if you prefer. Or is it simply a figment of Darien's imagination? You decide. Just sit back, relax, and follow Darien on his journey. Just remember, it doesn't end when you've reached the last page of this book. I am hoping you'll find this read fulfilling enough that you'll want to pick up *Part Two – Into the Wasteland* when it is released this next year to see where Darien's journey takes him.

Acknowledgments

I am forever grateful for the circumstances and the weave and texture of each event that has shaped my life up to this point—even the tears that drove me into dark places, for they made me stronger and led me toward the light. Mildred and Wilbur, thank you for the gift of life and for finding me a family that carved out a place for me. Edna, who became the only mom in my life, I am forever grateful for your secret connection to "new thought" ideas, for your stoic yet positive sayings planted a seed in my mind although it took another twenty-five years to sprout and take hold in my life.

Many individuals have had a profound impact on my life, and all for good, though they didn't always appear that way at the time. I will simply list your names. You know why you are among them: Bob Jr.; Sylvia, Fran, and Annie; Hank and Donnie G. (God rest his soul); Polly; Cleo, who taught me to love all aspects of myself; Dolph, who befriended me during my darkest hours and literally rescued me from the edge; Mark G., my way-shower into recovery; Eric Butterworth, the first minister to teach me about my own divinity and to introduce me to the energy of Love; Carmen, for introducing me to the love of my life; Paula, my love, my soul mate, and my best friend; Ron and Ronnie, true friends through the ups and downs of the past forty years; Joan Mazza, who showed me the basics of writing and who made me believe I could write and get published; Gay Lynn, who showed me what joy looks like; Rev. Tita, who showed me what spiritual excellence and passion are; Rev. Marge, who sees beyond my shadows and gives me so many opportunities to demonstrate that I AM; Donna and Pat, who bring out my "kid" and an inner joy; and to all those unnamed members of my spiritual family at Unity of The Villages, namaste.

And my acknowledgments wouldn't be complete without mentioning my "Florida 80" friends from LifeSpring and my gratitude for those who facilitated my discovery of the power of release work and in daily asking the question: "What's next?"

Prologue

He stretched his tiny arms up toward the walls of the sack that enveloped him, yawning and scrunching his eyes more tightly together as he squirmed and tried to shift his delicate legs into a more comfortable position. As he moved and pushed against the barrier that imprisoned him, he heard a slight sound, a moan of sorts, followed by a series of vibrations, ones he did not understand but had become a pattern nearly always following his increased movement these days.

"It's kicking, Mama! I can feel it, and it hurts!"

"You've got nobody to blame but yourself. If you hadn't spread your legs for that damned street-corner cowboy, you wouldn't be in this mess."

"He said he loved me, and besides, he's taking good care of me."

"Good care of ya? Is that why you had to call me and Erin last week when he sure as hell nearly beat you to a pulp? You call that love?"

"He was just upset 'bout losing his job. He had a few too many beers that night and lost his temper."

He couldn't comprehend the meaning of the sounds, but he certainly sensed the dark energy that surrounded him. And it seemed to be getting stronger as time went by. He didn't yet have the understanding or the ability to express what he felt, but if he could, he would have said, "I scared! I afraid! Make it go away!" But he couldn't.

What was happening to him? He did not know. But he did know he was changing. He could feel the Life Force surging through his entire body, evolving and developing. He could sense the changes taking place within him, the pulsing of new pathways that served as lifelines feeding his internal organs, structures within the thin layer of elastic skin that enveloped him. He could feel, without yet understanding, the tingling sensations that followed yet other pathways that channeled neural impulses and signals to and from his brain and all his other body parts. Where he had once felt like a floating blob, he now sensed firm structures developing within his body: a flexible central core and extensions that he was now able to move in various directions. Pulsing organs seemed to work together in a harmonious rhythm that followed a soft beating, emanating from an area close to the middle of his body.

But despite all the anxiety as a result of the world beyond his tiny, dark, liquid space, he also felt a kind of peace every now and then, as if an unseen force was protecting him. There were moments, particularly when he was experiencing harsh, loud sounds and even an occasional blow to whatever it was that was carrying him around, when he would feel a soothing energy wrap itself around him, keeping him safe and quieting the fear he felt.

And in those brief moments when he felt safe and protected, he also sensed … no, *heard* … a voice that whispered softly, "I am here, Darien, protecting you. I am with you, so fear not." Instantly, he would feel a warm wave of peace spread throughout his mind and body and that, once again, he was connected to something greater and more powerful than the energies that swirled around just beyond the womb that carried him.

As more time passed, he became aware of a surging series of eruptions that seemed to be pushing him toward a small sliver of light in his otherwise darkened sanctuary. He heard new sounds from within the shadowy cavern that had served as his world, whooshing water sounds. Loud screams followed by pressure against his little body, as if something was forcing him toward that still-closed opening. Now he felt new sensations on his head as he found himself being both pushed and pulled through that opening. A brilliant, blinding white light enveloped him as cold air chilled his bare skin. Then he heard himself scream as he entered a new, frightening world.

Chapter One

April 1943:
The First Day of the Rest of His Life

Four-year-old Darien O'Hara gripped her hand as he struggled to keep up with the plump little lady whose side-to-side waddle added to the difficulty of walking next to her.

"Where are we going?" He was pretty sure he knew and already felt fearful of the answer, but he asked anyway.

"To stay with that nice lady again. The one with the young boy."

Darien heard her words and felt his tummy do flip-flops as he followed her onto the bus. Vague but disturbing images flashed through his mind: big people shouting at one another and banging doors; a lady staggering and cursing, her words slurred, her breath smelly—like medicine. He quickly squeezed his eyes shut, willing the memories to disappear. They did, and he breathed a sigh of relief. While he wondered why such images filled his mind since they had nothing to do with the nice lady and her older boy, he was glad the memories disappeared.

He watched as the chubby lady handed some coins to the bus driver, whispered something to him, and then led Darien to a seat near the rear of the bus.

"Are you going too?" he asked.

She ignored his question. "Remember, don't talk to strangers, and don't leave this seat until you hear the bus driver call out your name."

Darien repeated the instructions silently as the lady shoved his single piece of luggage into the overhead rack. She stooped down and gave him a peck on the cheek before she turned and exited the middle door of the bus without looking back.

What Darien didn't know was why he was now being shuttled off to another home. He didn't know that the plump little lady was just one of a series of well-meaning individuals who had served as foster parents for a few weeks—sometimes for several months—offering him little more than room and board.

The year was 1943, a time when most American men were serving in the military, spread out over Europe and the Asia-Pacific theater, as World War II was being waged against Nazi Germany and Japan. During this time, thousands of young mothers found themselves without husbands and with only modest means to support themselves and their young children. Having just experienced the Great Depression that ended a few years earlier, many could no longer afford to keep their children, as they became war widows. Construction of institutions to house orphans and unwanted children was interrupted as government funds went toward the war effort. More and more people placed their children into foster care, which often meant the children lived with older couples or families who had room and could use the small payments offered to those taking on the foster care role.

Such was the case with Darien. He'd been taken in by several foster care families, even spending a brief time in an orphanage when there'd been no foster family available. The little lady who had just deposited Darien on the bus suffered from a bad hip and was finding it too difficult to continue taking care of a small child. So he was off to live with a younger woman who had an older boy to help in the care, someone Darien already knew because she had briefly taken him in on several previous occasions.

Darien clutched the sides of his seat and stretched to catch a glimpse of the little, waddling woman out the bus window. He spotted her retreating figure and kept his eyes fixed on her. He heard the bus gears screech and groan and felt the forward motion as they pulled out from the curb and onto the street. By then, she was but a speck in the distance. She, like the others, would become a forgotten memory, pushed into the recesses of his mind—yet another brief moment with a kindly stranger before being passed on again.

How many foster homes had he lived in, some for only a few weeks, others for several months? Confused and anxious, he no longer could recall for certain. He only knew each trip to a different family left him feeling very uncertain and sad. Separated. Alone and lonely. And afraid. Darien retreated into a very private place that gave him some comfort and temporary escape from a sense of dread that haunted his daily life. He needed only a few moments there before he could return to the outer world around him, ready to take on what was next. And what puzzled Darien was that, when he went into that secret place in his mind, he had the sense he wasn't alone, that he was somehow being protected, and that made him feel good. It wasn't that he saw people—he didn't—but nevertheless, he *felt* a presence, like someone or something was standing just behind him, out of his line of sight. But when he sensed this presence and turned around to see what it was, there was nothing, no one there. Today he did not sense that presence, and it left him feeling anxious and uncertain.

Within a few minutes, he was out of the city. The countryside of western Massachusetts blurred past him as the bus rattled along, jostling him from side to side. He had taken the ride to Hammerville several times before, so the images were not unfamiliar. He saw towering blue spruce with their sharply defined boughs, the softer, more graceful pines that struggled for light in between and beneath them, and the tall oaks and occasional clusters of birch that bordered the paved road linking Bartlow and Hammerville. The pastoral landscape would have, under other circumstances, stirred a sense of peace in Darien, but today it did not. Instead, he felt familiar twitches that began in his toes and traveled up his legs through his torso and out through his fingertips. Disturbing thoughts of being left alone and of never knowing the security of a permanent family flooded his mind. How long would his stay be this time? he wondered.

Darien closed his eyes and pressed himself back into the seat. It was happening again. The feelings that started in his tummy and worked their way up, sometimes causing him to throw up. He closed his eyes even tighter. *Bad, bad, go away! Come again another day!* A rhyme an older boy had taught him in a place he couldn't recall.

An elderly couple sitting across the aisle from him had noticed Darien board the bus and had seen him being deposited onto the bus by the chubby woman. They had quietly observed him and had sensed his fearfulness. They nodded at each other, seemingly exchanging thoughts without a word, until the sliver of a woman leaned across the aisle and lightly tapped Darien on his arm and said, "What a grown-up little boy you are, riding this bus all by yourself! I'll bet your mother is very proud of you." The gray-haired lady offered a genuine smile.

Darien opened his eyes and shyly looked in her direction, uncertain what to say. He caught the twinkle in her very blue eyes and was reassured by her smile that he needn't be afraid. He stated what he'd been told about his mother: "I don't have one." He said it matter-of-factly with no hint of emotion.

She closed her fingers around his arm and lowered her voice to a whisper. "I'll bet she's looking down on you right now and feeling as proud as punch over you being such a courageous little tyke." The lady traveler patted his arm once more and then sat back, still taking in his handsome, round face and light blue eyes framed by baby-blond hair, which she was pretty sure would turn to light brown by the time the boy reached adolescence.

Darien had no idea what she meant. He'd been told he didn't have a mother or a father, so the idea of someone who didn't exist looking down at him from somewhere above made no sense to him. Confused, he remained silent until she looked away, and he could close his eyes and make the world disappear.

He felt the bus stop several times over the next hour, and he heard the shuffling of feet and the opening and closing of doors, but he kept his eyes tightly closed and silently repeated the words that helped protect him.

The bus slowed down and came to another stop. This time, he opened his eyes just enough to see, and the view out the window came into focus. He saw the center of the small town with the funny name. He watched as the only other passenger, an elderly woman carrying a suitcase in one hand and a handbag in the other, rose and stepped out the open side door. He looked across the aisle and noticed the elderly couple had gone. He felt a slight bit of sadness and closed his eyes again.

Darien remained in his seat as he'd been instructed when he boarded in Bartlow, some twenty miles away. He heard the bus driver call out his name, and he peered over the top of the torn leather seat in front of him as a familiar face came into view.

"Hi, Darien. It's me, Mrs. Edwards." The tall lady strode toward the center of the bus and stopped in front of him.

Darien remained mute, pushing himself firmly against the back of his seat.

"I'll get your suitcase," she said, ignoring his silence as she reached up and pulled down a scuffed and worn piece of Samsonite from the overhead rack. "Take my hand, Darien, and come along."

He studied her for a moment. She looked much the same as he remembered from his last visit: tall and bony, with salt-and-pepper hair that made her look much older than her thirty-four years. Not even the two small, ivory barrettes, positioned slightly above each ear in an effort to keep the hair off her face, and the ruby-red lipstick were able to hide the weariness that showed in the heavy lines around her eyes and mouth. Yet Darien was still able to sense a softness just behind the austerity that defined her on the surface. Finally acknowledging her command, he stood and took her hand, following in silence as she led him to the front of the bus.

"Don't be afraid. It's a big step, but I won't let you fall. Just step down slowly, one foot at a time."

Darien looked down from the top step and clenched his teeth. The steps were high for a child his age to easily navigate by himself. On his previous trips to Hammerville, Mrs. Edwards had picked him up and carried him down the steps. She apparently thought he was now old enough to navigate the steps on his own, with just a little support from her.

He clutched her hand even harder and cautiously stepped out and down to the first step, quickly bringing his other foot to the same level and catching his balance. His chubby legs trembled even as he gripped the chrome handrail with his other hand. He stepped out again tentatively until he found himself on solid ground. He let out a sigh but continued to squeeze the lady's hand as he followed her to a wood-paneled Ford station wagon parked a few yards from the bus stop.

He came to a halt when they reached the car and studied the wagon for a moment as he waited for her to unlock the car door and slide his luggage onto the backseat. While the metal fenders and hood of the car were a shiny deep burgundy, the cabin, doors, and roof were constructed of highly polished, two-toned wood, and he remembered how excited he had been the first time he rode in it a few months earlier. He recalled Mrs. Edwards exclaiming to her sister how grateful she and her husband were to have been able to purchase such a "grand automobile."

Prior to his enlisting in the navy, her husband, Stanley Edwards, had worked at a Ford dealership as a master mechanic, and he'd been given the opportunity to purchase the brand-new wagon for a very good price given that he was a highly regarded employee of the dealership. They had even promised they'd hire him back into his old job after he completed his service obligation.

Darien's gaze now wandered beyond the car, taking in the surrounding town center. A row of storefronts lined the main street of the town. He remembered being in one of them on an earlier visit—the soda shop and stationery store where Mrs. Edwards had treated him to an ice cream cone. It had melted all over his hand, and she had reminded him to lick it quickly to keep it from dripping onto his clothes and the black-and-white linoleum tiles of the store.

"We mustn't dilly-dally, Darien," he heard her say, breaking into his thoughts.

"Don't dilly-dally, Darien." He giggled at the sounds of his own voice repeating her reminder.

"And don't you be fresh with me!" She frowned.

Despite the frown, he caught a glimmer of a smile that followed with a twinkle in her eyes that reassured him she wasn't *that* angry.

"Yes, ma'am." He stepped through the open car door and crawled onto the backseat, next to his suitcase. He kneeled on the seat, facing toward the rear of the car, and gripped the top of the backrest tightly, as Mrs. Edwards climbed into the front seat. She pulled her purse into her lap and reached in, pulling out a cigarette and a silver Zippo lighter that bore a navy insignia on it. She lit the cigarette, inhaled deeply, placed her bag back on the seat next to her, and then drove off.

Darien now had an unobstructed view out the back and side windows of the station wagon. His anxiety lessened as he caught sight of vaguely familiar structures lining both sides of the street.

There were the old, multistoried Victorian-style estate homes across from the town's common and the three churches that lined both the north end of Main Street as well as Cottage Street that paralleled Main on the other side of the town common. Darien recalled being in the one with the tallest steeple when he'd been left with the Edwardses for a weekend earlier the same year. He didn't remember much of that visit other than how uncomfortable the thinly padded wooden pews had felt and that he'd been bad. He recalled her words.

"Stop fidgeting, Darien!" She had firmly pressed one hand on his thigh to keep him from wiggling.

"These seats are hard," Darien had responded, not so quietly.

"Shush!" She placed one finger to her lips.

He sat out the rest of that Sunday service in silence. Penance, she had called it.

Before he knew it, they were slowing down and turning onto a gravel driveway at the bottom of the hill. The station wagon came to a stop, the engine sputtering as the ignition was turned off.

"Does this look familiar, Darien?" She turned around to face him and pointed at the small cottage-style bungalow. Covered in a chalky-white asbestos siding and crowned by a deep blue shingled roof, it sat on top of a large tract of well-maintained lawn that continued at a lower level in the rear. Several mature trees—a mixture of maple and oak and one pecan tree—provided spots of dappled shade across the yard. A dense woodland surrounded the property. It was a pleasing sight for Darien, for he so loved being in the country.

"Yes," he replied to her question.

"I'm happy the cat doesn't have your tongue any longer!" Her last words burst out with added force as she broke into a coughing spasm. She crushed out the butt of the cigarette, dropped it into the ashtray on the dashboard, and reached into her handbag for a handkerchief. Covering her mouth with it, her face grew red as she began coughing until she was able to catch her breath and breathe more easily.

"Huh?" Darien said in response to her comment about the cat.

"Not 'huh.' *What*, Darien. 'Huh' isn't proper English. You say 'what' when you don't understand something." She reached toward him and adjusted the collar of his outside jacket as she continued. "Anyway, it's just an old saying people use when someone is asked a question and they don't answer."

He nodded. "Can I get out now?"

"*May* I get out now, Darien."

"Can I?"

Mrs. Edwards sighed and shook her head before nodding.

Darien climbed out of the backseat of the car and ran down to the sandbox that had been constructed for the Edwards' only child, Billie, when he was just about Darien's age. Darien had found it on one of the prior times he'd been left with Mrs. Edwards and her son and he loved playing in it. Although it was not more than five feet square, the sand was very fine and he felt safe within the raised wooden borders. Billie had left some of his old metal toy trucks in the sand, and Darien very quickly became lost in his imaginary world where he visualized himself as a truck driver who hauled sand from one place to another. *Vahroooommmmm, vahrooom* were the sounds he made, mimicking the noise of a truck making its way up a steep, sandy hill as he guided the toy truck up a small mound of sand he'd created.

Mrs. Edwards stood quietly for a few moments, staring down at Darien, now totally engrossed in his own world. She chuckled to herself and said, "Darien, make sure you brush off all the sand after you're through playing. And I don't want you going into the woods by yourself, do you hear me?" She waited a second or two for an answer, but she could tell he was totally absorbed in what he was doing. She repeated herself, this time in a louder, more commanding voice, and got his attention.

Darien looked up at her and replied, "Yes, ma'am," and then refocused on uprighting the truck he had caused to overturn and tumble down the slope, accompanied by crashing sounds as only a little boy can make. For the next hour or so, Darien was free of any worry or anxiety, managing to escape it all in the little sandbox that lay at the edge of the surrounding woods. Of course he couldn't see Mrs. Edwards come to the dining room door and look out every now and then to make sure he was still in the sandbox and hadn't ventured into the woods. And he also couldn't see who else was watching over him.

Chapter Two

Later That Same Afternoon

When Darien tired of playing and came into the house, Mrs. Edwards showed him to the room he would share with Billie and pointed out the twin bed he was to use, although he remembered which one from his previous visits. She beckoned him into the kitchen and motioned for him to sit down on one of the wooden chairs arranged around the small drop-leaf table.

"I want to talk to you, Darien."

He climbed up on the seat and sat, fidgeting from side to side as he waited in silence.

"You're going to be living here with us. With me and my son, Billie." She reached over and brushed a lock of blond hair back from his eyes. "And with his father when he comes back from the service."

Darien peered up at the tall, bony woman standing over him, looking for something, perhaps a glimpse of reassurance.

"Forever?"

"Time will tell."

He liked the tone of her voice, deep for a lady, but warm and reassuring. Still, her *words* were not so reassuring, and he felt uncertain of what to say next.

"You can call me Mom if you like," she said.

Darien bowed his head slightly but maintained eye contact. He remained silent. He didn't know just what that meant and wasn't sure he wanted to call her that. Not yet, anyway. He vaguely recalled having once heard an older boy talking about his mom and dad, but as far as Darien knew, he hadn't ever had either one in his life, so he wasn't sure what he should say.

"You don't have to, Darien. Not if you don't want to."

He nodded but said nothing.

"We're going to love you and take care of you just like you were our own son."

Darien cocked his head to one side, confused. He didn't quite know what these words meant either. Certainly nobody had ever spoken in that way to him before, and for some reason, the words made him feel scared and sad at the same time.

"Do you know why you've come to live with me and Billie?" She folded her hands between her legs and leaned forward.

He shook his head.

"Because your mother—your *real* mother—can't take care of you, and she asked me to."

More confusion. As far as he knew, he didn't have a mother, and Darien had no memory of a *real* mother. He didn't know where she had been since he was born or where exactly *he* had been before coming into the Edwards household. He had no clear memories of those who had taken care of him. Except for the plump little lady in Bartlow and this lady, of course.

All he could recall were vague images of stainless steel countertops, the scent of oranges, and light streaming through a vast expanse of windows. Another blurry image of looking up at the legs of lots of big people, milling around in a darkened room, the clinking of glasses and ruckus laughter and a medicinal smell that filled the room. And he remembered once sitting in front of a large picture window overlooking a city street, alone. The thoughts brought on a familiar feeling he didn't like.

"Do you have any questions?"

He shook his head.

"Well, if any come to mind, you just speak up and ask me, okay?" She waited for a moment or two, stood, and turned away to continue with her work.

He remained in the chair several minutes longer and studied Mrs. Edwards as she prepared their supper.

Tired of watching her peel potatoes and shuck peas, he glanced up at the large round clock on the wall. He whispered as softly as he knew how. "The little han' is on the number thwee and the big han' is on thix. That mean itth thwee and a half o'clock. No, that not right ..."

"Close, Darien, *very* close!" Mrs. Edwards broke in, overhearing his whispers. "It's three-thirty, or thirty minutes past three is another way of saying it."

"Thwee-thirty," he repeated.

"Very *good*! You remember what I taught you the last few times you were here, don't you?" A smile crossed her face.

"Uh-huh." He'd pleased her, and that made him feel good. He felt a yawn coming on and raised both hands to his face but was unable to hold back the funny sound that escaped his mouth.

"Why don't you go lie down? I'll wake you when Billie gets home, and maybe he'll play with you until supper. How does that sound?"

"Okay." Darien hopped off the chair and scampered out of the kitchen and into the bedroom he was to share with Billie, closing the door behind him.

Chapter Three

Still Later the Same Day

Darien removed his shoes and crawled onto the twin bed Mrs. Edwards had pointed out to him earlier, pulling a portion of the cream-colored chenille spread over him. Both of the yellowed canvas window shades in the room had been rolled almost all the way down, blocking out the afternoon sun and leaving the room in near darkness.

He stared up at the ceiling as thoughts flitted across his mind. He replayed what Mrs. Edwards had said to him earlier … about treating him like a son and loving him. She'd never talked like that during any of the earlier times he'd stayed with her and her son. So why now? Questions popped into his mind. *Will they really keep me forever?* He hadn't ever met Mr. Edwards, although Mrs. Edwards had pointed out a black-and-white photo of him in his dress navy uniform. Darien had thought the man looked very handsome, but there was something about his steely blue eyes that made him feel uncomfortable. *Will Mr. Edwards like me?* He tossed and turned as worry over the answers to these questions kept him awake several more minutes.

Darien felt his eyelids grow heavy as he lowered his vision to the paper border lining the room just below the ceiling and mindlessly traced its repeating pattern of curlicues. As he felt himself drifting into sleep, he heard the voice.

"You are not alone, Darien. I am here whenever you need me." The words echoed in his ears and seemed to vibrate throughout his entire body.

He sat up suddenly and peered at a shadowy form in the far corner of the ceiling. He blinked his eyes several times. *Who is that?* He felt himself trembling all over.

"Bad, bad, go away! Come again another day!" He whispered the words and then squeezed his eyes shut for an instant. He opened them again but couldn't make the image go away. It just floated up there, staring down at him, saying nothing more. As Darien continued to stare back, frozen where he lay, the image began to give off a pulsating light that contained every color Darien had ever seen, and it seemed to last forever. The glow was mesmerizing and a calm overtook him. The vision became a blur, and within moments, he drifted into a sound sleep.

★★★★

Darien was roused from his short nap by the feeling of something squeezing his toes. He raised his head as he rubbed sleepy eyes with both hands and squinted to see what it was, his heart beginning to race as he feared the worst. *Had it come back?*

"Wake up, Darien!"

He recognized the voice and let out a sigh of relief when he saw Billie Edwards sitting at the end of his bed. The young boy seemed much older looking than him and showed off dimples when he smiled. At ten going on eleven, Billie stood nearly five feet tall with broad shoulders on a wiry frame that lent proof to the fact he was active and loved sports. Dusty blond hair that was long enough to cover one eye completed the look of a young boy about to become a handsome young man in a few years.

"Hi, Billie," he said, still rubbing one of his eyes as he yawned and propped himself up with one elbow.

"Mom told me to get you up and play with you. You wanna?"

"Okay."

"Whadya wanna play?"

"I don't know."

"How about cowboys and Indians?"

"Okay, if you want to." Darien didn't have the vaguest idea what the game of cowboys and Indians was, but he was sure Billie would show him.

Billie pinched one of Darien's toes once more, harder this time so it hurt.

"Ouch!" He jerked his foot away, breaking Billie's hold.

"Get your shoes on while I go tell Mom where we're going," he said, turning his back on Darien. "I'll meet you outside, near the front porch!" Billie jumped up from the bed and was gone.

Darien pushed the bedspread off and pulled one foot up to inspect his toe more closely. The pinch had hurt and he wondered why Billie had done it. He pulled off the sock and scrutinized the little toe. It was slightly red, but the pain had already gone away, so he slipped the sock back on, tumbled out of bed, and quickly laced up his sneakers. Then he was off to learn about cowboys and Indians and to find out more about ten-year old Billie as he followed him off the front porch and down the driveway into the backyard.

They both reached the lower yard, but Billie continued on into the woods while Darien hesitated at the edge of the woods that bordered the back of their house, remembering a warning from Mrs. Edwards during a previous stay with the Edwards family. "I'm not supposed to go there, Billie!" he shouted. Waiting for a response, he adjusted the red-and-white kerchief Billie had fashioned into a band around his head, touching the blue jay tail feather to make sure it was still tucked under the makeshift headband.

"It's okay, Darien, 'cause you're with me and I'm older than you."

"She won't be mad at me?" Darien still wasn't moving beyond the cleared area that now served as their backyard lawn.

"Don't be such a fraidy-cat! Come on!"

Darien watched Billie stride forward through the underbrush, his right hand on a toy pistol dangling in its holster at one side and a coil of clothesline rope in his other. He wasn't looking back any longer. Darien charged after him, leaving all fear behind.

Chirping sounds echoed across the woods. Darien shot a glance upward as he scanned the branches of the maple and elm trees that provided lacey umbrellas of shade for the undergrowth around him. He stopped and listened intently to locate the direction and source of the sound, but it kept changing. He realized it must be a pair of birds calling to each other. He became captivated by the exchange, which rose above the sporadic sounds of snapping branches in the distance and the gurgling waters from a nearby stream.

The rustling of leaves close by grabbed his attention. He looked down to see a chipmunk dart through the dried fall foliage that lined the floor of the woods. It was all so exciting and wondrous! He had found a place that seemed to hold magical qualities where he felt safe. But a few seconds later, a sharp command broke into his reverie, and the old churning in the pit of his stomach returned.

"Come on, slowpoke. You gotta keep up with me!"

"I'm coming." He pressed forward in an effort to catch up with Billie and was nearly there when he tripped over a hidden stump, falling noisily into the dried leaves stacked high from seasons past.

"You're supposed to be an Indian, stupid! Indians don't make noise when they walk through the woods, for cripes sake!"

"You swore, Billie!"

"Did not!"

"Did too!"

"You keep that up and I'm not gonna play with you!"

Darien didn't know why, but he began to cry. He buried his face in his arms and sobbed, making no effort to get up from the pile of leaves that now partially covered him. A few seconds passed before he felt himself being raised up and hugged. He opened his eyes to find Billie's face so close their noses were nearly touching.

"Don't cry, Darien. I didn't mean what I said. Honest."

He couldn't ever remember anyone holding him like that, and it felt good. Warm and safe. He stopped sniffling, pulled back slightly, and wiped his nose on the sleeve of his jacket. "Okay."

"And just so you know, *cripes* isn't a swear word. If I'd said *Christ*, it woulda been, but I didn't say that. Now get up so we can play!"

Chapter Four

Reflection Time in the Kitchen

Virginia Edwards settled back at the maple wood drop-leaf kitchen table in the hand-painted chair she always occupied for lunch or supper. It was located nearest the doorway to the dining room where she would have a view of the side door to see anyone who might come calling, as well as being close to the stove where she generally kept the leftover meals in case Billie or Darien wanted seconds. Her hands were still wet from having washed her coffee cup, and she wiped them on the lap of her gingham housedress. She reached over and took a machine-rolled cigarette out of the small brown humidor she kept on the kitchen table when her husband was away and lit it up. Taking a deep inhale on it and then letting it out so the gray haze encircled her head, she fell into thought about this decision she had made … to take in this little boy she'd cared for before.

On two prior occasions she'd been asked by his mother, Martha O'Hara, to "babysit" him for a few days and she had said yes. Their paths had crossed at the state institution where they both worked, Virginia as a nurse and Darien's mother as an attendant. While Virginia hadn't been exactly eager to take on the responsibility the first time she was asked, she felt badly for both the mother and the child. She knew how difficult it was to raise a child by herself and could only imagine how hard it might be to be the only breadwinner, given that Martha O'Hara had told Virginia the father had disappeared. He had possibly run away by enlisting into the service in order to avoid any responsibility for the child, but she wasn't sure. She just knew she hadn't heard from him again once she told him she was pregnant with his baby, and that had been nearly five years ago.

Virginia had accepted the idea that Darien was essentially a bastard child and had agreed to take him in for three days, the first time. And then it had been for two weeks. Only this time it was with the option of adoption, of making it a permanent transfer of responsibility. Darien's mother had met another man who wanted to marry her, so she told Virginia, and he didn't want any "baggage" coming along with her.

Virginia had nearly lost her life during the birth of her son, Billie, and while she'd desperately wanted another child, her doctor advised her against even trying. He couldn't promise that she wouldn't have complications during delivery, even if she were able to carry the baby to full term, and those complications included the possibility of her not surviving the delivery process.

She and her husband, Stanley, had slowly adjusted to the fact they wouldn't have but the one child. She thought her husband was likely relieved since she very much wanted a daughter and he'd remarked on more than one occasion how much more it would cost to raise a girl.

Virginia had raised the topic of another child on several occasions, suggesting they perhaps adopt one as soon as Billie was old enough to start school, but Stanley resisted the idea, coming up with reasons why the timing was never right. And then he'd decided to enlist in the navy and it seemed adoption, at that point, was out of the question.

Now with him being away, Billie being in school, and she alone, she'd decided to look for work and quickly found a nursing job at the state institution that was within walking distance of their home. And that was where she had met Martha O'Hara, Darien's mother

It had only taken Virginia Edwards one look at Darien and her heart almost jumped out of her chest the first time Martha brought him by the house for her to meet him. He was such a beautiful young boy, so innocent looking. And he also looked so very sad, a longing look that tugged at her. During the two times Darien was left with her, those maternal feelings she had locked away as something that would never be satisfied with a second child were ripped out of the secret place deep inside her, and she allowed herself to feel them once again. Maybe they could have another child. And she decided that perhaps Darien was God's way of preparing her for that time when she and Stanley would finally go looking for an orphan to adopt. At that point, she hadn't really even considered the possibility that Darien might be that child.

When Martha asked if Virginia and her husband would consider adopting Darien, Virginia had tried to remain calm and unemotional. "I'll have to discuss this with my husband," she said in a reserved manner. She would call him that evening at the naval base where he was stationed in the Philippines. She would need to give him a little time to think about it and she'd definitely have to give him a chance to meet Darien before she committed to anything. But inside she was nearly bursting with excitement.

While Virginia hadn't made any adoption commitment to Martha, she had agreed to take Darien in once more and care for him on a temporary basis, telling her any such decision would have to be made after her husband came home on a furlough and could have the chance to meet Darien and get used to him. What she'd told her husband was that she was taking Darien in again for "a little while" and that maybe he'd get to meet him during his next time home. She made no mention of adoption, thinking it wisest to approach that topic after he'd had the opportunity to meet Darien and realize what a wonderful little tyke he was.

Virginia Edwards thought about what she'd just told Darien earlier … about his living with them and their treating him like a son. She hoped she hadn't gotten his hopes up too high in case Stanley didn't warm up to the idea after he met Darien and they would have to send him back to his mother. She knew that would be traumatic for him, even at his age. And for *her* as well.

She loved her husband deeply but had already seen how stern he could be with their son. He had a way with children that could be hard for a young person to understand. Billie never let on, of course, but she saw the little ways he registered fear around his father when he would challenge Billie to be the best, to never be a coward or afraid of anything. To be a man. And he didn't ever hesitate to take Billie over his knee and give him a few whacks with his belt when he sassed his mother.

Billie had talked back at his father once and had been given a look that was like steel. She knew because once or twice she'd been on the receiving end of that look and it had frightened even her, although he'd never hit her and she felt certain he never would. But children were a different matter. In his view, children needed to be disciplined, severely if necessary. "Let 'em know who's in charge, who's paying for the roof over their head, the clothes they wear, and the food they eat." Darien was clearly a sensitive child, and she wondered if Stanley would be able to understand a child with such a different disposition. She recalled what he'd said of his own father: "You damned well better not give him any lip cuz when you did, he'd beat the hell outta you! I got it on more than one occasion when I was growing up, and I soon learned I didn't need to like him, but I damned sure better show him respect. And I did."

Billie seemed to have learned the same lesson but with fewer incidents of having to face his father's wrath. Or, as her husband put it, "some discipline to set him straight!" She wondered now if Darien would have to face similar punishment, and if he did, would he come through it for the better or for the worse? Only time would tell.

Chapter Five

Late April 1943

Two weeks had now passed. Darien trailed along behind Billie out to the sidewalk and watched him as he strapped the fishing pole to the handlebars of his bike.

"Can I go fishing with you?" It was the second Saturday Darien had asked. He felt certain Billie would say yes this time.

"You're too little!"

"But I wanna go." He felt the tears building and about to come trickling down his cheeks. He turned his face away and brushed at them. He wasn't going to cry, no matter what.

"Where I'm going is too deep for you. You might fall in and drown. I wouldn't be able to save you."

That did it for Darien. He was frightened of deep water, remembering the one time Mrs. Edwards had taken them to a place they called Middle Pond and he had been too afraid to wade past his knees. Billie splashed him and tried to drag him into deeper water. He screamed and Mrs. Edwards heard him. She had punished both of them, Billie for tormenting him and Darien for making so much noise, by marching them into the station wagon and driving home in silence.

You go fish with your big friends! Darien stood, silent, his arms folded in front of him as Billie pedaled off. *I've got my own spot where I can fish,* remembering the rippling sounds of a stream he heard when Billie had taken him into the woods that first time. *I don't need you!*

He only had to convince Mrs. Edwards to let him go into the woods by himself. Today was the day he would ask her. He waited for the right opportunity. He didn't have to wait long.

In less than an hour after he'd gone to his room to use his coloring books and crayons, Darien sensed someone behind him and looked up over one shoulder.

"It's too nice a day for you to spend it cooped up in your room coloring, Darien." Mrs. Edwards leaned into the room, holding a mop in one hand and a cigarette in the other. "Get your jacket and go outside for some fresh air. It'll put color in your cheeks," she said, breaking into a wheeze as she inhaled deeply on her fourth cigarette in an hour.

This was his chance. "Can I pleeeease go into the woods? I'll be careful. Please, Mom?" It was only the second time he'd called her that since coming to live with them a month ago, but he'd begun to feel like a part of the family and he remembered how her face lit up the first time he'd called her that. He was hoping it would happen again and she'd say yes.

She stepped into the room, placed the mop against the doorjamb, and walked to the window that faced the woods, motioning with one hand for him to follow. Ashes fell from the cigarette she was holding, and she quickly reached out with the other hand to catch them before they fell to the floor. She stuffed them into the pocket of her apron and pointed out the window. "You see out there, beyond the sandbox? There's a stream that cuts through the woods, right out there."

"Yes!" He felt his excitement growing with each second.

"You're to go no farther, understand?"

"Yes!" he replied quickly, barely able to contain himself.

"And make sure you keep away from the edge of the stream, do you hear?"

"Yes, ma'am … I mean, Mom," he said, no longer able to restrain his excitement as he jumped up from the floor and danced around in circles. Unable to resist, Darien raced over to her and wrapped his arms around her legs. He buried his face in her skirt and then pulled back to look up at her, giving her the biggest grin he knew how.

Surprise registered in her eyes followed by a broad smile. He felt her hand on his head before she turned, picked up the mop, and retreated into the kitchen.

"You be back here before the five o'clock whistle blows!" he heard her say over the clatter of dishes.

"I will!" Darien waved his arms to move the odor of the cigarette smoke away from him and quickly collected up the crayons and coloring books strewn on the floor. He crammed them into the bottom dresser drawer, the one his mother had told him and Billie was just for his things. No one else's. Then he pulled on his jacket and bounded through the dining room and out the side door.

"Bye, Mom!" he shouted, not waiting for a reply. The screened door slammed behind him as he broke into a full run, taking the easier way down the gravel driveway that led to the lower backyard level.

Darien made a beeline to the spot that had captured his heart that first time in the woods. He found the small clearing and heard the sounds of the stream that cut through the wooded property not more than twenty yards beyond the opening. He raced to within a few feet of it and stopped abruptly.

Late spring rains added to the melting snow from higher ground had turned the normally placid stream into a rushing brook that was now at least four feet wide and looked very deep to Darien. He watched, mesmerized by the force of the water as it propelled small branches and other forest debris downstream. Deep water kept him from going closer. He could appreciate the sounds from a safe distance, he thought, but his resolve did not last long.

Darien crouched down, his short legs spread wide for better balance and his forearms resting across his knees. He stretched his neck up as high as he could to see over the embankment of the brook. Patches of trillium and tall weeds blocked his vision. He turned around and briefly looked back in the direction of the house. Good! No sign of Mrs. Edwards. He returned his attention to the tumbling waters and inched his way a little closer, pushing aside the foliage until he had a clear view.

He scrutinized all the activity in the stream. There, in an isolated area of relatively still water, he spotted a school of minnow. He clapped his hands together and giggled as he watched them dart to the surface and then disappear back into the lower depths of the pool. A strange-looking insect with elongated legs skimmed across the surface of the water and was gone in an instant, swallowed up by a minnow large enough to splash the water as it snapped up the feast and dove to the bottom.

Feeling a little braver, Darien edged even closer until his feet were nearly at the waterline. He reached over to one side and picked up a dried branch no more than two feet long. He broke off most of the smaller branches, creating a makeshift walking stick. Darien evaluated his handiwork. *Maybe this is what the Indians did a long time ago. Right here, where I am now.*

He leaned over and looked down, marveling at his own reflection, distorted though it was by the rippling waters. He poked the stick down into the stream and laughed at the sight of the tiny minnow darting off in all directions to avoid the ragged point. He strained forward, bending over the water to get closer to the underwater activity. Then he felt his weight shift abruptly. He cried out, as he pitched forward, his hands flailing in front of him. He tried with all his might to regain his balance, but it was too late. He raised both arms out in front of him, hoping to break his fall into the water. His hands broke through the surface of the water, and he opened his mouth to scream.

Suddenly, he felt an invisible force lift him from his fall into the moving waters, catapulting him back up into the air and onto solid ground. His landing was gentle, as if the force had carried him up and then set him down. Darien struggled to his feet and looked around in a daze, unable to comprehend what had just occurred.

A voice came out of nowhere. "You are safe now, Darien." It resonated, as if amplified by a megaphone.

He turned around, almost losing his balance again, as he searched for its source behind him. It sounded like it had come from the area of the clearing, but he saw no one.

And then he looked up and let out a gasp. There, hovering in the air near the top of a boulder by the clearing was a man with an olive complexion and jet-black hair, pulled back. He bore a trimmed mustache and goatee and was dressed in a robe.

The man's garment had long, elegant sleeves that hung almost to the ground where the rest of the material flowed down, covering his feet. The iridescent fabric in its vibrant blue, green, and orange-red hues shimmered in the sunlight. Golden threads, woven through it, created a design, one Darien could not quite make out.

Had the man not been so magnificently dressed like some kind of very special prince Darien would have been frightened, but he wasn't. Instead, he felt drawn into a state of pure wonder.

The man on the ceiling! He recalled the vague, shimmering image he'd seen that first afternoon of this most recent stay with the Edwardses. Still, he was in shock, unable to speak.

Almost as if knowing this, the man crossed his hands at his chest and bowed slightly before he spoke again. "I am Sundeep, and I've come to serve and guide you." He grinned and then leaped, effortlessly, as if in slow motion, down from the top of the boulder to within a few feet of where Darien was standing.

Darien remained silent, unable to believe his eyes. *Who is this man? A magician? Or a friend of Billie's, dressed up as a trick to fool me?* He continued to stare, cocking his head to one side and then the other as he looked for something that would give it away as a prank.

"I am who I say I am, not who you think I might be."

He knows what I'm thinking, like Mrs. Edwards does.

"You're right, Darien. I do read your mind, just like your mother does when you don't voice your own thoughts." The man who called himself Sundeep smiled with eyes that soothed Darien somewhere deep inside, like the softness of lips brushing across his forehead. Gathering up the many folds of his robe, Sundeep gently lowered himself to the ground, ending up with his legs crossed beneath him.

He repeated what he'd said moments earlier. "I've been chosen to work with you. I'm always available."

"Is this some kind of trick of Billie's?"

"No, Darien, not a trick. I saw the danger you couldn't see and came to protect you."

Darien considered this for a moment. He was finding it hard to understand what had happened. He knew he had lost his balance and had nearly fallen into the water, but his memory of what had happened next was blurred. Only a vague sense of having been wrapped in some invisible arms and safely swooped back up onto the ground. How did he do that?

"I've been at your side since before you were born, watching over you, my gifted one."

Gifted one? Darien turned all around but saw no one else there but Sundeep. He furrowed his brow and glanced back at this wondrous form before him.

"I'm speaking of you, Darien. Your name means many things, and one of them is The Gift. One day you will know just what a gift you are, and you will rise up and shine with a light so brilliant, my robe will seem pale by comparison." Sundeep clasped his hands together in front of his face and rocked silently with his eyes closed.

The words of the stranger who called himself Sundeep were beyond Darien's ability to understand.

"I never seen you before."

"You saw me the day you arrived here for the final time. Just before you went to sleep."

He didn't know what Sundeep meant by *final* time, but he remembered the glowing image he'd seen in his room the day of his arrival over a month ago. *But that didn't look like a person,* he thought to himself.

"I didn't want to frighten you any more than I did, so I didn't fully materialize."

"What?"

"I just appeared different, Darien."

"You can change how you look?" Darien's eyes widened as he continued to listen to Sundeep, transfixed by this gentle man with amazing abilities.

"Yes, and so will you be able to one day. There is a part of you, deep inside, that is your spirit. Right here." Sundeep touched him on the chest.

Darien rocked from side to side, his hands now fidgeting behind his back. The words made no sense, but Sundeep's deep, resonant voice kept his attention.

"You don't know this yet, but you have magnificent powers. They come from that spirit within you that knows no limits. You need only call upon it and trust yourself."

Darien frowned and shook his head.

"I know this is all hard for you to understand, and that's all right. You will, in your own time. Until then, just know I will appear whenever you wish."

"How?"

"Close your eyes and silently make the wish to yourself."

"Like the wish I make every night before I go to sleep?"

"Yes, like that."

Darien wondered if Sundeep knew what his wish was. *He probably does. He knew I was thinking about Mrs. Edwards.* He wondered how wishing could make things come true or even if it really could. *But even Mrs. Edwards has said so.* He remembered part of the song she sometimes sang to him at bedtime: "When you wish upon a star ..." He couldn't remember the rest. If only his wish could come true. His thoughts returned to Sundeep's ability to appear and disappear.

"Could Billie and Mrs. Edwards see you if they were here?"

"No, Darien. I'm here just for you."

He lowered his gaze and considered Sundeep's words. He looked up and smiled. "And I just wish and you'll be here?"

"Yes, but you must wish with your heart, not just your mind."

He didn't know what that meant, but he heard a distant voice somewhere in his head ask, "How?," and the word tumbled out of his mouth.

"Practice, Darien. Practice. It may not happen the first time, but you keep trying and wish really hard, and it will happen."

"Will you visit me when I come here?"

"Yes, when you wish it with your whole heart. And now I must go, Darien. And so must you, for it is nearly time."

"Tomorrow, Mr. Sundeep. I'll be here again tomorrow."

Darien blinked several times. Sundeep had performed a magical dance in the air above and then disappeared. Not more than a few seconds later, he heard the whistle sound five long blasts. *Better hightail it home,* he thought, remembering Mrs. Edwards' words when she'd instructed him about being on time for meals.

There was a bounce in his step as he retraced his way back to the house. *I have a special friend. Just for me.* Tomorrow could not come soon enough.

Chapter Six

One Day Later

The next day was Sunday. After breakfast, Darien and Billie both crowded into the small bathroom off the kitchen and brushed their teeth. It wasn't so much a matter of their having forged a close bond of brotherly love as it was one of practicality and water conservation. They relied upon natural springwater that flowed into a well located on the property, and the hot water tank was small, probably too small for a family with two young boys who invariably managed to arrive home from their outdoor activities dirty or covered with grass stains from Roughhousing on the lawn. On more than one occasion, Mrs. Edwards had come home to find she had no hot water to run a wash or to sponge bathe. She was not a happy camper, and although Darien sensed that she tried very hard to hold her temper in check, she more often than not failed. The tirade that ensued always made Darien feel anxious and guilty. He'd been a bad boy. That was certain.

Darien finished brushing and waited for Billie to make room for him to spit into the small sink. Then they heard the good news.

"I know you two will be very disappointed, but we won't be attending church services this morning," Mrs. Edwards said from the other side of the partially closed door.

Darien's eyes widened, and he quickly covered his mouth to stop the outburst of joy he was feeling. He never really looked forward to going to church. There were very few other children there, and it was nearly always stuffy and the pews were most uncomfortable. He did like to hear the giant organ played by the elderly woman who sat behind it, peering over her sheet music to see the soloists, and he absolutely loved to listen to the family of singers who rotated duties as soloists. He had heard Mrs. Edwards say that the older man had sung with the Metropolitan Opera chorus when he was younger and had trained his two daughters to sing. Yes, Darien loved the music but found the sermons boring and had to work very hard not to fuss and fidget, something Mrs. Edwards wouldn't tolerate. And now, for some unexplained reason, they didn't have to go. Well, he certainly wasn't going to ask any questions. He just closed his eyes for a second and said a silent prayer of thanks. He snuck a sideways glance at Billie and snickered.

Billie crouched down and leaped into the air, a grin on his face, his clenched fists raised above his head in a triumphant salute.

Darien jumped also, but since he was not on the throw rug, he came down with a loud *thud!* when his feet hit the linoleum flooring.

"I heard that and know what you two are up to!" Mrs. Edwards' voice grew closer and her head popped through the door as she opened it enough to peer in. "You're both free to go out and play today, but don't think this is going to be a regular Sunday thing, hear me?" She was smiling and tousled Billie's hair as the two of them passed her to return to their room.

Darien felt her touch the top of his head as well when he moved by her. *She likes me too!*

He waited for Billie to dress and leave, pretending to be busy scanning one of Billie's comic books. Darien wasn't sure why he avoided dressing and undressing in front of Billie. He only knew he felt embarrassed of his own body, like it didn't measure up to Billie's, and that made him feel inadequate. Once alone, Darien dressed himself and glanced around the room to make certain all his toys and coloring books were put away before leaving. "Orderliness is next to godliness," he whispered to himself, recalling Mrs. Edwards' words when he had first arrived.

Darien heard Billie holler something to their mother and then caught sight of him out the window as he wheeled his bicycle off the front porch into the driveway and head up the street.

Left to himself, Darien headed for the kitchen where he heard sounds of running water and dishes being stacked. He spotted Mrs. Edwards looking out the window above the sink as she placed the last plate on the drying rack.

"I made my bed, Mommy. I'm going to go outside and play."

"Where?"

"In the woods."

"You like being in the woods, don't you?"

"Yup."

"Make sure you listen for the cowbell when I ring it."

"Okay." He knew the signal that lunch or dinner was ready.

In no time, he was near his favorite spot in the woods. Darien's first thought was *I hope I see Sundeep!* But another idea passed across his mind. *Pick some posies for Mommy!* As much as he wanted to see Sundeep, he felt drawn to the idea of surprising Mrs. Edwards with a bunch of wildflowers. Without further thought, he raced off in the direction where he'd seen some his first time in the woods with Billie.

Sure enough, not far from the place where Sundeep had visited him the day before, he spotted bursts of deep purple pushing up through the dried leaves. As he brushed away the covering of leaves, small clusters of long-stemmed, delicate violets appeared, surrounded by green arrow-shaped leaves. Excitedly, he snapped off each tiny flower at the base of its stem and transferred it to his other hand.

When he'd collected enough of the fragile blooms, he picked a handful of the green leaves from their base and added them to complete the arrangement. He looked around several times to be sure Sundeep hadn't appeared while he'd been busy picking the flowers. *Silly me. I didn't wish with all my heart yet!*

Satisfied Sundeep was nowhere around, he stood and raced back toward the house with his gift.

Once there, Darien crouched and peered from behind the entryway into the kitchen. He remained silent, although he was certain she would hear his breathing and the heavy pounding of his heart. He listened. No sounds of her. The coast was clear.

Darien reached down and gently placed the nosegay of violets on the linoleum-covered floor, propping them up against the threshold that separated the kitchen from the adjoining dining room. She would see them, he was sure, when she came back up from the basement. He turned and ran back through the dining room and out the door into the mid-morning sunlight, cringing slightly as the screened door slammed shut behind him.

He scurried down the stone steps to the backyard and into the woods. He raced to his special sanctuary, crashing through the underbrush until he reached the shady, moss-covered opening just this side of the small freshwater stream that meandered through the wooded property. It was time to say his special magic prayer.

Chapter Seven

Meanwhile, Back at the House

As Virginia Edwards straightened up the downstairs guest room, she thought she heard something at the upper level and climbed the stairs that led to the kitchen. "Hello?" she called out as she reached the top step and swung the door open. There was no response, so she closed the door behind her and moved toward the dining room to see if anyone was at the side door. Since it was almost May, the door was open, and she could see through the outer screened door. No one was there. Something near her foot caught her eye, and she looked down. There on the floor, propped up against the threshold, was a small bouquet of violets.

She bent over, picked them up, and lifted them to her nose to take in the delicate scent. "Oh, how lovely! Darien, you're such a thoughtful little boy," she said aloud, taking in a quick breath to hold back the emotions she was feeling. She pulled out the clean hanky she always kept in the side pocket of her housedress and dabbed at her eyes as she walked back into the kitchen and took a clean glass jelly jar out of the cupboard. She stepped to the sink and turned on the faucet, filled the jar to within an inch of the top, and placed the bouquet into it.

Once she had rearranged the bouquet so the green leaves all encircled the cluster of magenta blossoms with their vivid yellow-gold centers and found a perfect spot for them on the windowsill over the porcelain kitchen sink, she leaned forward and stared out the window overlooking the wooded lot bordering their property.

She loved the view. She looked past the small bird feeder Stanley had mounted on a post just outside the window. He had erected the feeder so she could enjoy the chickadees and bluebirds that visited it daily. As she washed dishes or peeled potatoes over the sink, she would watch them peck away at the peanut butter she or Billie would slather onto the piece of birch wood Stanley had used to serve as a feeder.

Now her mind was elsewhere as she gazed into the woods. Memories from more than ten years earlier surfaced, and she floated into them, experiencing all the subtle feelings that came with them.

Raised as one of eleven children, a younger brother and nine sisters, all but one being older than she, Virginia grew up in Hammerville, raised in the very same farmhouse where her parents still lived across the street from the home she and Stanley had decided to rent from one of her brothers-in-law.

She had left Bellevue Hospital's School of Nursing, located on the west side of Manhattan, New York City, only a few months shy of graduation in order to marry Stanley. When asked why she decided not to wait until after graduation, she simply replied to one of her older sisters, "I love him, and I just didn't want to wait any longer."

Her parents had been deeply disappointed when they found out that she had dropped out of school with so little time left before she would graduate.

Virginia and Stanley had quietly eloped and spent their honeymoon in a dreary hotel off Broadway near midtown. It didn't matter to her. She was deeply in love with her high school sweetheart and worshipped the ground he walked on. But that didn't prevent her from recognizing his shortcomings, although it took several years of marriage for her to see these things.

Stanley was a hardworking young man who, having a fiery temper, was also a scrappy hell-raiser who wasn't afraid of anything or anyone and who also had a lust for life and for Virginia. And she for him. This was born out by her willingness to spend what little free time she had with him holed up in one of the nearby cheap hotels where he would reserve a room once a month as soon as he completed the two-hour drive from Hammerville to New York City. While she didn't really feel guilty about their sleeping together and having sex, she wasn't about to let her parents know. Young women of her day did it, but they didn't talk about it.

Their early years of marriage were deeply fulfilling for Virginia, and she quickly let go of any shame she felt about walking away from school when Billie was born the following spring. He was the most beautiful baby she'd ever set eyes on and well worth the difficulty she had giving birth, during which she had almost died.

For the next six years, Virginia filled her time being a mother and a wife, happy to be both, although the reality that she couldn't risk becoming pregnant again weighed heavily on her. She made every effort to hide her sadness about that from her husband, but it was there nonetheless. So she busied herself with worthwhile hobbies like learning how to sew and make clothing for herself and, later on, for Billie. These efforts served to reduce the financial burdens she and Stanley shared raising a child in a time when good jobs were scarce and where he had to settle for manual work as a truck driver.

Virginia recalled how he had worked for the town, hauling dirt and rock on a major tri-county project to create a dam being built as part of the construction of a major reservoir that ultimately became known as Quabbin Reservoir, which provided water for all the neighboring towns as well as for Boston and its surrounding communities, located some eighty miles away. She admired his work ethic and determination to provide as much as he could for his family.

As soon as Billie began first grade, however, Virginia was free to find work and she did, almost immediately, as a nurse at the nearby state institution that housed over two thousand patients, most of which were individuals with severe mental disabilities ranging from low IQ to Mongoloidism and schizophrenia. But, sadly, it also was a place that housed orphaned children and teenaged young adults who were turned over by their parents to be wards of the state. And while they may have had the potential to succeed out in the world given half a chance, they soon took on all the habits and characteristics of those around them who were more seriously challenged, mentally and behaviorally.

While the administrative staff who had hired Virginia was aware that she hadn't graduated from nurses' training, her knowledge and abilities became very obvious from her application and during the interview, so her lack of a diploma was overlooked and she was hired on the spot. The job was an absolute godsend for the Edwards family. Within a few months, Virginia and Stanley had managed to scrimp and save up enough to offer to purchase the house from the brother-in-law, who agreed to an arrangement that enabled them to buy the house with him holding the mortgage for them.

A coughing spasm racked Virginia Edwards out of her memories, and she pulled a second handkerchief ... a more used one ... from beneath her sleeve and held it over her mouth to catch the spittle that came up and into the cloth from deep within her chest. She held it up closer to the light coming through the window and inspected it. It was dark and filled with clotted pieces of phlegm. She frowned and balled the cloth up and walked over to the bathroom, a few steps away. She lifted the lid on a white whicker hamper where all the dirty laundry went and dropped it in, observing it was nearly full and making a mental note to run a wash that evening.

She glanced up at the kitchen wall clock. It was getting close to lunchtime, so she busied herself with laying out slices of white bread, lettuce, tomatoes, and egg salad that she'd made the night before. And she thought again about Darien. She looked over at the bouquet of violets, now sitting prominently on the kitchen windowsill. She shook her head and smiled absently.

Chapter Eight

Back in the Woods: An Answered Prayer

Darien bent down and sat back, resting his weight on the heels of his sneakers. Pressing his hands together in front of him, he closed his eyes tightly and prayed, "Please, Sundeep, come and let me see you!" He repeated this over and over, to himself, for what seemed like several minutes. He opened his eyes and waited, scanning the area as he looked for his special friend.

After several moments, Darien caught a glimmer of colors out of the corner of one eye and heard a now-familiar voice.

"And how are you today, Darien?"

"I'm happy, sir." Darien stood and turned to face Sundeep, who was leaning against the large boulder behind him, a big smile on his face.

"I know why, and please, call me Sundeep." He stroked the sides of his goatee and then pulled on both earlobes, seemingly unaware of these hand movements.

"How do you know why I'm happy?"

"Because I see your heart and it's open and filled with joy."

"Why? I don't always feel like that."

"I know, but when you give of your self, you feel the gift of joy in your heart. Like you just did a little while ago, when you gathered the flowers and left them for Mrs. Edwards to find."

"You were here and saw me?" Darien asked, a puzzled look on his face. "I didn't see you."

"I don't need to be visible for me to be with you and see you."

Sundeep's answer seemed to satisfy Darien, but he still wondered about his earlier statement about seeing his heart opened and filled with joy.

"Then why don't I always feel happy?"

"Because the words and actions of others sometimes cause you to feel sad or frightened."

"Why?"

"Because you feel alone."

The thought made Darien feel sad, and he reached up and wiped away a tear on his cheek.

Sundeep leaned forward and touched Darien's arm. "Remember this, Darien. You're never alone. Not really. Even when it seems like you are, I'm always here with you."

"Even when I can't see you?"

"Even then."

Darien felt comforted by that thought and by Sundeep's gentle touch on his shoulder. Any fear or doubt he might have had when he first saw Sundeep was gone. He felt safe in a way he couldn't put into words. He thought about his new home and family. He didn't feel safe with them. Not yet, anyways, and not like this. He wasn't sure why. He only knew, right now, in Sundeep's presence, he felt good. He felt happy, and he felt free.

Darien squealed with delight when Sundeep suddenly leaped up several feet into the air and did three somersaults before his feet hit the ground. Darien clapped his hands together and laughed. "Do it again, Sundeep! Do it again!"

Sundeep chuckled and obliged by doing a triple back-flip, effortlessly. "Do you know how to play leapfrog, Darien?" he asked, not even breathing hard.

"Show me."

He did, and when Darien tired of that, Sundeep showed him how to play hide-and-seek, although Darien was certain Sundeep cheated a little bit. The two of them played until it was time for Darien to go back to the house. Sundeep hugged him gently and disappeared in an instant, leaving Darien in a total state of amazement. He could not remember ever being so happy. But would it last? he wondered.

Chapter Nine

July 1943:
The Navy Man's Coming

"Darien O'Hara, eat your cereal!" Mrs. Edwards towered over him, her hands on her hips and her legs spread in a determined stance.

"I don't like it! It tastes terrible!" He held the spoonful of Wheatena to his mouth, his hand shaking from the rage he felt inside. *I'm not gonna eat it,* he thought but dared not say aloud.

"That's perfectly good cereal, and you need it to grow up healthy and strong."

"But it's cold and rubbery!"

"It wasn't when I served it to you an hour ago! Now eat it, Darien! Do you hear me?" She was nearly shouting at this point as she flipped her head back and brushed a strand of damp hair from her eyes.

"I said, eat it! Right now! Because if you don't …" She reached over to the counter beneath the cupboards and grabbed hold of the large pitcher she used to make ice tea or Kool-Aid. She turned on the faucet at the kitchen sink and began to fill the pitcher with water. " … I'm going to make you wish you had. Now, one last time, eat that cereal!"

Darien folded his arms in front of him and scowled. "No!"

Without further warning, Mrs. Edwards took hold of the side of the vessel with her other hand and hurled its contents at Darien. In an instant, he was drenched and screamed even louder, now pounding his legs up and down as he launched into a major temper tantrum. "IhateyouIhateyouIhateyou!"

Ignoring his rage, or perhaps more fueled by it, she grabbed the long wooden spoon that hung on a hook next to the gas stove and raised it above her head. She took in a deep breath and said evenly, "One last time. Eat your cereal or you get this across your backside!"

He had pushed her as far as he could without suffering a swat with the dreaded wooden spoon. Darien had seen her use it on Billie once when he had misbehaved. He let out a whimper and forced himself to take in the last several jiggly spoons full, gagging and fighting the reflex to throw them back up.

"When your father gets here, you won't be acting like this, young man!" These were her final words as she placed the spoon back on its hook and watched him finish off the last traces of the cereal.

She was, of course, referring to *Mr.* Edwards. She didn't know who Darien's real father was, she had said solemnly on an earlier occasion when he had asked her about his mother and father.

"You didn't really have a father, but Mr. Edwards is going to be your father now."

These earlier words came to mind as he pushed away from the kitchen table and folded his napkin. *What does she mean, "He's going to be my father"?*

"Did I hear you say Pop's comin' home?" Billie, who had remained out of sight but had heard the entire incident play out from his spot in the bedroom, bounded into the kitchen as he pulled up his pants and tucked in his shirt.

"Isn't that wonderful, Billie?" Mrs. Edwards' mood had changed instantly, and Darien sensed it.

She's happy. Billie's happy. But I'm not. Darien felt a wave of nausea rise up from the pit of his stomach. He put one hand over his mouth and took in a deep breath.

Mrs. Edwards eyed Darien, now seeing him standing there, dripping wet and shivering. "Go to your room and change into dry clothes," she said, tossing him a frayed towel that was hanging on the back of the bathroom door. She made a movement as if she were going to kneel down and reach out to Darien but then stood back up and simply smoothed his wet hair off his forehead. "Go, Darien. Wipe yourself dry and change your clothes, dear."

Darien looked up at her, uncertain if she was still mad at him or not, and then took the towel and walked out of the room and into his bedroom, still within hearing distance of Billie and his mother.

"When's he coming home, Mom?"

"In a few weeks, dear. Isn't that wonderful?"

Darien wasn't so sure. He would have to wait and see.

Chapter Ten

Arrival Day

Billie was now out of school for the summer. Mrs. Edwards had kept both boys busy during the week before her husband's arrival, helping her prepare the house and yard in preparation for his homecoming. And now the big homecoming was just two days away.

"Everything must be perfect for your father, boys. As he would say, you gotta have things shipshape! A place for everything, and everything in its place."

Darien looked to Billie for an explanation.

"That means, pick up your toys and get 'em out of sight. And then you're gonna help me cut and trim the lawn later, okay?" It was more an order than a request.

"Okay." Darien stepped out onto the porch and surveyed the lawn and shrubbery in front of the small bungalow home, remembering that the backyard was even larger. *I bet if I wished Sundeep to come he'd do his magic and have this work done in no time!* He closed his eyes and was about to recite his prayer when he was interrupted.

"Stop your daydreaming, Darien, and get moving!"

"Yes, Billie, I'm comin'." He'd have to wait for another opportunity to have Sundeep visit. He headed back toward the room he shared with Billie. Thoughts about meeting Billie's father surfaced and with them came shadowy memories of other places he'd lived for short periods of time. *The old couple. The big house with lots of other kids. The place I'm alone with no one to play with.* He thought about Billie's father. *Will he make me go away?* He didn't like the feelings that followed these thoughts, so he pushed them away. *I'm gonna work with Billie.* That thought made him feel happy. He moved into action, picking up his pajamas and folding them neatly before he slipped them under his pillowcase and straightened out the chenille bedspread, making sure he smoothed out a wrinkle he'd created when he pulled the spread back to deposit the pajamas beneath his pillow.

Next he rearranged the top half of the dresser he shared with Billie, giving special attention to organizing his shoe horn, brush and comb, and the little jewelry dish Mrs. Edwards had told him he could use to hold his "going to church" cufflinks and tie clip. Darien was especially proud of these items because to him they were what big boys and grown men used on their long-sleeved shirts. That completed, he joined Billie, who was already outside pushing the lawn mower on the front lawn as he finished the final section of uncut grass.

Darien already knew what he was to do and picked up the grass clippers Billie had set out on the sidewalk. Walking over to the edge of the newly mowed lawn near the side door, he knelt down on his knees and began to carefully trim the taller grass along the edge of the concrete sidewalk that led toward the walkway to the front door. He quickly retreated into that wonderful, very private place in his mind, one where there was nothing to fear or worry over. It was as if he were transported to another place as he became one with the movements of his hands, both working to squeeze the clipper blades together, slicing through the bits of grass and stray weeds.

Much time had passed, perhaps as much as fifteen or twenty minutes, when he was stirred back to an awareness of where he was and what he was doing. He had sensed someone standing over him and looked up to see Billie. At the same time, he realized he had completed trimming one whole side of the sidewalk and was now working on the section of the main sidewalk that led out to the driveway. He looked at what he'd done and smiled. "How'd I do, Billie?" he asked, hoping to hear some praise.

"Not bad, but you missed a spot. See?" replied Billie, pointing. "Pretty good, though," he added, seeing Billie's smile begin to fade. "Especially for someone your age."

Darien gave him a big, big smile as he moved over to the spot he'd missed, cut the few wisps of grass, and then moved on to where he'd left off.

★★★★

"Today's the day, boys. I'm going to leave now to pick up your father at the bus station." Mrs. Edwards smoothed the front of her dress and adjusted her pearl earrings while Darien and Billie stood and watched her gather up her handbag and car keys and move toward the door.

Darien hadn't ever seen her look so pretty as she did now, with her hair newly curled and red nail polish on her fingernails. She'd even applied extra rouge to her cheeks and was wearing a flowered cotton dress that swirled around as she took steps toward the dining room door.

"I shouldn't be more than an hour. You two behave yourselves while I'm gone."

"We will," Billie said as he wrapped one arm around Darien's head and proceeded to grind the knuckles of his other hand into his hair. Darien scrunched up his shoulders and pulled away but didn't utter a sound. He hated it when Billie gave him nooggies.

"Billie, you behave! Do you hear me?" Mrs. Edwards wasn't smiling.

"I was just kidding with Darien, Mom. See?"

Darien gave little resistance when Billie pulled him back into a bear hug and planted a big, noisy kiss on his ear.

"All right. We'll see you in a little while." She laughed, turned to leave, and then stopped.

"You're not to answer the door for anyone unless you know who it is," she added, looking at Billie.

"Yes, Mom. Bye."

Darien wished she hadn't warned them about strangers, for now his active imagination was off and running and he didn't like the feelings that came with the thoughts. He hurriedly recited the magic words that always seemed to push away the scary thoughts and feelings. *Bad, bad, go away! Come again another day!* Within moments, he felt better and hurried to join Billie, who was now in the living room, sitting on the carpet, his head bent toward the cloth-covered speakers of the small Zenith radio.

After the two of them listened to a Saturday morning episode of *Sergeant Preston*, Darien followed Billie back to their room and changed into the clothing his mother had laid out for him.

"Why do I have to be all dressed up?" Darien tugged at the starched, white collar of the shirt he was already outgrowing. He looked down as he inspected the Buster Brown shoes she'd bought for him the week before. "Gotta see your face in 'em," he mumbled to himself, recalling what Billie had said one Sunday when they were getting dressed for church.

Picking up one foot, he attempted to bring up the shine by wiping the shoe on the back of the other trouser leg, but he lost his balance and pitched forward.

Billie roughly grabbed for his arm and pulled him back into a standing position. "Where were you when the brains were passed out? Behind the door? If you can't keep your balance, hold on to the darned bedpost or something!"

Darien didn't understand Billie's words, but he felt them. He folded his bottom lip over his top one as he felt tears well up. *I'm not going to cry!* He turned away from Billie and focused his attention on getting his shoes shinier as he looked for something to wipe them with.

"And you're wearing your Sunday best clothes because Pop's coming home." Billie pulled on a pair of corduroy trousers, tucked in his freshly ironed shirt, and then stopped suddenly. "What are you doin' now?" His voice was raised.

"Shining my shoes." Darien continued to make small, circular motions with the piece of white cloth he'd spotted on Billie's bed.

"Jesus Christ! That's my darned handkerchief, you idiot."

Darien was unable to duck in time and felt the sting of Billie's hand across the top of his head. He screamed, more from fright than actual pain, and began to bawl as he rushed out into the dining room. As he did, he heard the side door open and turned toward it.

"He's home, kids!" It was Mrs. Edwards.

"What in hell is all the racket about?" It was not a voice he recognized.

Darien froze in his tracks and looked up at the small, wiry man dressed in a navy blue uniform and shiny black shoes. He looked down and saw his reflection in the round patent leather mirrors.

"This is Darien, honey. Darien, this is your father."

He remained motionless, observing the silent exchange of looks between the two adults.

"Pop, you're home!" Billie yelled as he raced out of the bedroom, pushed past Darien, and stretched up to hug his father.

Darien slinked backward a few steps and silently watched the man pick Billie up and wrestle him to the floor.

The man beamed with pride as he reached for his duffel bag, pulled something out, and handed it to Billie. "Just a little souvenir from the Islands, Billie boy."

Mrs. Edwards leaned down and whispered in her husband's ear, something Darien was unable to hear. She looked over at Darien, and they made eye contact, but only for an instant. She quickly looked back at her husband.

He ignored her and kept his eyes on Billie, smiling broadly as his son opened the crudely wrapped gift.

"Wow, Pop! A silver letter opener!"

"Handmade, Billie, by the Gooks."

"Honey …"

"What!" Mr. Edwards scowled as he got up from the floor and brushed off his dark blue trousers. He turned and stared at Darien, who had stepped even farther away from Billie and his parents.

"So you're name is Darien, huh?"

"Yes, sir." He clasped his hands behind his back and rocked from side to side, barely making eye contact.

"Well, I tell you what, Dar-ee-en," he said, emphasizing each syllable of his name. "Tomorrow I'm going to take you outside and see just what kind of boy you are. How's that sound?"

Mr. Edwards was smiling, but his unblinking stare seemed to pass right through Darien. *What happens tomorrow?* Darien felt emptiness at the bottom of his stomach, and that definitely wasn't a good sign.

Chapter Eleven

The Next Morning:
Strike One

Early the following morning, Darien quietly got out of bed, still sleepy and covered with perspiration from a restless night of frightening dreams. He was not yet old enough to grasp the connection between these repetitive nightmares and the thoughts and worries he had on his mind as he fell asleep each night. On these occasions, he always awoke feeling dazed and confused, with no memory of the unsettling dreams. And so it was this morning.

He was careful not to wake Billie, who still lay asleep on the bed next to him, snoring, with one leg hanging over the side. Although the canvas shades were fully drawn, Billie could see that it was daylight outside, and that gave him enough light to change from his pajamas into the play clothes he'd neatly placed on the floor next to his bed. He slipped on his socks and shoes and gave it his best effort to properly tie his shoes. He tiptoed to the bedroom door and opened it.

"Glad to see you're an early riser!" The man who was going to be his father stood there, just outside his door, his arms folded across his chest.

He's smiling, but why don't I feel happy about it, like when Mrs. Edwards smiles at me? Darien wondered where Mrs. Edwards was and peered past the man into the kitchen. He saw the door to the bathroom was closed and could hear water running.

"Here's your jacket. Put it on," Mr. Edwards said as he pointed toward the door leading to the outside and waited for Darien to follow his instructions.

Darien obeyed, taking the flannel jacket and slipping an arm through one of the sleeves as he whipped it behind his head so he could stick his other arm through the other sleeve, uncertain what would happen next.

Once out on the sidewalk, Darien waited while Mr. Edwards strode past him and down the stone steps to the lower level. Darien watched as he opened the garage door and disappeared into the darkness of the basement that adjoined the garage. A few minutes later, he reappeared as he walked up the driveway, carrying a worn-looking, rusty tricycle. He set it down on the tarmac driveway and motioned to Darien.

"Get on it, Darien!" Mr. Edwards said, pointing at the strange-looking contraption.

Darien whimpered and remained rigid in the spot where he stood. While he was familiar with Billie's bicycle, he'd never seen an object like this. Standing next to it, the seat somehow seemed much higher and the handlebars too far away for him to safely reach.

"What the hell's the matter with you? It's just a tricycle. Now, get on it!"

"I'm … I'm scared!"

"I said, get *on* it! There's nothing to be scared about!" Mr. Edwards scooped Darien up and set him down on the seat so hard, it hurt. Darien winced but said nothing.

"Now put your hands on the handlebars and your feet on the pedals. No, not like *that*! Like *this*!" He lifted Darien's small feet and forced them onto the pedal bars and then grabbed hold of both of Darien's hands and wrapped them around each side of the handlebars.

Darien felt a shove from behind. He screamed, tears flowing down his cheeks as he found himself propelled forward along the driveway. *I'm gonna fall!* he thought, his feet slipping off the pedals. He stretched to put his feet back on solid ground, but the turning pedals scraped his bare legs and he screamed even louder. "No! I'm afraid!"

Unable to stop the gathering momentum of the tricycle as it moved forward down the slope of the driveway, he lifted his legs into the air to avoid the sharp edges of the pedals and gripped the handlebars even more tightly as he let out a scream that didn't stop until he had reached the bottom of the driveway and had traveled a few feet up onto the lower level lawn, where his ride was slowed to a stop. He hunched over the handlebars and began to wail.

Mr. Edwards, unable to get to Darien in time to stop the tricycle from going down the driveway slope, had run after him and arrived at the lower level just as Darien came to a stop.

"What's the matter with you, boy? You a damned sissy?" His new father pulled him off the tricycle and roughly set him on the driveway, glaring down at him.

Darien stared up at the man who threw him one last look of disgust over his shoulder as he marched back up the driveway and into the house. The tears stopped, replaced by sniffles that lasted for another several minutes as he rubbed the reddened skin of his leg. He knew he had done something wrong. "I made him mad. I'm a bad boy," he repeated over and over to himself. Darien knew one thing for certain. He would avoid that man as much as he safely could for the rest of the two weeks he was there. He hoped and prayed Sundeep would somehow make that happen.

Chapter Twelve

A Little Bit of Magic

The next week and a half passed without further incidence. No one acknowledged having heard Darien's screams or that the incident had even happened. Darien and Mr. Edwards had no unpleasant exchanges. In fact, it was almost as if Darien weren't there, judging from the number of times the two of them exchanged any words. And that was just fine with Darien. During the next ten days, he spent as much time as possible by himself in his room, either drawing or looking through the storybooks he'd been given. He was sure Sundeep had something to do with the situation, even though Darien hadn't seen Sundeep during that time.

Two days before Mr. Edwards was to return to his naval assignment in the Philippine Islands, the "navy man," as Darien overheard Mrs. Edwards call him, had taken Billie to a Little League softball game and Darien was allowed to spend part of the afternoon in the woods. He could barely wait.

He silently mouthed his prayer just once as soon as he reached his spot in the woods. *Please, Sundeep. I need you.* Tears flowed down his cheeks as he waited.

No more than a few seconds passed before a sparkling swirl of light appeared out of nowhere, nearly blinding Darien, and just as suddenly, Sundeep appeared before him.

"Dry your tears with this special handkerchief, Darien. It will take away all the hurt you're feeling." Sundeep handed him a shimmering piece of cloth and knelt next to him.

Darien took the cloth, wiped his eyes and cheeks with it, and looked up at Sundeep. He felt better, but the old thoughts returned. "I'm a bad boy. They don't like me."

"Darien, your new mother loves you. Very much. You need to know that."

"She yells at me."

"Her job, taking care of both her son, Billie, and you, all by herself, isn't easy. She misses your new father when he's away and that makes her cranky."

"He's not my father! I don't have one."

"Life is difficult, Darien. Too confusing for a young boy like you to understand. But one day you will." He stroked Darien's head and continued. "He's going to learn to love you, just as much as she does, Darien. So will Billie."

Darien wanted to believe Sundeep, but he didn't. He shook his head and lowered his eyes to the ground. He wondered what it was about him that made it hard for them to love him just as he was. He let out a sigh.

"It has nothing to do with you, Darien. It's about Mr. Edwards. His father was much like he is, and Billie has learned from him. It's the only way he knows how to be. He's just a very stern and disciplined man, and this is new for him, having you join his family."

Darien didn't understand and frowned, cocking his head to one side.

"You just need to remember one thing, Darien. You are a wonderful and smart little boy who deserves to be loved and happy." Sundeep cupped Darien's chin and lifted his face so he had to look Sundeep square in the eyes.

The look Darien saw made him feel warm all over. It was a good kind of warm. "I am?"

"Yes, you are. No matter what happens to you, remember that. And try to *be* that. *Be happy.* If you do that, things will get better. Others will be happy too. I promise you."

Darien looked down at the ground and poked at a small beetle that had emerged from under the layer of dried leaves as he pondered what Sundeep had told him. He knew when Mrs. Edwards and Billie were happy, he felt happy. Except when he felt left out. *If I'm happy, they'll be happy with me.* That seemed to make sense. Armed with this new idea, he felt good again. He decided he would be happy, no matter what. He raised his gaze back to where Sundeep had been sitting. But he had disappeared.

Darien stood up, looked around again, and slowly walked back toward the house. As he stuffed his hands into his pants pockets, he felt something and pulled it out. It was the handkerchief Sundeep had given him. He looked at it and smiled as he carefully folded it into a small square and tucked it into his back pocket. This was proof that Sundeep was indeed real, not just someone he'd imagined. He made a mental note to be sure to put the cloth in his special bureau drawer where no one else would find it and to remember to carry it with him each time he got dressed. If he felt he had to cry, he could use it to make the tears disappear.

Darien was on his best behavior for the remainder of time the four of them were together as a family. He smiled a lot but spoke only when spoken to.

For some reason, a magical one, Darien was sure, Mr. Edwards seemed less angry toward him. He remembered having overheard Mr. and Mrs. Edwards in a long conversation the same evening of the tricycle episode. Darien had been in bed, not yet able to fall asleep. He couldn't hear all of what they were saying, but he heard his name mentioned. Since then, Mr. Edwards had even smiled at Darien once or twice. Still, Darien was happy when Mr. Edwards left two days later. *Things'll be better. Sundeep said so.*

Chapter Thirteen

A Year Rolls By and New Things Happen!

Things *did* get better. Through the rest of the summer, Darien became comfortable with the living arrangements at the Edwards household. Navy Man was gone with no furloughs planned until the following summer, and that made Darien quite happy, although he knew he mustn't let Mrs. Edwards or Billie know the reason.

He didn't mind that Billie spent much of his time away from the house, usually playing softball or swimming at the town lake with older boys. Darien felt most comfortable and happy by himself, exploring the backyard woods or coloring the pictures in the coloring books Mrs. Edwards had given him shortly after he had first arrived.

And he enjoyed even more the brief times he was able to spend in the woods with his secret friend, Sundeep.

When September rolled around, even bigger changes took place. The school year began for Billie, which meant it was just Mrs. Edwards and Darien at home. In the months that followed, Darien spent time every morning after breakfast with Mrs. Edwards, learning to tell time, how to count to twenty, and write his name. Now he was learning his ABCs. And while he spent time playing in the woods with Sundeep, he made sure he did things to help Mrs. Edwards whenever he could. He learned how to carefully clear the kitchen table of dirty dishes, one at a time so he wouldn't drop any, and to walk them over to the sink and hand them to Mrs. Edwards. He was even able to wipe down the checkered vinyl tablecloth, pushing the crumbs into a cupped hand with the other, just like she did.

On this particular August morning, nearly a year later, a slight breeze made the unseasonably warm, ninety-degree temperature seem cooler. "Perfect for drying," Mrs. Edwards had told him as the two of them stood in the backyard hanging damp clothing on the clothesline.

Removing a clothespin she'd been holding between her teeth, she stretched to slip it over a corner of the bedsheet that hung on the line and said, "Hand me another clothespin, Darien."

He removed several of the wooden clips from the cloth bag beside him and handed her one. "Here it is, Mommy."

He liked calling her that now and she seemed to like it too. She smiled broadly when he did and that always made the flutters in his stomach go away.

She took the clothespin from him and pressed it onto the line, securing the far end of the flapping sheet. She paused and looked at Darien long enough for him to feel a little anxious. He hadn't done anything wrong, he was sure, but then feeling anxious seemed to be normal for Darien. He couldn't recall more than a very few times when he'd felt anything but. It was a kind of subtle quiver at the pit of his stomach, sometimes accompanied by a strange feeling that seemed to emanate from beneath his skin, a kind of vibration that was almost numbing in nature. And he felt it through every pore of his body. He felt it but came to accept it as normal and never once had the thought to mention it to anyone. He looked up at Mrs. Edwards.

She kneeled down and took one of his hands between hers and smiled. "Darien, I have two very big surprises for you. Would you like to know what they are?"

"Yes!" He felt excitement replace the anxiety.

"Your father and I spoke on the telephone last night, after you'd gone to bed, and we've decided to adopt you."

Tears spilled down one of her cheeks as she spoke, and he felt the anxiety return. *Adopt me? What does it mean?*

She patted his hand and continued as she wiped away the tears with the back of her other hand. "You're going to become our son, forever. Part of our family. Billie will be your real brother. We're going to make it legal and official."

"You mean I'll never be taken away? I really can stay forever?"

"Yes."

Sundeep was right! Darien let a wide grin creep across his face.

"And that's not all," she went on, pressing a finger on the tip of his nose and winking at him. "You're going to begin school next month. First grade, Darien! Isn't that wonderful?"

"Like Billie?" Darien wasn't sure what he was feeling now. A little excited, yes, and also a little scared about going someplace new and strange.

"Will you go with me?"

"Of course I will. I'll drive you to school and pick you up each afternoon."

This must be how she feels when she says she's on cloud nine! Darien reached out and hugged her and then twirled around in circles until he felt so dizzy he had to sit down to make everything stop spinning. As soon as that happened, he thought about Sundeep and the feeling hit him. It was like a warm vibration traveling through every part of his body. It was followed by a very strong thought: *He already knows!* Darien looked around, but there was no sign of Sundeep.

A puzzled look crossed Mrs. Edwards' face. "Something wrong?"

"No, Mommy." He reached out and hugged her again. Sundeep was one secret he'd have to keep to himself.

★★★★

The adoption occurred later that same month and was a turning point for Darien, an event that said to him, "You belong, Darien. You're a part of this family." While he didn't fully understand the significance of the signing of legal papers that late-summer day, Darien knew it meant something pretty important.

"Darien, dear! Come out from under there." It was a lady's voice, but not that of his mother.

He peered up from under the large maple dining room table and recognized his mother's legs and the familiar gingham housedress she wore. Next to her was a set of trouser legs and slightly scuffed brown work shoes. There was one other set of men's pants and highly polished shoes, visible from his hiding spot, but they weren't the black patent leather shoes Mr. Edwards always wore when he came home. Also, *he* wasn't supposed to be home for another few months. Darien surmised they belonged to the man his mother had let in earlier that morning, the one carrying a handful of documents and an official air about him. Next to him was a pair of very pretty legs, exposed to the knee. He recognized the shapely legs as ones belonging to one of his soon-to-be aunts, and then he caught a glimpse of her face smiling back at him from beneath a fold of the tablecloth she had lifted.

Darien crawled out, pressed against his mother, and wrapped one arm around her legs. He glanced up at his aunt and allowed a tiny smile to show on his face.

His mother picked him up and hugged him without a word. He saw tears in her eyes when she set him back down again. *Was she happy or sad?* he wondered. It wouldn't be until later that same day, when he would visit with Sundeep in his special place in the woods, that an answer would be offered.

After the official-looking man had left, Mrs. Edwards served his now-official aunt and uncle some coffee and cake, and they exchanged happy chatter about how wonderful it was that the Edwards family now numbered four. Darien sat quietly and dutifully smiled at each remark directed his way, barely aware of what was being said, his mind more focused on waiting until he could be excused and head out to his special place in the woods.

When his aunt and uncle finally left and he'd helped his mother bring the dirty dishes into the kitchen, he asked for and received permission to go out into the woods and explore, so long as he was back in time to help set the table for supper. He squirmed but couldn't hold back a big smile as Mrs. Edwards bent down and gave him a final hug and a wet kiss on the cheek. He raced out the dining room door and headed out toward the woods, knowing Sundeep would be there even before he spoke the special prayer aloud. And he was not disappointed. Without any greetings or fanfare, Sundeep spoke, providing an answer to the question that had lingered in his mind after seeing Mrs. Edwards shed tears at the end of the signing of papers in the dining room.

"When people feel joy in their hearts, Darien, it's because something they wished for and desired very deeply has come true."

Darien had thought about this for a few moments and then moved toward Sundeep. "If I told you what I wish for with all my heart, would you keep it a secret, Sundeep?"

"From your lips to my ears and no further. I promise!"

Darien stretched up on his toes, pulling Sundeep down by one arm until he could cup Sundeep's ear with his hands. It was barely a whisper. "I don't want to feel sad or scared anymore."

Sundeep gazed down at Darien for several moments before speaking. "Your wish is God's desire, Darien."

"Really?"

"Really."

"When?"

"When you are ready to accept it as yours."

"I don't understand."

"I know, Darien, but you will one day. Just know that you can have whatever your heart desires and that God knows what that is, even before you ask."

Sundeep was right. He didn't understand. He wondered if he ever would.

Chapter Fourteen

September 1944:
Oh, the Terrors of First Grade!

Nearly a month later, Darien was about to begin his first year in school. The suppertime conversation about it the evening before his first day left Darien feeling a mixture of excitement and anxiety. Excitement because his mother had told him he'd learn to write and spell more than just his name, that he'd learn addition and subtraction, and that he would also be able to draw and sing in school. That appealed to Darien because he loved to draw and was becoming quite good at it. At least that's what she told him. She'd said he would be meeting lots of new children his own age. When he heard that, he felt a wave of anxiety start in his stomach and move very quickly up into his throat.

By the end of the evening, he was feeling much better, but he had mixed feelings about this next step in his life. What would school be like? How would the other children treat him? Would they like him? His mother had told him there would be girls in his class, and he had no idea how to talk to or treat a girl. He wasn't even sure he'd know what to do with other boys his age. After all, the only boy he really spent any time with was his older brother, and they didn't spend that much time together, except for breakfast and evening meals and when they'd both listen to the radio or to records on the phonograph, which wasn't very often. He'd met a few of his cousins and friends of Billie, but none were his age. He thought about asking his mother the questions that now caused him to feel anxious, but he didn't want her to think he was being a sissy (though he feared it might in fact be so, based upon the remark by Mr. Edwards when he first arrived to live as part of the Edwards household nearly a year ago), and so he said nothing when she came into his room and told him it was time to go to sleep. She kissed him on the forehead, turned out the light, and closed the door, leaving him to run these questions over in his mind, again and again, until sleep overcame him.

On this first day of school, his teacher, Miss Holloway, had called out the names of each first grade student alphabetically and asked each one to stand by their seat and introduce him- or herself.

Darien studied each of the first-graders as they rose and introduced themselves. His legs began to shake when he heard "Patty Deveroux" called out and a petite blond-haired girl rose. He knew his alphabet and was pretty sure he'd be hearing *his* name very soon, and that thought scared him something awful!

Sure enough, the next name she called out was his, but she insisted that he stand at the front of the room next to her desk where all the other first-graders could see him. Now he wished she hadn't. He slid out from his chair desk and timidly approached the front of the class. He turned and faced the other children, his head down. Perspiration began to collect on his forehead and slide down his cheeks.

"This is Dar-ee-an Edwards, class. Isn't that right, Darien?" She bent forward, slightly exposing the cleavage of her ample bosoms to the rest of the class. A lone titter erupted somewhere in the back of the room, followed by a chain of giggles. She straightened up and clapped her hands together twice, her smile disappearing at once. "Be still!"

Darien was uncertain about the reason for the laughter but feared he was the cause and turned to look at his teacher, hoping for an answer.

She fingered the material at the top of the polka dot dress she was wearing and ignored his silent plea.

"Is there anything you'd like to share with the rest of the class, Darien?"

He wished Sundeep had taught him how to disappear, but he hadn't, not yet, anyway. He stood there, shifting his weight from one leg to the other. He remained silent, unable to say anything. *I guess the cat's got my tongue,* he thought.

Miss Holloway tapped her foot for a few more seconds and sighed impatiently before breaking the silence. "Well, children, Darien just moved into town this past year to live with the Edwards family, and I want all of you to welcome him and make him feel at home."

"Yes, Miss Holloway," the class replied in staggered unison.

Darien felt his face flush. He hated being the center of attention and didn't want to be there in front of the class any longer. He took a step to return to his seat when he felt her hand close around his right arm, bringing his escape to a halt.

"Tell the class your good news, Darien." She beamed as she waited for his answer.

He stood, frozen in silence. *What good news? What was he supposed to say?*

"Very well!" she said after several seconds had passed. "Class, Darien has been adopted into the Edwards family. Can anyone tell us what that means?"

A hand shot up at the back of the room as Darien felt his heartbeat quicken.

"Yes, Michael?"

"It means his real parents didn't want him anymore and the Edwards felt sorry for him." The tubby young boy threw a sideward smirk toward the boy to his left and then sat back, eyes wide with innocence.

A mixed chorus of gasps, titters, and whispers filled the room as Darien burst into tears and fled toward the rear of the class and into the coatroom where he found a dark corner. He curled into a tight ball and rocked himself into another place faraway and safe. Not even the prying hands of Miss Holloway could bring him back to this world until he was ready. And a half hour later, after the school principal had called his mother, not even her appearance made a difference. He didn't so much as open his eyes until he was safely home, tucked away in his bed.

It was there, left alone to nap for the rest of the morning, that Darien recited his special prayer to make Sundeep appear. He only had to repeat it once, and Sundeep's presence filled the room with a soft and comforting blue light. Darien whimpered and reached out to Sundeep, who sat cross-legged at the foot of his bed. The whimpering turned into soft sobs, but Sundeep remained at the foot of the bed and simply sent out a comforting wave of energy that felt to Darien like he was being held very gently and rocked. He continued to lie there until he composed himself and sat up.

"Your first morning at school has been challenging, but you are stronger because of it." Sundeep leaned forward and smoothed back a strand of hair that had fallen over one of Darien's eyes.

"Why weren't you there to stop that boy from saying those things?"

"I was there, looking over your shoulder."

"Then why didn't you make him be nice to me?" Darien sniffled and wiped his nose with one sleeve of his pajamas. He put on his best pout, but it seemed to have no effect on Sundeep.

"No one, not even I, can make someone be something they're not until they're ready to be different. This was a lesson for that boy, just as it has been for you, and you came through it with flying colors!" Sundeep smiled and lifted Darien's face by the chin.

"I acted like a scaredy-cat and ran!"

"You protected yourself in the only way you knew how. You needn't feel ashamed of that, ever."

Darien hung his head and sighed. *Mr. Edwards wouldn't say that.*

"Your father just wants you to stand up for yourself, but he doesn't yet know there's a power greater than anything he could ever imagine, one that is always present for us to call upon. It has many names, but I like to simply call it Love. That is a lesson for *him* to learn when he is ready. You just need to know this: you are never alone and can never be hurt by the ignorance of others unless you give their words and actions power over you."

A gentle knock on the bedroom door grabbed Darien's attention, and his heartbeat quickened when the door swung open. He looked back toward the foot of his bed, afraid his mother would see Sundeep, but he had already disappeared.

"Talking to an imaginary friend again?" She bent over and straightened out the edges of the spread. "You're a little old for that, don't you think?" She smiled, not waiting for an answer as she left the room and closed the door. It was more a reminder than a question, one that followed Darien into a troubled sleep.

Darien returned to school the following day and did his best to not draw attention to himself. He made sure he listened to his teacher's instructions and directions and followed them exactly. No one said anything to him about his being adopted or about his running into the clothes closet the prior day. They were clearly being on their best behavior. Even Miss Holloway had seemed to make a point of not asking him any questions, and Darien suspected his teacher had discussed it with his mother, for she, too, had not asked him about it. For that he was thankful.

As the months went by, Darien grew to enjoy going to school, and while he felt very shy and awkward among the other children at first, he slowly made friends with several of his classmates. By the end of that first year, he had a best friend who lived close enough for the two of them to play together after school and on weekends.

At home, Darien was also becoming comfortable and a little more sure of himself. He had learned what he needed to do and say to please his new mom: be polite, pick up his toys, eat everything on his plate, do his homework (when there was any) and, most important of all, not yell or scream even if Billie was teasing him.

Mr. Edwards, or Daddy, as Darien had been told to call him, had visited them several months after the adoption. Darien had been surprised by how much nicer he treated him. He suspected his mother had something to do with it, for he'd overheard them talk about that very thing on more than one occasion when he came home on a furlough.

The result was that Daddy seemed gentler somehow and more tolerant, although he still never made much physical contact with Darien unless it was to playfully spar with him when he'd coax him into putting on a pair of boxing gloves and exchanging jabs. That was something that frightened Darien, but he was getting good at covering up his fear.

"When the going gets tough, the tough get going." Running away probably wasn't exactly what Mr. Edwards had in mind when he'd said that, but that was what Darien would do when he failed to get out of the way and felt one of his father's right hooks to his shoulder or chest.

"Where you running to, boy?"

"Have to pee bad, Daddy." He would slam the bathroom door behind him and then stand in front of the sink and let the water trickle into the basin, enough to be heard if someone were listening on the other side of the closed door. A few minutes' wait, he had learned, was enough for his father to lose interest in the sport of making a man out of him.

One thing Darien noticed, particularly when World War II was over and his father had come back home permanently, discharged from service, was that he didn't really treat Billie all that differently when it came to showing affection. He didn't ever hug either one of them like their mom sometimes did. *Maybe that's how you're supposed to be,* Darien thought. *Men aren't supposed to hug.*

Chapter Fifteen

November 1946: Time to Give Up Childish Things

"It's been awhile since you've asked to see me, hasn't it, Darien?" It was more a statement than a question.

Darien jumped at the sound of Sundeep's voice behind him and stopped raking the pile of shiny brown horse chestnuts he was gathering beneath the massive tree that dominated the side yard of the Edwards' bungalow. He turned to face him. This was an unexpected visit. *I didn't do my prayer for you.* He looked away from Sundeep and dug a toe into the moist covering of leaves, still wet from an earlier rain shower. *It's been months since I prayed for him to visit, but I have other friends now. Richie and Teddy.* But of course he didn't admit to that.

He glanced up over his shoulder toward the house, looking for any sign of his mother standing at one of the bedroom windows that overlooked the backyard. He saw nothing and felt relieved.

"I've been busy with my chores and schoolwork." He looked at Sundeep but could not meet his steady gaze. He felt the clamminess of his hands and hoped Sundeep didn't know. He was uneasy when he didn't tell the whole truth.

"I understand, Darien, and I'm happy you've found friends at school. That you're getting along so well with your father and Billie."

He knows about my friends. And Daddy and Billie! Darien swayed back and forth and stared at Sundeep, still amazed at how his friend of the woods sometimes appeared so transparent that Darien could actually see right through him.

Sundeep moved closer and motioned for Darien to sit down next to him. Darien didn't move and shifted his weight onto one leg instead.

"It's time for me to speak of certain things. You're no longer a little boy, Darien. You're nearly eight. There are beliefs you have that will be challenged, even ridiculed, by other older children and adults."

"You mean like Santa Claus and the tooth fairy?"

"Yes, like that."

"I already know they don't exist. But I pretend I believe 'cause Billie told me I wouldn't get as much presents at Christmastime if I didn't. And I like finding money under my pillow." He crossed his arms and looked away again.

"But Santa does exist, Darien. Just not the way you've been told."

"What do you mean?" He was curious now and moved closer to Sundeep, choosing to sit down on the low stonewall that separated the main lawn from the wooded area to the west of the property.

"Santa Claus represents the spirit of giving ... of love. And he represents prosperity and abundance." Sundeep gestured, spreading his arms out wide. "There's a Santa in each of us, Darien. Christmas celebrates the birth of Jesus."

Darien had heard Jesus mentioned when he'd gone to Sunday school, but he didn't remember what was said about him. He watched Sundeep's gestures.

"It's a time when Christians express that love and prosperity toward others with gifts."

"Uh-huh." Darien yawned and unconsciously found himself rapidly lifting his heels up and down as his legs moved to an unheard rhythm.

"People around you will want you to grow up and give up childish things, as they like to call them. They do this because that's what they've learned to do. But you mustn't forget the ability you have to hear and see me, for that gift will grow and develop as you get older."

"I feel funny praying to make you appear. Other kids don't do that."

"You're not just another kid, Darien."

"But when I ask them if they have a special friend that can appear and disappear, they laugh at me."

"And that makes you feel different, doesn't it?"

"Yeah. And I wonder if maybe I'm crazy and just imagine seeing you."

Sundeep smiled and pointed. "And what about that handkerchief you have in your back pocket?"

Darien reached for the pocket Sundeep was pointing at and touched it to make sure the cloth was there, the one Sundeep had magically materialized and given him months before. Darien had to admit he hadn't imagined *that*. The handkerchief was proof.

"Imagination is a wonderful gift from our Creator. Your thoughts are just like an oak seed." Sundeep was animated now, moving his hands together and raising them upward and apart in a sweeping motion. "When it is nurtured, it becomes a full-grown tree. So in a way, you do create the world around you, and that includes seeing me."

"I created you?"

"You're able to see me because you believe I exist, that you can call me into your world when you pray for that to happen. That's the power of faith. The power of believing."

Darien shook his head. Sundeep's words still didn't make sense to him.

"Don't struggle to understand. Just remember, and one day, you *will* understand." Sundeep leaned closer. "What I'm about to say to you is even more important, so listen closely."

Darien sighed and shifted his weight to find a more comfortable position.

"Don't be fooled by appearances. Things aren't always what they seem. You are at a very impressionable age. Your future is going to be influenced by those very close to you. No matter what happens, no matter what is said or done to you by others, you're a very special young boy." Sundeep paused and extended one hand to Darien, lightly touching him on the chest. "You have within you the power to overcome anything. It is always with you. Remember that." Sundeep gently touched Darien on one hand.

"*You* are a good boy, and you have a very bright future. Don't let anyone else tell you differently."

Sundeep stood up, leaned forward, and effortlessly lifted Darien into the air. Holding him at eye level, he continued. "I will be with you, Darien, always. Even if you don't see me, you can hear me, if you wish to. It will be up to you, for you have that choice."

Holding Darien with just one hand, Sundeep touched his own chest with the other hand and then laid it upon Darien's. Darien felt a wave of heat flow through his entire body and, for just an instant, experienced being catapulted into a blinding white light. For that moment, he felt totally at peace. A few seconds later, he was on the ground by himself. He heard the rustling of leaves and opened his eyes. He froze when he saw his mother standing over him, her hands on her hips.

"Who were you talking to?" She looked around, a curious look on her face. It was obvious that no one else was there now.

Darien wasn't sure what to say. He didn't want to lie, but he was sure she wouldn't believe him if he told her. He fidgeted with his hands behind his back and remained mute.

"Was it that imaginary friend again, dear?" She crouched down next to him and took one of his hands in hers. "A pretend friend, maybe?" She smiled and raised her eyebrows.

Darien continued to stare at her for a moment, weighing what he should say before he answered. He decided to tell the truth. "He's real, Mom, but no one else can see him but me."

She lifted her head back and laughed and then covered her mouth as she squeezed his hand.

Darien didn't understand. He had told her the truth and she was laughing. He felt his bottom lip quiver. He tried to pull his hand away, but she held on.

"I'm sorry, dear. I wasn't laughing at you, but that's what an imaginary friend is—someone you make up in your mind. So of course no one else can see them." She rose and pulled him up with her. "Come along now. It's time for us to prepare supper."

Darien picked up his rake and followed along in silence, leaving behind the pile of shiny chestnuts. The only sounds to break the stillness were a distant birdcall and the intermittent tap of raindrops overflowing from the end of leaves in the foliage above him.

Darien silently traced his way up the grassy embankment behind his mother as they made their way back into the house. *Did Sundeep really just visit me or did I just imagine it? And why do I feel so sad?* He didn't know just why, but he knew it would be a long time before he saw Sundeep again. And that thought made him feel sad.

Chapter Sixteen

Growing Pains

If there was ever a time Darien wished he could disappear, it was when his mother took him into the bathroom and forced down his pants to look at his penis.

"Please, Mom, no!" He squirmed as she pulled down his shorts and then his Fruit of the Loom briefs. He closed his eyes tightly, but he could feel the tears flowing down his cheeks, and it felt like his skin was on fire.

"Dr. Willard said I have to make you do this. Now take it in your hand and try to pull the skin back over the head."

"It hurts when I do that!" He gingerly pulled at the foreskin to slide it back over the tip of his uncircumcised penis, but it was too tight, so he stopped.

"Honey, I know it's very uncomfortable for you, but you have to do it. It'll hurt a bit, but the skin will stretch and then you can clean your self really well. Please try again."

"It hurts!" He tried to pull away as she moved his hand aside and took his penis between her thumb and forefinger. He squirmed, pushing himself against the back of the toilet tank.

"Sit still and let me do this! It's for your own good. If we don't stretch the skin back, we'll have to have the doctor circumcise you! Do you want that?"

Darien remembered her telling him this meant a doctor would cut off part of his penis. At least that's the picture he'd formed in his head from the lengthy and frightening explanation she'd given him. He felt himself quiver all over. "No," he whined.

"Well then, just hold your breath and let me do this for you. Just a couple of times is all, okay?"

It wasn't okay, but he knew he'd live through it, just as he had each time before. He would let her, but he wasn't going to look while she did it. *Out of sight, out of mind.* He loved her, but he also hated her for doing this for the humiliation he felt each time she did this to him. Darien sat there on the toilet bowl, his legs spread slightly so she could do what she had to do. He squeezed his eyes shut and grimaced as he turned his head down and to the side, covering his face with one hand. His entire body shook. Clenching his teeth together, he held his breath until the ordeal was over.

Later that evening as he lay in bed, unable to sleep, the episode replayed in his mind and he began to cry. *There's something wrong with me. I'm different, and there's nothing I can do about it.* And with that declaration, other thoughts came flooding into his head: *My real parents didn't want me! Mom and Daddy don't either because I'm not like Billie! They just keep me 'cause they have to. I'll never fit in.* Exhausted, he drifted into a deep, deep sleep and dreamed of flying far, far away. And next to him was his friend, Sundeep.

They soared high above the treetops as the night breeze fueled their astral flight. Darien angled his arms to go higher and higher. He arched his back and zoomed down through the star-filled sky, feeling free as he passed dozens of other beings, all diving and swooping through the air around him.

He leveled off and slowed down, hovering as he waited for Sundeep to catch up with him. They exchanged knowing glances. It was as if he could feel what Sundeep was feeling and thinking. No words were necessary. They lingered there for a while, their eyes fixed on each other as they floated on the air, until Darien felt himself fade into peaceful oblivion.

He slept soundly that night. When he awoke the next morning, he remembered nothing of his night flight.

The next day began well for Darien. He felt unusually refreshed as he strode off to school, lunch pail in hand, but that changed later in the day as he sat in his homeroom class and jiggled his legs from side to side, getting up courage to ask permission. He raised his hand, already feeling a growing sense of embarrassment as the teacher, Miss Orlando, stopped her lesson and looked over the top of her large-framed glasses at him.

"What is it, Darien?" She placed a finger in between the pages of the book she was holding and closed it, pressing it up against her bosom as she embraced it with the other hand.

"I have to go to the bathroom, ma'am." He was already standing when she asked the question and was rocking from side to side as he shifted his weight from one foot to the other. Although he kept his gaze down, he knew the other children in the room were all looking at him, and that only added to his discomfort.

She checked her watch. "You can't wait until recess?"

"I don't think so, ma'am." He could have, but he wanted to go before all the other students in the elementary school were let out of their classrooms for the afternoon break. He couldn't let her know that he absolutely hated it when he had to go to the bathroom and stand at the urinal with others around him. Fear would grip him, and in that state, he was unable to pee.

His uncircumcised and undersized penis was an embarrassment to him, and it was an ordeal that lasted until he was alone and could relax.

"Very well, but be back here in five minutes." She waved at him, flipping the fingers of one hand in the air.

Darien hurried out into the hall and raced for the bathroom. He reached to push open the door, but it swung wide before him. He stopped abruptly to avoid running into the older boy in his path.

"Whoa! Where's the fire, buddy?"

"Sorry." Darien avoided direct eye contact, feeling embarrassed, although not sure why. He walked passed the boy without looking back and entered the restroom. It was then he realized one of the upper grades must have been let out early. Several youngsters stood at the line of sinks, talking and laughing as they washed their hands.

He looked over and eyed the two stalls in the far corner of the tiled room. The doors were closed on both, and he could see feet showing from beneath. *Darn! Now I'll have to use the urinal.* Flashes of his mother peering through the bathroom door when he peed into the toilet and he took too long because he was playing with himself crossed his mind as he edged into the room. He tried his best not to look at the adolescent boys lined up at the urinal, their hips thrust forward.

One of them looked over his shoulder at Darien and laughed. Darien was sure he knew why. *Why wasn't I circumcised when I was a baby, like other boys?*

His question had gone unanswered when he first asked his mother earlier that year. *No one cared* was his own answer.

Darien surveyed the far end of the urinal and saw two boys standing there. He considered trying to hold it until they had all left but knew he had to be back in his classroom soon. And besides, he couldn't hold back the urge to pee much longer.

He walked toward a vacant spot along the trough, some distance from the other two boys, and unzipped his fly. He fumbled as he worked to pull his penis out through the flap of his briefs and then strained forward so as not to urinate on his trousers. He stole a glance at his uncircumcised penis but quickly looked up at the blank wall in front of him when a third boy walked up and stood next to him.

He hated it when that happened, for no matter how hard he tried to release a stream, nothing came. He stood there, growing more self-conscious, until the boy finished and walked away. Breathing a sigh of relief, he was able to relax and empty his bladder. *Next time I'll wait until a stall is empty,* he promised himself as he finished and headed back to his class.

Chapter Seventeen

Late Fall 1947:
Fun for Billie, Not So Much for Darien

Now that Darien was old enough to walk home from school with a friend from up the street, his mother had returned to work as a nurse attendant at the nearby state school, an institution that housed people who were mentally insane, mentally handicapped, or were otherwise unwanted by family. This included babies who were Mongoloids or were handed over to the state by parents who could no longer manage them and viewed them as either dumb or incorrigible.

Billie was also old enough to watch over Darien and be home with him after school on those days he didn't have junior varsity baseball or basketball practice. On one of those days, Billie came home from baseball practice earlier than usual. Darien was happy to see him. He sometimes grew bored and restless at home by himself for the couple of hours between the end of the school day and his mother's arrival home from work. Maybe Billie would play with him, he thought.

He watched his older brother shed his school clothes and put on a T-shirt and an old pair of dungarees. Billie was growing into a young man, now almost fourteen. Darien thought he was a dead ringer for a young movie star he'd once seen pictured on a *Life* magazine cover. He frowned as he searched his memory for a name. Dean! James Dean. That was it.

"Want to wrestle, Sport?" Sport was what Billie called him, and Darien loved having a special nickname.

"Sure, but not too rough, Billie."

His brother got down on all fours, assuming the starting position for the man on the bottom. Darien got down on his knees next to him and wrapped his arms around Billie's midsection. He waited for the countdown from Billie.

"At the count of three: one, two, *three!*"

Darien gripped him as tight as he could and tried to pull him over onto one side and wrap a leg over his brother's, but Billie was much stronger. Darien knew he wasn't using all his strength to get out from under him. He knew because his brother just remained on all fours, not moving an inch as Darien struggled to gain the advantage. Unable to do it from a kneeling position, Darien raised one knee up from the living room rug and attempted to climb onto Billie's back. He panted and huffed, growing tired and still unable to move his brother. And then it was over in an instant, as he felt Billie twist out from beneath him. Before he could react, Billie was on top of him and had him pinned to the floor.

"One, two, three. Beatcha, Sport!" Billie kept his hands firmly on Darien's shoulders and raised himself into a kneeling position, but he didn't get up. He remained over him, a curious smile on his face. Darien was certain he was still kidding around, but he hadn't a clue what was going to happen next.

First the tickling routine came. Darien reacted with a giggle, for he was very sensitive. Now Billie was trying to strip his T-shirt off. He resisted, but Billie easily forced his arms in the air and pulled the shirt off. In the next instant, he saw Billie reach for his shorts.

"Hey, cut it out!" Darien struggled to keep his pants from coming off, but Billie successfully stripped both his shorts and underwear off at the same time. Now Darien was stark naked.

Darien thrashed about, kicking up toward his brother's face, but Billie ducked to one side, rolled over, and stood up, dragging Darien to his feet.

"Stop!"

"What's the matter with you? Can't take a little teasing? Poor little Darien." There was a mocking cadence to his brother's voice. He pushed Darien toward the front door now, and as panic set in, Darien let out a series of shrieks.

Billie ignored him, his arms tightly around Darien's chest as he used his own body weight to physically shove Darien, still screaming, out through the door and onto the front lawn.

A wave of rage came over him as Billie pushed him onto the ground and then raced back into the house, slamming the door shut. Darien heard the deadbolt click and felt his heart pounding in his chest as he got up and ran toward the door. He pulled at the door handle and shook it with all his might. It wouldn't open.

"Billieeeee!" He let out a long, plaintive wail before he crumpled onto the lawn in tears. He lay there sobbing for several minutes, wishing he were dead.

Darien lifted his head and craned his neck to look over the lawn embankment and down the street in the direction of the state hospital where his mother worked. He couldn't see anyone and didn't hear any cars in the distance. Thank God!

He looked down at himself and quickly covered his private area, painfully self-conscious of his smooth, pale skin. He also had no pubic hair like his older brother. The comparison only made him feel more despondent.

Darien heard the lock click again and the door open. He looked up and saw Billie standing there with an apologetic expression on his face.

"I'm sorry, Sport. I was just having fun with you."

Darien lowered his head and folded his arms in front of him, ignoring his brother. *I'll make you feel bad. One of these days I'll never come back, and then you'll be sorry.* And then another thought came to him. He looked up at Billie and glared as he felt the heat of anger rise up within him. He knew what he would do.

Darien stood and charged past Billie and into the house. Within less than a minute, he raced back and stopped abruptly, still naked, in front of Billie. He waved an envelope at his brother.

Stamped on the cover was a large colorful "First Day of Issue" imprint. It was part of a prized collection Grandpa Ferris had begun for him a year earlier when he had discovered he shared the old man's passion for collecting stamps and coins.

"You see this?" Darien wiped away tears. He felt his chin tremble as he choked back the tears that welled up in his throat. He grabbed the other corner of the envelope and tore it in two. "Now see what you made me do!" Darien looked at the two pieces of the envelope in his hands and realized what he had done. It was permanent. Destroyed. A one-of-a-kind. The rage only deepened, filling his chest with a fiery sensation. "I hate you! I HATE YOU!"

Only the second time he screamed it as loud as he could.

"Lower your voice! Mom's coming home any minute, and she'll hear you!"

Billie was right. Darien had barely enough time to slip his clothes back on when the side door flew open and she appeared in the dining room, breathing heavily, as she pulled off her woolen coat and threw it over a dining room chair.

"What's the matter with you, young man?" She was looking at Darien. "Were you trying to wake up the whole neighborhood? I could hear you all the way over to building C!" She shook her head and made a hissing sound as she exhaled.

Darien just stood there, saying nothing, his shoulders drooped. There was no point in trying to explain what Billie had done to him. Big boys don't tattle on their brother. He watched her silently as she stomped out of the room and into her bedroom and closed the door with a slam.

"Go to your room and think about your behavior!" she added loudly enough for Darien to hear her through the closed door.

He retreated into the bedroom he shared with Billie, closed the door, and flopped down on his bed. He'd messed up again.

Chapter Eighteen

A Few Weeks Later:
Darned If You Do, Darned If You Don't

"Three strikes and you're out, kiddo!"

Darien had heard his father say this to him on more than one occasion, and now, for some unknown reason, the words surfaced in his mind. He tried to block out the unsettling idea when the telephone rang, breaking into his thoughts.

"I'll get it, Mom." He rose from the living room couch where he'd been sketching and moved toward the phone in the adjoining dining room, nearly tripping on the edge of the faded living room rug.

"Let me get it, dear. I'm expecting a call from your father." She appeared from the kitchen, off the other end of the dining room, and dropped a dishtowel onto the small, corner writing desk as she reached for the phone.

Darien plopped himself back onto the couch. He picked up his sketchpad but put it back down, his mind now going over the special plans his mother had made for the next day. He broke into a smile.

It was to be a special event, the Eastern States Exposition, or fair, as his mother called it. It had everything from craft projects and paintings to livestock on exhibit. There were to be rodeo contests, amusement rides, carnival games, and concession stands. And his favorite relative, Aunt Sarah, the lady with the pretty legs, was going with them.

He glanced at his mother, sensing something wrong. She frowned as she nodded her head, either in agreement or understanding, he wasn't sure which.

"Yes, I understand." She looped a finger around the black telephone cord and moved it up and down its length.

"Of course. Yes, I'll ask him and will let you know later today. If you'd be so kind to wait for just a moment while I get out a notepad and pencil so I can write down the hospital telephone number and the room number." She reached into a cubbyhole at the back of the desk and selected a pencil from a jar filled with half-used pencils and the one prized Parker pen and pencil set that she had given her husband as a Christmas present the year after he was discharged from the navy. It was in celebration of his having secured a job as a mechanic at a Ford dealership some twenty-five miles away in the city of Springfield. "Thank you for waiting. If you'll give me the number, I'm ready to write it down." When she had the information written down, she glanced over at Darien and added faintly, "Good-bye."

Darien watched her as she lowered he head, slowly placed the receiver back into its cradle, and then stared off into space, her head moving from side to side. She sighed deeply and attempted to smooth away the furrows between her heavy brows. She hesitated, glanced over at Darien, and then walked to where he was sitting.

"What is it, Mom?"

"That was a nurse at the Bartlow Hospital. Your mother, your birth mother, is not well. She's asked to see you."

"Why?"

"She has cancer, Darien, and isn't expected to live much longer. She wants to see you before she dies."

He stiffened for a second as he tried to figure out what response was expected. He felt strangely disconnected from himself, from the news. *I don't even know her. Why would she want to see me? What do I say?* He remained silent, unable to make up his mind. "Do I have to go?"

"That's up to you, dear, but if you want to see her, we'll have to go tomorrow. I've already scheduled the day off from work and can't take another one."

Seeing her or going to the fair. Darien studied his mother's face, looking for clues as to what to say. He thought about various things she had taught him and had emphasized whenever she was explaining what was right and what was wrong. Be honest. Be mannerly. Be grateful for what you have, and always share what you have with others. And always try to please others, particularly your parents. *I have to do the right thing. Mom wants me to see this person or she wouldn't ask me,* he decided.

"So what's your answer, Darien?" She stood up and waited for a response.

"See her." He was barely able to get the words out. He automatically looked away as he did any time he wasn't telling the truth.

"Please look at me when you're speaking, Darien. I can't hear you."

"Go see her in the hospital." His heart wasn't in it, but he hoped she wouldn't notice. He waited for her reaction, but there was none. Not that he could make out, anyway. She just stood there with her arms folded and a flat expression on her face.

"Very well. I'll call your Aunt Sarah and tell her we won't be going to the fair." She turned and abruptly walked out of the room.

The next thing he heard was the closing of her bedroom door and then faint sobs. He approached the closed door and considered knocking so he could say he was sorry but thought better of it and slumped his shoulders as he moped back into the living room and flung himself onto the couch. *Darned if I do, and darned if I don't.*

Chapter Nineteen

The Next Day:
Two Strikes Out!

Darien couldn't remember ever having been in a hospital, and he had never seen a dying person before. He didn't want to look at her now, stretched out in the hospital bed, her skin pale and a vacant stare in her eyes. What do you say to a complete stranger who's dying but you don't feel anything about it, except afraid? That's how Darien was feeling as he stood just inside the darkened hospital room, his eyes pleading for permission to leave.

The only mother he now knew stood behind him, gently nudging him into the room. "She wants to spend some time with you, Darien. Just you."

"Please, Mom, stay in the room with me!" It was a whispered plea.

"Be brave."

"But Mom!"

She shook her head and backed out the door, shutting it behind her. Darien stood there, the only feelings those of his trembling legs. He inhaled a large breath, trying to slow the beating in his chest. He caught a whiff of a rancid odor in the room and felt a wave of nausea.

Be brave.

He looked around the barren room. Pale green walls in need of a fresh coat of paint gave it a neglected look. A narrow window opened out on the parking lot, now wet and dreary looking from the morning rain. A small metal bedside table and an adjustable serving cart, pushed to one side, were the only other pieces of furniture in the room along with the single hospital bed with her in it.

Darien timidly approached the foot of the bed and stared. *Make this be over quick.*

The woman stirred as Darien's presence registered in her eyes, and she struggled to get into an upright position. Her sunken chest rose and fell as she took in shallow breaths, the cords in her neck rigid. Raspy sounds escaped from her throat. She motioned him over to her side, turning her head away as she coughed and attempted to clear her throat.

"Nice boy." The words were slurred and barely audible.

He stepped closer, near enough for her to reach him. *Gosh, but I hate this! What am I supposed to do?* He stood there and allowed her to take his limp hand in hers. Lifting his gaze from the frail form outlined by the sheets, Darien took in the gaunt face with the haunting expression. Was she in pain or silently begging for something?

"I didn't have a choice … giving you up, I mean." Her words were faint, but he could hear them. He just didn't understand what they meant. In the several years that had passed since his adoption, not once had his new parents ever made any further mention about his birth mother or who his father might be. And he hadn't asked. He hadn't known what the questions should even be. It seemed to be a topic best avoided … buried in the past. He accepted the unknowing in silence and grew used to the empty feeling that sometimes rose up from his stomach when he wondered about that time in his life. The feeling was there now, but he was too numb to do anything about it.

She continued to hold his hand and gently caressed it with the other. The silence hung in the sterile room, broken only by an occasional murmur he couldn't make out. He remained there, motionless, until he could bear the oppressive feeling no longer. He yanked his hand away and dashed out of the room, into the waiting arms of his mother. Thank God it was over!

Or was it? He raised his head and peered up at her. Her face was not so boney and lifeless as the woman lying in the hospital room, but there was that same pained expression. Her arms were around him, but he sensed a tension in her hug. *What did I do wrong now?* She took his hand but said nothing and strode toward the elevators.

The silence of the drive back home made the trip seem twice as long. He glanced over at her several times. He even touched her arm lightly, but she looked straight ahead. He had done what he was supposed to do, deciding to go see the woman in the hospital when he'd really had his heart set on going to the big fair. *Why does she seem mad at me?*

He sneaked one last peek in her direction. Now she was scowling and her lips moved, hinting at some private conversation she was holding with someone. Or preparing for one *they* would be having when they arrived home.

She slammed the car door when she got out and marched into the house. More silence. Darien went straight to his room and sat on his bed, dread building with each passing moment. He strained to hear the sounds coming out of the kitchen where she was. They sounded normal. He could hear the clatter of dishes as she took them from the cupboard and set the table for supper. *Oops! That was supposed to be my chore!* He jumped up and raced into the kitchen.

"I'll do that, Mom." He reached for the napkins, but she grabbed them from his hands.

He let his hands drop to his sides. "What's wrong, Mom?"

She set the napkins down on the table and stared back at Darien, shaking her head. "Do you realize how much your father and I have sacrificed just so you and Billie could have the things you need and want?"

She's mad all right. He just didn't know why.

"What did I do, Mom?" He sighed and sank onto the chair next to the stove as he lowered his head, preparing to find out. There was silence. He raised his head and saw her taking him in. Only this time he saw sadness, not anger, in her eyes.

"What, Mom?"

She took out a Kleenex from her housedress pocket and dabbed at the corner of one eye. "I just don't think you love me, Darien."

He didn't know what love was or what it felt like, but he knew he *should* love her. He wanted her to believe he did, even if he didn't feel it.

He'd done something wrong yesterday, he was sure, although he didn't know what. Now today he'd screwed up again and he couldn't figure out how. *Maybe there's something wrong with me.* He thought again about his father's statement. *How many strikes have I already had?* He could think of several that might count. He knew for certain he'd had at least two. *When will the next one come?*

"I'm sorry, Darien. I guess I expect too much from you. Let's forget the whole matter and finish setting the table. Your father will be home soon and so will Billie." She bent forward, lifted one corner of her apron, and wiped away tears from her face. She straightened and turned to stir the day-old stew.

Darien stood up and walked over to the small cabinet on the far side of the stove. "All three pieces of silverware, Mom, or just a fork and knife?"

"All three will be fine, dear," she said evenly.

She didn't seem upset any longer. But Darien still wasn't sure.

He thought about all that had happened that day—their hospital visit to see the woman who'd given birth to him and his own behavior during all of it. *I shouldn't have got scared and been such a crybaby about it!* "Just be brave" was what she'd said. "Don't show those kinds of feelings." He considered his mother's reactions to nearly everything—just going on as if nothing had happened. What had his mother said once? "Peace at all costs. Act as if nothing is wrong." Yes, that is how he would deal with things from now on.

He checked the table setting twice to make sure it would meet with her approval and then glanced up at his mother. "Did I do it right?"

"Perfectly, dear. Perfectly."

Chapter Twenty

The Beginnings of Tissue Damage

Darien gingerly removed his shoes and socks as he prepared for his ritual Saturday night bath. Seated on the toilet seat cover, he lifted one foot up and set it on his other knee and bent over to examine the sores between his toes. The skin around them was reddened and oozing a pus that reminded him of the stuff that accompanied the huge boils he had been prone to for most of his time he'd been living with the Edwardses.

This condition was different, however. The sores were extremely painful and seemed to be getting bigger and bigger, spreading all around the toes and leaving raw, exposed flesh between them. He hadn't wanted to tell his mother because then she'd maybe make him go to see their family doctor and he didn't like doctors, particularly after the time he was forced to see the local dentist because of an abscessed tooth.

The dentist had been a mean-spirited Japanese man who had no patience with scared little kids and had forced Darien to sit in the chair and have the abscessed tooth pulled out with an ominous-looking pair of dental pliers without benefit of any pain medication. Darien had let out such a blood-curdling scream that his mother heard him out in the waiting room and rushed into the room where she likely imagined her young boy being brutalized. She realized he wasn't, but Darien was never taken back there again and instead was driven into a nearby city to a dentist that a friend of hers had recommended.

Darien glanced down at the white socks he'd just removed and saw the pinkish stains at the tip of them, telltale signs that his mother would surely see when she did the wash. Now he had to tell her, and he wasn't looking forward to it. With her being trained in the field of nursing, he knew she would closely inspect the condition and probably try some of the home medications she kept stored in the bathroom medicine chest. He hated the attention and, more to the point, knew she'd end up taking him to see the family doctor.

Then an idea came to him. Perhaps if he tried to wash out the socks he could remove most of the stain and she wouldn't see it. He quickly dropped them into the sink and ran water over them as he took hand soap and, placing a sock on each of his hands, scrubbed them together. He rinsed them out and examined them again. He'd gotten most of the stain out, he thought, so he lifted the clothes hamper and buried them under the top pile of clothes. He felt better already. Maybe the condition would clear up by itself. He certainly hoped so. He managed to hide the condition from his mother by making sure he kept colored socks on until he went into the bathroom for his weekly bath. He even kept socks on while he slept at night, saying his feet were cold if he didn't. The real reason was he didn't want the sores to stain the sheets because she might see it when she stripped the beds every Saturday to do the laundry.

But a week later, the condition had only grown worse. He had difficulty walking without a great deal of pain when he bent his toes and the area above his toes were now beginning to swell to the point where his shoes were tight. He had successfully masked his discomfort at home, so his mother didn't seem to notice, but his fifth-grade teacher noticed his limp and called him up to her desk.

"Darien, you've been limping a bit over the past few days. What's wrong?" she whispered to him, not wanting the class members in the front to overhear the conversation.

"Nothing, Mrs. Legrand," he said, trying hard to appear okay.

"I'm not so sure that's the case, Darien. Sit down here next to me and take one of your shoes off." She waited, giving him a look that said she wasn't going to take no for an answer.

Darien sat and bent over, slowly untying the laces of one of the shoes. Pushing it off with the other foot, he paused and then sighed, knowing her continued stare meant also take off the sock. It stuck to the ooze as he began to pull it off. As soon as it was fully in sight, Mrs. Legrand uttered a hushed "Oh my goodness!"

"Is the other foot as bad as this?" she asked, bending over a little closer to see the wounds. "Does your mother know about this, or have you been hiding it from her?"

When he looked away, she had her answer.

"Put your sock back on, and if you can, put the shoe back on as well. Then I want you to pick up your books and things and head down to the nurse's office and wait for me." She checked her watch. It was nearly two-thirty, almost time for school to let out. She knew Darien's mother worked until five and that it was also likely Darien's older brother would be at senior varsity basketball practice. She had no way to contact his mother at work and she didn't want Darien trying to ride his bicycle home now that she knew that his feet were in such a condition. She also didn't want to call his father who she knew worked in a nearby city and wouldn't take kindly to the idea of his having to leave work to pick up Darien.

The next best idea was to call the bus driver who handled the route closest to where Darien lived. Maybe he hadn't left home yet, and she could catch him to request that he include Darien in his pick up and delivery to their home since it was on their route. She gave her class instructions to continue their reading assignment and to behave while she stepped out of the room and then hurried off down the hallway to the nurse's office.

Darien was already seated in the empty office; the nurse was only there in the mornings. Mrs. Legrand stepped by Darien around to the nurse's desk and sat, reaching for the telephone as she did so. She scanned the desktop until she found the single page listing of all the school staff, which included the names, addresses, and telephone numbers of the school bus drivers as well as all other individuals who were paid by the school system. She quickly scanned through it until she found the name she was looking for and dialed the number listed. It rang five or six times before she heard someone pick up on the other end.

"Alfred, this is Sally Legrand. At middle school. Yes, I'm glad I caught you. When you get here to pick up the kids, Darien Edwards is going to be getting on your bus. Yes, he lives very close to you, actually. Yeah, I'd appreciate it if you'd drop him off at his house on your way home. No, I don't want to get into it right now." She turned away and faced the window behind the desk and lowered her voice to barely a whisper. "He's sitting beside me so I can't really talk. There's just a good reason why he needs to be driven home today. Okay? Wonderful."

She swung back around and hung up the phone. "Darien, you're going to go home today on the bus. Mr. Johnson, the bus driver, is going to take you home at the end of his run. He lives quite close to you. I'll arrange for one of the other boys in your class to put your bicycle in the storage room until your mother says it's okay for you to ride it back and forth to school. Okay?"

"Won't she be mad at me for leaving my bike at school? I mean, I think I can ride it okay. My feet only hurt a little." Darien was now feeling very nervous and upset about the whole situation. He knew that even if his mom wasn't mad, his father would be and he'd hear about it.

The bike was an old secondhand one his father had bought from a family friend and had given to Darien the year before as a Christmas gift. It had seemed like the best gift he could have received, for once Billie showed him how to ride it and keep his balance, it gave him a new sense of freedom. He could go on rides in his grandfather's orchard across the street and along the dirt road that connected his street to another main road east of where they lived. The dirt road ran through a heavily wooded section of property that was owned by an uncle. Darien loved to ride or even walk through the surrounding woods and would spend hours by himself, dreaming about when he'd be old enough to leave home and make a home for himself, always visualizing a modest shack in a woodland setting that was filled with birds and animals and they all were his friends. No humans. Just animals. It gave him a feeling of peace as the images floated into his mind. And they also brought with them thoughts of Sundeep. He realized it had been a very long while since he'd seen or even thought about him.

Remembering how much better and more hopeful he always felt about life after one of Sundeep's visits, Darien wished he could make him appear right there in the nurse's office, but of course that wouldn't happen with Mrs. Legrand being there. And then his mind quickly returned to his worry about what his father would say about leaving the bike at school.

Mrs. Legrand spoke, interrupting his thoughts. "I'm sure both your mother and father will understand. And I'll call them early this evening and explain why you've been sent home on the bus. So don't you worry, Darien."

He nodded. *Maybe I'll have time before Mom gets home to let Sundeep know I need to see him,* he thought. That buoyed his spirits a bit. Darien could hardly wait to get home.

Chapter Twenty-One

Believe It or Not

The bus ride from the school to the end of the normal route Alfred Johnson drove took less than forty-five minutes, and in another five minutes, Darien was deposited outside his home. With his schoolbooks tucked under one arm, he carefully stepped off the bus and waved a good-bye over his shoulder as he made his way up the sidewalk to the side door.

He stooped down, lifted the mat, and picked up the skeleton key that was always left there. In a community this small, nearly everyone knew one another and the idea of someone breaking into someone else's home just wasn't a concern that was ever raised by the Edwards or anyone else, for that matter. People rarely locked their doors in fact, but because the state institution was located just on the other side of the railroad tracks, barely five hundred yards away, Darien's parents had decided it was best to be safe. Patients committed to living in the institution occasionally jumped over the fence or simply walked out of one of the gates that were also not locked. And while they never gave Darien a reason to be afraid of them, he suspected that might be the reason his parents decided to start locking the doors. That was enough for a bit of fear to register in the back of his mind.

Darien stole a quick glance around him, particularly off to his right in the direction of the backyard and the thickly wooded section of trees and underbrush that blocked most of the railroad tracks and the institutional buildings that lay beyond the chain-link fence surrounding the institution grounds. That was where he feared any escapee would hide and from where he would suddenly appear if he were trying to run away. Or worse yet, wanted to break into their home. But he saw no one and quickly unlocked the dining room door and entered, closing the door behind him with a slam.

Dropping his books on the dining room buffet, he continued on into his room and shed his light jacket and sat on the edge of his bed to take off his shoes. Leaving his socks on, he got up and limped out of the bedroom and into the kitchen where he took a glass out of the cupboard, set it down, and reached into the refrigerator for a quart container of Kool-Aid his mother always kept there for him and Billie. He filled his glass and then went into the living room where he slumped onto the couch and set his drink down. It was time.

He closed his eyes and quietly murmured the prayer Sundeep had taught him, but nothing happened, so he repeated it again, a little louder. "Please, Sundeep, come and let me see you now!" Still nothing. Darien squinted more tightly and decided to place his hands in a prayer position in front of him. "Pleeeeze, Sundeep! I really need to see you and talk with you!" He felt a tear at the edge of one eye and brushed it away with the back of one finger. And then he felt a breeze, as if someone had opened a window and a burst of wind had entered from outside. He felt like he wasn't alone any longer. He opened his eyes, and as he turned, he saw Sundeep sitting next to him.

Darien felt his heart flutter with excitement and then begin to slow down as he felt a calm wash over him. Without thinking, he leaned toward Sundeep and the two of them moved into an embrace that Darien wished would last forever. But after a few moments, Sundeep let go of Darien and sat back with a look of deep concern.

"You've been having some challenges, haven't you, Darien?" he said, more a statement than a question.

"I'm okay. Really," Darien replied, attempting to convince Sundeep as well as himself.

"Your body doesn't agree with that and is trying to tell you something." Sundeep reached over and laid a hand on one of Darien's feet.

Darien cocked his head to one side, confusion on his face. He could not fathom how his feelings had anything to do with the condition of his feet. "I don't understand," he said.

"Let me try to explain. Ever since you were just a tiny embryo lying in your birth mother's womb, you've had to protect yourself from being hurt by the people and situations around you. Feeling like you didn't have enough power by yourself to make things change, you've simply been holding all those emotions and fear and, yes, even anger inside. Do you understand what I'm telling you so far?"

Darien knew that was what he did every time he felt hurt or rejected or powerless to change a situation, whether it be with his father or Billie or kids at school or even his mother, whom he loved dearly but sometimes hated for how she treated him when she got angry. "Yes, I think so."

"Those emotions have a great deal of power, Darien. Left unexpressed or not understood, they remain bottled up inside you, and they begin to express their power in a damaging way. Like by causing your earaches and the high fevers you sometimes run and even by eating away at your physical body, like this condition you have between the toes of your feet. And those dizzy spells you have when you're alone, when you begin to twirl around in circles and it feels to you like some outer force is doing it to you and you can't stop it until you fall down."

Darien's eyes widened in disbelief. "How do you know about that?"

"Darien, I told you a long time ago. I am *always* with you."

"Then why don't you *do* something and *stop* all those bad and crazy things from happening to me?" He was becoming angry now and it showed, as his voice grew louder.

"Because these things that happen to you, at least a many of them, are ways your body is trying to release all those negative and damaging emotions and thoughts. Your body is trying to get your attention and maybe even the attention of your parents. It's telling you to let go of all those thoughts and emotions that don't feel good."

Sundeep became still, bent forward, and laid his hands on both of Darien's feet. He closed his eyes and began to murmur some kind of chant Darien couldn't quite hear or understand. Within seconds, he began to feel tremendous heat all around his feet. The warmth seemed to permeate his skin and enter into the entire foot. It then began to travel up into his legs and through his entire body, out through his fingertips. He even felt a surge of heat vibrate up into his neck and head and seemingly out through the top of his head. Or was it now the other way around? Was it also flowing *into* his head and down through his body and meeting the other heat flow near the center of his body? Around his heart? He wasn't certain, but he knew this: all the pain had disappeared from his feet!

Darien stooped down and pulled off one sock. The swelling had disappeared and the oozing sores between the toes appeared to be drying up. The crevices of raw flesh were getting smaller. He felt excitement grow within him as he pulled off the other sock. That foot also looked much better than it had just a few minutes ago. He stared at Sundeep in disbelief. Unable to express himself, he sat in silence.

Sundeep opened his eyes and brought his hands back into his lap as his gaze met Darien's. They held it for several moments before he spoke again. "What just happened, Darien, is explained in many ways. Some would call it a spontaneous healing. Others would say it was a miracle, and some would insist that it hadn't really happened, that it wasn't as bad as what you and I saw just a few minutes ago. They would say we were exaggerating because they couldn't believe such a thing unless they saw it happen with their own eyes. And even then they might not believe it. They would convince themselves that it was some kind of magic, an illusion.

"What most people don't realize and don't believe is that, as children of God, of the One Source, the Infinite, we are all created in the image of God, perfect and whole and complete in every way. But many, many people believe they are born in sin and that we need to spend this life making up for those sins. We are in truth one with God and all that is. And all that God is is good and perfect. There is no separation, except in our minds. When we start to see ourselves as separate from God, we lose that connection and become limited. We start to live our lives as limited beings, only operating with our basic senses.

"We understand according to what we can see, hear, smell, taste, and touch, and a large part of that understanding is based upon what others tell us, particularly when we're as young and impressionable as you are. But there is much more at work here, many more powers you have within you. And if you'll learn to use them, you will be amazed at how your life can be transformed and changed!" Sundeep stopped talking and watched Darien trying to absorb and understand all he'd just said.

Darien's concern now wasn't so much about the healing but about what was he going to do when his mother came home and there was nothing wrong? How was he going to explain why he'd ridden home on the bus instead of riding his bike home? And what about the call his mother would be receiving from the teacher? His mother and father would both believe he'd somehow lied to the teacher and made up a story to get attention. Then he'd be in *big* trouble!

Darien was *very* confused. Yes, he'd seen the transformation of the wounds on his feet take place, right before his very eyes. But had it *really* happened or were his eyes deceiving him? Had Sundeep somehow cast a magic spell over him, causing him to see what wasn't real? As much as he wanted to believe Sundeep, Darien was filled with doubt. He could hear the voices in his head telling him, "You're too old to continue believing in magic or miracles! And stop believing that this secret friend, this so-called 'Merlin,' even exists except in your mind!" He hadn't been told that in so many words, but the message his mother gave him was just that. Like Billie had told him, Santa doesn't really exist. *And neither does Sundeep!* Darien thought.

Darien glanced down at his feet and let out a gasp. Both his feet were swollen and puffier than before, and the raw flesh oozed a yellowish pus that looked more infected than it had before Sundeep had appeared. It was when he looked over to where Sundeep had been sitting that he realized he wasn't there anymore. He had vanished into thin air.

Darien let out a sigh and hung his head. He couldn't recall a time when he'd felt more alone. For all the hope that Sundeep had inspired and instilled in him over the past few years of his time as part of the Edwards family, he now felt lost and isolated in a world where he just didn't seem to fit in.

Darien reached down and gingerly put his socks back on, stood up, and painfully made his way back into his bedroom to lay down on his bed. He felt more tired than he could ever remember feeling before. He would let himself fall to sleep and wait for whatever was going to happen to him when his parents came home. And he was certain his dreams would not be about flying free in the sky with his friend, Sundeep. No, the hope for any of that had disappeared in the living room just a few minutes ago.

Darien allowed the pain in his feet to replace the ache he felt in his heart as he drifted off to sleep and into a darker kind of dream that would remind him of his true reality, one he would keep tightly sealed off from anyone else.

Chapter Twenty-Two

A Day Later: Another Trial

The episode with Darien being sent home from school on the bus and his parents receiving the call from his teacher that evening had unfolded as he had feared. They were upset, mostly because he had hidden the condition from them for so long but also because his father felt he'd acted like a sissy and could have ridden his bike home if he'd had any backbone and told the teacher that. His mother was more understanding and had the last word; she would take him to their family doctor and get it treated.

The next day she called the doctor and was told he could squeeze in an appointment to see Darien that very afternoon. Then she called the school office and let them know Darien would be absent and gave them the reason. Later that day, the family doctor, Dr. Willard, examined both of Darien's feet and diagnosed it as a case of impetigo, a common bacterial skin infection. He prescribed a topical cream to be used daily and then asked Darien to unbutton his trousers and slip his pants and underwear down so he could give him a shot of antibiotics to get a jump-start on destroying the bacteria.

Darien complied with the order and squeezed his eyes shut so he wouldn't see the needle. He held his breath and only winced a little as he felt the prick of the needle jab into his buttocks. As soon as it was over, he hoisted his shorts and trousers back up and buckled his belt.

"He needs to stay off his feet for a few days and let those toes air. No socks for at least the next three days," he said as he helped Darien put his socks and shoes back on. "You'll need to wash them each morning and apply more fresh salve, but it should clear up by the end of the week, and then you can let him return to school."

"What could have been the cause of this condition, doctor?" His mom broke into a coughing spell and pulled a handkerchief out of her sleeve and covered her mouth. It continued and she turned away, coughing into her hanky as her face grew red and the tendons in her neck bulged to the surface. "Excuse me, please. Just a little cough. Nothing serious, doctor. Now, as I was saying, I'm familiar with the medical term impetigo from my nurse's training, and I understand it is contagious on contact. So I should make sure I wash my hands well after I bathe his feet and put on the salve, right?"

"Yes, and so should he if he's going to be in contact with anyone else in the family, although by the time you let him go back to school, that shouldn't be an issue for other kids in his class."

"Is this how he …" She again broke out into a convulsive, racking cough and had to stop talking until she could catch her breath.

"How long have you had that cough, Virginia? That doesn't sound good. Maybe you should make an appointment to see me about it."

"Oh, no, it's really nothing, Dr. Willard. I just need to catch my breath, that's all." She took a couple of deeper breaths and then continued. "I was just asking how he contracted it. From someone at school? Maybe I should remind the school nurse of this."

"It could be the case, but it could also be if he was under extreme stress. Has anything happened that might've been a stressor for him? At school or at home?" The doctor paused and laced his hands together in front of his rather portly midsection as he leaned back in his chair.

"No. At least I can't think of anything," she said before turning to Darien who now had his head down as he avoided eye contact and looked at the white-tiled floor. "Did something happen at school, Darien? Something you didn't tell me about?"

Darien lifted his gaze until he was looking directly at his mother. *What makes you think it has to be something that happened at school?* he thought. "No, Mom. Nothing," he said. He then looked away again and pretended to focus on the medical certificates that lined the walls of the room.

If Darien had been asked again to be completely truthful, he couldn't have explained even if he tried. After all, how do you explain feelings and senses you have when even *you* don't understand them? And how do you talk to your mother or father about thoughts that enter your mind? Thoughts about wishing you were dead because sometimes you feel like it would be better for everyone if you were? Thoughts that tell you you're a misfit. That you don't *really* belong. No, those were thoughts you keep to yourself.

The doctor shifted his attention back to Darien's mother and said, "Well, it's possible he could've picked it up from someone at school or even from another friend or someone he came in contact with. It's hard to pin down the source of such conditions. Just make sure he keeps to himself and washes his hands real well if he happens to itch his feet. And he shouldn't do that anyway. Okay, Darien?" he added, looking at Darien. He finished writing a prescription for the medication and handed it to Darien's mother.

"No, sir. I won't." Darien stood up, wanting to leave and end this visit.

Mrs. Edwards stood and thanked Dr. Willard as she headed out after Darien. But then she stopped and turned around to face the doctor, who had followed her out into the waiting room. "If you'll send us the bill for the visit and shot, we'll mail you our payment next month, if that's all right?"

"That'll be fine, Virginia."

"Thanks, Dr. Willard. Maybe we'll see you and your wife at the Eastern Star banquet in a few weeks." She quickly turned without waiting for an answer and disappeared out the office door, picking up her pace to catch up to Darien who was already beginning to walk along Main Street in the direction toward home. Catching up with him, she took his hand and slowed him down to her pace, still trying to catch her breath.

"You're wheezing, Mom. Are you sure you're okay?" He was a little worried, particularly because of the doctor's remark. Over the past several weeks, Darien had noticed she'd been having some difficulty breathing. At least that's how it looked when she'd lift her shoulders as she tried to take in air, sometimes even gasping a little. And then it would seem to go away and she'd appear fine. But now he wondered as the two of them continued their mile-and-a-half walk back home, both in silence, each deep in their own private thoughts. Concerned, Darien kept sneaking a quick peek at her every block or so to make sure she wasn't still having trouble with her breathing.

Over the past year, Darien had begun to notice differences between his mother and the mothers of other young children his age. She was taller and bonier than other mothers and women friends of hers. And it didn't escape his awareness that some of her housedresses seemed too big for her … like maybe she'd lost weight.

An unusual observation for a boy his age, it would seem, but Darien had learned to pay attention to little things in the Edwards household, mostly because he felt he needed to do things perfectly. He figured out if he watched others do certain things, he could learn from those details and also do them right. It was a way for him to win favor, particularly with his father, who seemed to notice any little thing he did wrong, and he wanted to avoid that at all costs.

Darien glanced up at his mother again. She seemed okay now, and he tried to think about something else. Out of habit, he found himself thinking, *Bad, bad, go away! Come again another day.* And he felt a little calmer. It was his own form of prayer, sort of like "casting out the demons," a phrase he'd heard in church on more than one occasion.

They were almost home, and that nearly always felt good to Darien. For all the doubt and uncertainty he felt at times, he knew at some level that this was a good home, a good family, and that he was most fortunate to be able to be a part of it, even if he didn't feel like he deserved it. Darien knew this woman he called Mom was the main reason why he felt so fortunate. He had to believe she would always be there for him in her own quiet way. Whatever God was up there would look out for her and not let anything bad happen to her. That's what Darien hoped, anyway.

They reached the bottom of the hill, right at the intersection of the gravel road he so loved to ride his bike on and their street.

Darien picked up his pace and trotted on toward the house, leaving his mother behind. As he arrived at the front door and lifted the doormat to get the key, he heard his mother cry out. When he turned, he saw her collapse onto the sidewalk. He raced back down the steps and knelt down next to her as panic set in.

"Mommy, Mommy!" he screamed, taking hold of one of her shoulders and shaking it.

She rolled her head to one side and made an attempt to lift herself back up, but she was unable to and simply grabbed at her chest and wheezed as she tried to catch her breath. Between gasps, she managed to speak. "G-g-go over to Auntie S-S-Sarah's house … tell her … come over … right away!"

Darien saw her close her eyes and grimace as she fought to take in air. He started screaming as he stood up and ran toward the weatherworn farmhouse across the street. "Auntie Sarah! Uncle Eddie! Mommy's dying!" Tears now ran down his face as he raced up the hill to their front door and started banging on it wildly. The curtain that covered the glass window was pulled to one side, and Darien saw his aunt peering through the opening. "Auntie Sarah! Mommy's fallen down and can't breathe! She needs to get to a doctor!" he pleaded, now beginning to stomp up and down as he again pounded on the storm door.

The inside door opened wide and an attractive, young woman appeared, gesturing for him to step back so she could open up the storm door without hitting him with it. As she opened up the outside door, she turned and shouted out over her shoulder, "Honey! Something's happened to your sister! She's fallen down and is having some kind of attack. We need to get her to a doctor right away!"

Darien grabbed her by one sleeve and pulled on it as he tried to get her to run back with him to help his mother. Sarah Winters pulled her arm away and quickly ran ahead of Darien in long strides as she caught a glimpse of her sister-in-law lying on the sidewalk across the street from them. Within seconds, she was on the ground next to Darien's mother. She could see that Virginia was breathing, although with difficulty. Her eyes were open but didn't seem to be focused, as if she weren't able to see.

"Virginia, can you hear me? It's Sarah! Darien says you fell. Eddie's coming right over, and we're gonna get you to the doctor. You go to Dr. Willard, right? I think that's what you said the last time we spoke." Sarah grabbed Virginia's arm and checked for a pulse. She thought it was a bit erratic, but she wasn't a nurse and so wasn't sure. She looked over her shoulder toward her home across the street and frowned. Her husband was evidently still in the house. "Eddie!" she shouted. "Get over here!" Then she heard the sound of a car engine turn over and realized he'd pulled their car out of its garage and was driving over to save precious time. Within less than a minute, Eddie pulled into the driveway, put the car into neutral, and pulled on the brakes. He jumped out and ran around to the back door and opened it.

Without a word, he moved in next to Darien's mother and swooped his sister up in one motion and carried her to the car. He carefully slid her onto the backseat and positioned her so her head and upper torso rested against the seat and the other door. He gently bent her legs and placed her feet on the floor so he could close the door.

"Sarah, I'll take her up to Dr. Willard's office while you take Darien to their house and help quiet him down. You should call Dr. Willard and let him know what's happened and that I'm bringing Virginia in to have him take a look and see what needs to be done. And if you or Darien can find his father's work number, you should call him and let him know this may be serious." He kissed her lightly and then walked around to the driver's door, got in and, releasing the brake and putting the car in reverse, backed out onto the street and roared off up the street.

Tears streamed down Darien's face as he watched the car disappear up the roadway and out of sight. *Will I ever see her again?* he wondered. The thought was more than he could handle, and he began to whisper his chant, "Bad, bad, go away! Come again another day!" Darien buried his face into the waist of his favorite aunt as they made their way into his house. What he could not see was the energy force of Sundeep floating along behind him, holding the crisis in a healing light very few get to see.

Chapter Twenty-Three

The Loss of Innocence

Darien awoke with a start, and it took him a minute to orient himself. The last thing he recalled was seeing his mother rushed away in his uncle's car and nothing else. He looked over and saw his Aunt Sarah sitting at the desk chair. She smiled and said, "Your mom is going to be okay, Darien. The doctor thinks he knows what the problem is and assures us she's going to get better. She just needs lots of rest, and he's given her some medicine that's going to help her get her strength back and also help her breathe more easily."

"Is she here, Auntie Sarah? Is she back home?" He got up and started toward the bedroom door.

"The doctor had her taken to Holyoke Hospital for a couple of days so they can run some tests and keep an eye on her to make sure the medicine is working. Your dad is there now, making sure she's getting the best of care, but he'll be home tonight after visiting hours are over."

Images of the shrunken form of his biological mother lying in her hospital bed immediately flooded Darien's mind, and he tried to hold back the terror and the tears. Soon the fear was crowded out by thoughts that only resulted in more tears. *Everybody leaves you, one way or another. You don't matter enough.*

You're the cause of this! If you were a better boy, this wouldn't have happened.

Darien reached into the breast pocket of his shirt, suddenly remembering the magical handkerchief Sundeep had given him a long time ago. It wasn't there! He quickly walked over to the closet door and checked the pockets of the other shirts he had hanging in there. Then he checked all the pockets of his jackets and even his pants. Nothing. It had disappeared! He went to the bureau and opened his drawers. It wasn't there either!

"What're you looking for, Darien?" his aunt asked.

"Nothing that important, Auntie Sarah," he said. His heart sank as he focused on just one thought: *Mom was right. I imagined all of it! Sundeep. The magical handkerchief. All of it!* He felt the life force drain out of him as he let go of all that had sustained him for the past years he'd spent as a part of the Edwards family. The kindness he'd felt and the wisdom he thought he'd heard from Sundeep had all been wishful thinking he'd dreamed up just to make himself feel better. He sighed and then turned around, crawled back into his bed, wrapped his pillow over his head, and mumbled, "I think I'll sleep some more, Auntie Sarah." And before she could ask him to repeat what he'd said, he was deep into sleep, insulated by the darkness he craved.

Chapter Twenty-Four

A Few Months Later

Several months had past. The bacterial infection in Darien's feet had cleared and Virginia Edwards was reasonably well again. She'd been able to return to work and now had a lot more energy and stamina. Tests at the hospital revealed she had two conditions: the early stages of what was diagnosed as an asthmatic condition and pernicious anemia.

When asked if she smoked, she finally admitted that while she only smoked a few cigarettes a day in the presence of her family, it was quite another matter when she was walking to and from work or when she was alone in the house or out grocery shopping by herself. In those situations, she was a chain smoker. The nurse then asked additional questions. What brand did she smoke? Lucky's or Pall Malls, she had told them, although more often than not, she rolled her own and used Raleigh's Cigarette and Pipe Tobacco. That she didn't tell them, though. Nor did she tell Dr. Willard during one of his follow-up home visits.

She made an effort to cut way back on her smoking, but it was a tough habit for her to break, so she settled for lighting one up only on very special occasions, like when she and Darien's father were having a highball with friends or when the urge just became too great. Then she would slip out the side door, walk down to the lower level, and enter through the cellar door into "the cave," as Darien called it, where she'd prop herself up against a stool and light up. If either Billie, Darien, or her husband had been a fly on the wall down there, they'd have seen her routine after each cigarette fix: she would grind the butt out under one shoe and then pick it up, remove the outer paper, and shred the remaining tobacco into the coal bin and finally stir up the coal with a shovel until no signs of her secret remained.

If the truth were to be known, Darien had already discovered her secret one day when he was given the task of adding a couple of shovels of coal to the furnace and found the remnants of the tobacco and small bits of paper. But he knew better than to say anything to anyone. He had his secrets, and she had hers.

As for the anemic condition, she was given a prescription for vitamin B12 shots. Since she'd had nearly two years' training as a nurse, Dr Willard allowed her to give herself the shots, which she did every day without fail. She also began eating fried onions and beef liver (calves liver when she wanted to splurge and have a treat) at least once a week. Darien liked the taste of it and also asked to have it whenever she planned to cook it for herself. For the rest of the family, who hated the texture, taste, and smell of liver in any form, she fried minute steak, which she would prepare by shaking a liberal dose of meat tenderizer on it and then pounding the piece of meat with the edge of a small plate, crisscrossing it into the grain until a grid pattern was deeply imbedded into the gristly cut of beef. With a bit of Worcester sauce added they were quite happy with it.

It was after just such a meal that Billie and Darien, having finished their supper chores, stepped outside and trotted down the driveway into the backyard and sat down in two green Adirondack chairs. Neither of them spoke. Billie stared off into the wooded area that surrounded their property, mindlessly scraping away at the emerald green paint that was beginning to flake off the arms of the chair, revealing yet another layer of federal blue from the previous paint job several years ago.

Darien seemed preoccupied with trying to pick up a large dandelion weed with the tips of his two sneakers. But his mind was elsewhere, trying to figure out how to start the conversation.

Sensing that Darien had something important on his mind, Billie broke the silence. "I know something's on your mind. What is it?"

Still more silence.

"Come on, Darien. What do you want to ask me?"

"Is Mom going to get better? *Really* better?" Darien struggled to contain the tears he felt welling up in his eyes, quickly brushing them away with the back of one hand.

Billie remained silent a few seconds too long, and Darien began to sob.

"I knew it! She's really sick and isn't going to get better. She's going to die just like my other mother died!" He crossed his arms on one of the broad wooden chair arms and buried his head into them, no longer even attempting to hide his grief.

Billie leaned over and put an arm over his shoulder, patting him gently as he spoke. "That's not necessarily true, Darien. Yes, she's pretty sick, but she's going to get better. Haven't you seen an improvement already? The shots and the medication she's taking for her breathing are helping her a lot."

He didn't sound very convincing to Darien, but he wanted to believe what Billie was saying was true and his words of encouragement helped. *But what if Billie wasn't telling him the whole truth? What if she does die?*

"But what if you're wrong, Billie? Who's going to take care of us? Who's going to be our mother?" Darien couldn't imagine what life would be like without her. Well, he could, but the picture he saw wasn't one he wanted to live with. He'd have do a lot more work around the house, and he'd probably be expected to do a lot of the cooking, something he had watched his mother do but hadn't really done all by himself. Unless you counted the time he and Billie had tried to make a birthday cake for her. His brother had used baking soda instead of baking powder and the cake never rose, ending up as flat as a pancake and not very tasty. They'd had to dump it in the trash and then tell their father who begrudgingly agreed to drive back into the center of town and pick up a store-bought cake.

And then there was his father. What would *that* be like, Darien wondered, living under his rules with no one to speak up for him? There'd be no one to calm his father when he'd start laying down the rules and dishing out punishments that weren't fair. It wasn't a life Darien wanted to imagine, but he already had.

He lifted his head and looked around at Billie, who wore an expression that told Darien he was thinking. "What, Billie?"

"I was just thinkin'. Maybe Pop would marry someone and she'd be like our mother." And as soon as the words had left his mouth, his expression turned into a frown and then back into a smile.

"Whaaat?" Darien asked, unable to understand why Billie would be smiling.

"Well, I was just supposing. Suppose he married our Aunt Sarah? She's a very pretty lady, you know! I sure wouldn't mind her kissing me good night at bedtime, would you?"

"Billie! That's not even funny. You know what that is? It's … it's in—"

"You trying to say incest? Nah, that's between a sister and a brother or a father and his daughter. And besides, she isn't even related to us by blood. She married our uncle, and that ain't incest!" Billie continued to smile, knowing he'd stirred Darien up.

"Well, I think that's pretty awful of you to even kid about a thing like that." Darien stood up and walked back into the house. He just didn't understand Billie sometimes.

Chapter Twenty-Five

A Year Later: A Shared Secret

Frankie Carrington was a friend of Billie's who had become a comfortable addition to the Edwards household, often stopping in to visit Billie, especially in the midafternoon when the two of them would arrive home long enough for Billie to drop off his books and change clothes before they rode their bikes off to play ball or simply ride around until suppertime.

One particular spring afternoon, Frankie Carrington appeared at the door of the Edwards' home alone. When Darien answered the knock, he was surprised when he saw that Billie wasn't with him.

"Hi, Big Dee," Frankie said, a warm smile on his face.

"Where's Billie?" Darien asked as he let the tall young man in and guided him into the living room where he'd been flipping through a comic book he'd bought earlier that week. Darien sat down on the sofa and motioned for Frankie to sit down with him.

Frankie nodded and sat next to him. "Oh, he decided to stay in town and get some batting practice in with some other guys down at the ball field. He knew you'd be alone and asked me if I'd stop by and look in on you."

Darien rolled his eyes.

"Not like you need a babysitter or anything like that," Frankie quickly added. "Cuz you don't! I mean, look at you. You're what ... practically a teenager already, right?"

Darien was pretty sure Frankie knew he wasn't anywhere near his teens, but the suggestion that he looked older caused Darien to sit up a little straighter and throw his shoulders back a bit. The comment made him feel good.

"Well, I'm not there yet, but gettin' close," he lied.

There was an awkward silence as the two of them sat on the couch. Darien sneaked a furtive glance at the young teenager next to him. He reminded him in some ways of Billie: tall, even taller than Billie, handsome and broad-shouldered, with a large, angular nose offset by a strong cleft chin. And he played center position on their junior varsity basketball team, something that added to Darien's admiration of him.

Darien had developed a sense of safety around Billie's friend; he didn't feel anxious in his presence as he sometimes did with other older boys. In fact, he rather liked Frankie and looked up to him, much as he did Billie. Still, he wasn't sure what to say or do as he waited for Frankie to say something more.

As if reading Darien's mind, Frankie asked, "Do you feel like taking a walk in the woods? We could see if that old barn owl has taken up nesting in that big old dead oak tree out there on the property next to yours. Billie showed it to me once when we were out there," he said, pointing in the direction of the woods that bordered the Edwards' home.

"Sure! I'd like that!" Darien jumped up from the couch and waited as Frankie seemed to hesitate, as if weighing something in his mind. "Well, come on! You wanna be back here before everybody gets home for supper, don'tcha?" he added, starting to move toward the door.

"Sure, you're right. And it'll give us more time to explore out there, just the two of us," Frankie said as he quickly caught up with Darien and draped an arm around his shoulders.

Within ten or fifteen minutes, they were deep into the woods, well beyond the stream that had been the boundary for Darien. Older now, he had been able to easily leap across a narrow spot in the stream to the other side. The area was denser where Frankie was leading them, dense enough that Darien remarked, "I bet no one can even see us from the dirt road that cuts through over to my uncle's place." That somehow made it special for Darien, sharing time with his brother's friend. Made *him* feel special.

Lost in his thoughts as he wandered amongst the tall trees and navigated around an occasional cluster of bushes and hanging vines, he stopped and turned to find Frankie standing to one side of a tree, his pants down around his thighs as he strained forward, his hips thrust in the direction of the trunk he was urinating on. He was holding in one hand the largest penis Darien had ever seen, even in the dirty photo magazine Billie had once let him look at earlier that same year.

Darien wanted to look away, embarassed and not knowing quite how he felt. Was it guilt because a part of him was curious and wanted to keep staring? Shame because he was envious? For some reason he couldn't understand, he felt mesmerized, frozen, unable to do or say anything except to continue staring.

"Come on over here, Darien. It's not going to bite you," Frankie said, finished relieving himself but still holding his private part that was now standing erect. He motioned for him to come closer, but Darien remained where he was, several yards away. So Frankie called out to him again. "Darien, there's nothing to be afraid of. Why, in a few years yours will look just like it, ya know? Your body's gonna go through changes, *big* changes, you know what I mean? I'll bet yours is already almost as big as this. Now c'mere."

Darien knew this last part wasn't the truth, and he wasn't so sure it would ever be, but he was still very curious. He slowly inched closer, trying to appear casual about it, interested but not *too* interested. Every now and then he looked around, afraid someone just might be taking a walk in the woods and would see them.

When he was within a couple of feet away, Frankie reached out, grabbed Darien's wrist, and pulled his hand toward his member. Darien resisted, pulling his hand out from Frankie's grip, certain he knew Billie's friend wanted him to touch it.

"Hey, Frankie, I don't want to! That's what queers do! And ... I'm not ... I'm not like that!" He could already feel the tears begin to well up and flow down his cheeks as he stood trembling and confused. *Why would he do this? And why to me?*

Frankie reached for his trousers, pulled them back up around his waist, and zipped his fly. He quickly strode to Darien, closing the gap, and circled his arms around him as he bent down to Darien's height and looked him square in the eyes for a moment before he said, "And I'm not either! It's just what guys do sometimes with one another. It doesn't mean anything, and I wasn't going to make you do anything you didn't want to do! You hear me? And one more thing. Don't you ever, *ever* say anything about this to *anyone*! Cuz if you do, I'll just tell 'em we were out for a walk, and when I took a piss, you got all hot and bothered when you saw my dick." Frankie walked away, leaving Darien to make his own way back home by himself.

Darien never uttered a word to anyone, and Frankie stopped visiting Billie at home. But not a week went by when Darien didn't remember the episode and reexperience feelings of guilt and shame that ever so slowly morphed into unexplained moments of anger. Over time, as he reminded himself of an old adage he'd heard his mother say, "Out of sight, out of mind," Darien decided that as long as nobody knew about it, it would just be his secret. And Frankie's.

Chapter Twenty-Six

June 1951:
Darien's Big Day

Today was a big day for Darien. It was his birthday, and he was about to celebrate becoming a teenager. Thirteen seemed to him like a point of arrival. He was no longer considered a boy; he was officially an adolescent, though he preferred the term *teenager* because it sounded older, like more nearly a young man, which was only a hair's breadth from being an adult, something he looked forward to becoming. Because then he could go off on his own and do and be how he wanted to be. Follow his own rules, not theirs. Yes, that thought occupied more than an occasional moment these days. But for now, he would revel in becoming a teenager, for it had a sense of status, of importance, and with it came certain privileges. At least that's what he'd observed over the past five years of watching Billie.

Billie received an allowance once he turned thirteen. Of course he was expected to perform chores around the house, even bigger ones than before, like mowing the lawn, trimming bushes, and chopping wood during the winter months. Wood was cheap and readily available in the surrounding land that relatives owned and allowed them access to. And it helped keep down the use of the coal his father had delivered every

November. Billie was also told it was time for him to look for some part-time jobs and begin saving for things he might want to buy as he became older. Darien remembered their father telling Billie he would one day go to college and that he was going to have to help with some of the expenses.

Darien had also noticed that Billie began to take a larger interest in girls when he turned thirteen and had even been allowed to invite ones he was particularly interested in to come to the occasional Saturday or Sunday afternoon family picnics in the backyard. Darien knew he would be expected to follow in his brother's footsteps although he secretly worried about being able to fill those shoes. He recognized, after all, that he was different from his brother in many ways, and the constant comparison he heard from his father, and that he silently went through himself, left him anxious about becoming a teenager.

Darien was certain he could do well taking on more chores around the house for both his father and his mother, and he actually liked mowing and raking and making the flowerbeds look even better than they did. These were things he could do by himself, and that alone time gave him an opportunity to daydream and try to work through feelings he had that he couldn't talk about with either of his parents or with any friends, for that matter. But for some reason he felt a strong connection with Billie, despite the things he'd done to Darien. Maybe *because* of those things. He silently questioned if his brother was really all that he seemed to be on the surface, but Darien also thought they might be more alike underneath it all. And that idea helped Darien decide that maybe he could talk to Billie about certain things that had troubled him from way back when he first joined the Edwards family and was officially adopted as their son.

So on this special day, as he and Billie finished making up their beds before they were called to breakfast, Darien sat at the foot of his bed and got up courage to ask his first question as he looked over at his brother, who as now sitting at the small desk that separated their twin beds.

"Billie, what do you know about my birth parents? I mean, did you ever hear Mom and Pop talk about them and why they decided to take me into their home?"

"A little. I remember they said your mother couldn't take care of you anymore. It had something to do with a man she was living with. Mom met her ... your mother I mean ... at the state school where she works now. I don't know the details. I just know that she worked there as an attendant and that she asked Mom to take care of you a few times and eventually Mom decided to have you live with us permanently. That was while Pop was in the navy. Why do you want to know?"

The information Billie offered didn't add too much to what Darien already had heard from their mother, although he didn't know the two had worked together. And the bit about his birth mother living with some man just seemed to support the reference to his mother being a "trollop," something he hadn't understood when he first heard the term used to describe his birth mother. But later on, when he'd asked his adopted mother, she'd told him it meant "a loose woman," and he never questioned what that meant either, although he had come to the conclusion that it meant something pretty bad, something one didn't talk about out loud.

Billie interrupted his thoughts. "Why're you asking, Darien? What's it matter? This is your family now."

"But why did my own parents not want me? Why did they give me away like some a piece of furniture or like those Mongoloids and retarded people in the state school? Like I wasn't good enough to keep! What was it? Did Mom feel *sorry* for me or something? Is *that* why she took me in?" Darien was working himself into an angry place he didn't want to go, so he stopped asking questions and folded his arms beneath his chest and tried to slow down his breathing.

"I don't think that's the way it was, Darien, but I don't really know why your mother gave you up other than maybe this guy didn't want to support a baby that wasn't his. Or maybe she just couldn't cuz of her problems with alcohol. Mom did say something about her being a heavy drinker. And as far as why Mom and Pop decided to adopt you, Mom wanted another child ... a girl, actually ... but she couldn't have another one, so I guess when she had a chance to get you, she did." Billie stood, grabbed his gym bag off the hook on their closet door, and reached over and slapped the top of Darien's head as he headed out of the bedroom. "I'm going to be late for baseball practice if I stay here yapping any longer. See you tonight for supper. And by the way, make sure you don't go poking around the kitchen and spoil Mom's surprise for you, birthday boy."

Darien perked up at this final remark and smiled as he watched Billie disappear into the dining room. He knew he'd be getting a couple of T-shirts and probably a pair of shorts because he needed them and his mom always used his birthday or Christmas to give him things he needed. "To kill two birds with one stone," Billie had said to him on one of his prior birthdays when she'd given him a new pair of dungarees and a pair of sneakers. But that was okay with Darien. As long as his father also surprised him by giving him his first allowance. He guessed he'd have to wait until that evening to find out. He just hoped he wouldn't be disappointed.

Chapter Twenty-Seven

The Same Afternoon:
Old Memories and Getting Ready

Darien heard a car pull in. He jumped up from the desk and pulled back the curtain to the side bedroom window that looked out to their driveway. Darien saw his father get out with several packages under one arm and a shopping bag in his other hand. He couldn't quite make out the department store name on it, but he could take a good guess, as there were only two major clothing stores in the Springfield area where his father worked. Darien was pretty sure it wasn't Sears. *He must have stopped at Steiger's on his way home from work,* he thought.

He quickly moved back to the desk to avoid being seen at the window and resumed reading the final few pages of the assigned chapter from *History of the World—100 A.D.–1950.* But his mind was now trying to deal with conflicting facts: the massacres of the Saracens by Richard the Lionheart in 1191 versus the fact that his father had just brought in a number of packages that he was pretty sure had his name going on them sometime between now and when supper would be over. Darien knew his mother would invite everyone to finish their piece of his birthday cake, the one she'd made earlier that morning and had frosted and stored away in the cool downstairs cellar room before she'd gone off to work, and then join Darien in the living room to watch him open his birthday gifts. It was no contest. The packages were winning over Richard the Lionheart's acts of bravery, hands down.

He dog-eared the page, closed the schoolbook, and sat back. He knew almost with certainty one of the packages would be either a pair of Keds sneakers or penny loafers. He needed both, actually, since the rubber on the outside edges of both heels was wearing thin on the sneakers and a layer of the sole had worn through in the center of the outer sole of his loafers, something he'd tried to hide from his mother because he knew it would cause her to be upset, having to figure out how and when they would be able to pay for a new pair. It wasn't that she directly blamed him for this, but he knew money was tight, and it bothered him that he was responsible for causing her stress.

His father, on the other hand, never made any effort to hide his displeasure when he found out such things, and his comments could cut to the bone. One Sunday after church, when he was barely ten, Darien had accidentally fallen into the small brook out back while waiting to be called in for their special dinner. Sunday was generally the day when his mother put either a pot roast or large pork roast into the oven just before they left for church. He'd failed to change out of his best clothes and, as a result, soaked his loafers and the bottoms of his dress pants. He'd tried to sneak back into the house and get to his room without his father seeing him, but Darien ran right into him as he came out of the kitchen and spotted Darien. The squishing sound his shoes made gave him away, and he was read the riot act.

"What the hell is the matter with you? You know better than to go off playing in your dress clothes. Now look at you!

Your shoes are ruined, and your mother probably won't be able to get the water stains out of those pants, young man!"

Recalling this incident from three years before, the old feelings crept over him now, leaving him with an empty feeling, not something he should be feeling on his birthday. Especially not *this* one. He looked down toward the foot of his bed and fixed his attention on two pairs of shoes that were lined up under it. One of them was his pair of cordovan loafers. He reached down and pulled them out and onto his lap. He turned them over and studied the thin holes that revealed the first telltale signs that new half soles would soon be needed. And that meant an added expense for his parents.

Darien got up and opened the closet door and rummaged around until he found the shoebox where he and his brother kept shoe polish, polishing rags, and brushes. He took it back to the desk, opened it, and took out the thin can of cordovan polish, a rag covered with a similar color, and a sable shoe brush. He quickly began to spread polish on the shoes and followed that with a vigorous brushing, trying his best to raise the shine. Maybe not a spit shine this time, but if he gave them a good polishing, just maybe his mother wouldn't look any closer and see the condition of the soles.

When he was satisfied with how they looked, he carefully rearranged them under the bed next to the other pair of shoes. Then, smelling the aroma of his favorite dish, shepherd's pie, wafting into his room, he jumped up and headed out into the dining room. Seeing the table decked out with all the dinnerware and silver set up on the white tablecloth that was only used on special occasions, Darien broke out into a smile and headed to the bathroom to wash up before dinner. It was going to be a wonderful evening. He just knew it.

Chapter Twenty-Eight

A Birthday Celebration: A Teenager, Yes, but Not Yet a Young Man

"The casserole was terrific, Mom. Good enough for a second helping, if you're not planning on saving it for another meal." Darien ran his finger across his dinner plate and licked off the residue of mashed potatoes. Lifting the serving spoon from the dish, he held it in the air, waiting for her answer.

"It's your big day, Darien. If you want more, go right ahead. Your father and brother have already had seconds, and I'm full from the first serving." She pushed the Pyrex casserole dish closer to his plate and added, "As soon as you're finished with that, I'll clear the table and make room for dessert. How does that sound?"

Darien hesitated and then put the spoon back into the dish as Billie broke into a grin and said, "Mom's chocolate cake with chocolate frosting always beats having more of that, huh?"

"William! That was supposed to be a surprise for him," she admonished. "Just for that, you can help me clear the table."

Darien started to rise, but his mother motioned him back down.

"You just sit and let your brother take care of this. William? Come help me bring the dishes into the kitchen. Everyone keep your forks." She and Billie stood and began to stack the dishes and other silverware.

"Can I have coffee tonight, Mom? It is my birthday, after all."

Before Mrs. Edwards could respond, Billie said, "Yeah, if you want a cup of milk with a dash of coffee! You know that's how Mom makes it for kids!"

"I'm not a kid anymore, Billie! I'm now officially a teenager, a young man."

Mr. Edwards, who'd been silently observing the exchange, said, "Not quite. A teenager? Yes. But a young man? No. Not until you turn eighteen."

Darien felt his spirits drop. Another put-down. He decided not to react and turned back to his mother, who was now standing in the doorway between the kitchen and the dining room. "Never mind, Mom. I hate coffee-flavored milk, but I wouldn't mind some *chocolate* milk, if you have any of that Hershey's syrup."

"One glass of chocolate milk coming up for the birthday boy!" she shouted over her shoulder.

"I'm not a *boy*, Mom! I'm …" He hesitated, looked over at his father, and then continued his thought. "I'm a teenager on his way to becoming a young man!" He straightened his shoulders as he tossed his father a satisfied look.

"We'll see what kind of a young man you're becoming when I tell you what additional chores I want you to take over from your brother. On the way to becoming a man there are some responsibilities you need to be able to take on, my boy." The emphasis on "my boy" didn't escape Darien, and he became quiet. His confidence in the idea that the rest of the evening was going to be a fun celebration of his coming of age, even if it was only in moving from an preadolescent to a teenager, grew weaker.

Billie reentered the room, saving the moment and turning things around for Darien. "Pop, aren't you going to have Darien mow the lawn and in the fall do the raking and stuff? I'm going to be away at college most of the time, and even if I do come home on a weekend, I won't have time to do that anymore, what with studies and all."

"I can mow the lawn and trim around the plant beds," Darien responded, a little excitement returning to his voice. "I've done it once or twice when you asked me to, remember, Billie? Remember? And I also helped shovel the sidewalks and part of the driveway last winter. Tell 'im, Billie!"

"He's right, Pop. He's pretty good at it, as a matter of fact. For a *boy*." Billie gave Darien a friendly jab on the shoulder and quickly jumped away as Darien tried to give him a swat with the back of his hand.

"Hey! No roughhousing around the dinner table!" That was all their father had to say for both of them to turn serious.

"Yes, sir," they said in unison.

But Darien didn't want to pass up the opportunity to raise the issue of an allowance, so he hesitantly asked, "Since I'll be taking over those chores in addition to helping Mom with dishes and stuff, do you think maybe I deserve to start getting a weekly allowance? Like you've been giving Billie for the past five years?"

"You can start out with two dollars. That's what I gave your brother when he was your age. And if you do a really good job and take on other chores as well, maybe we can talk about an increase. But for now, it's two dollars. Fair enough?"

Darien broke into a big grin. "Sure, Pop!" He was already thinking how much that was a month.

His father said, "I think I see dollar signs in your eyes, young man."

There! He'd said it! His father had just called him a young man! But Darien wasn't going to push it. He was satisfied to have heard his father call him that.

The rest of the evening played out like every other birthday celebration in the Edwards household. Mrs. Edwards called out from the kitchen to have the dining room lights turned off as she paraded in and set the birthday cake down in front of Darien, all thirteen candles fluttering brightly as he made the traditional silent wish and then blew out the candles in one breath.

"That means your wish is going to come true, Darien!" his mother proclaimed. "So tell us what it was."

"Yeah, tell us!" Billie chimed in.

"I'm gonna keep it a secret. Particularly from you, Billie! You always try to mess things up on me," he replied a little too emphatically.

"Now, boys, let's not start anything, you hear me?" Mrs. Edwards said firmly. "Cut the cake, Darien. You get the first piece, and then cut ones for your father and your brother. I'll have mine in a little while, once the coffee is ready." She then disappeared into the bedroom she and their father shared and returned with several gifts brightly wrapped in birthday paper. She set them next to Darien, sat back down, and smiled at him expectantly.

"Come on, Darien. Get the show on the road!" Billie said.

Darien quickly tore off the ribbon and wrapping paper from the middle-sized box and began to ball up the paper but was stopped as his mother reached out and held him by the wrist. "Let's fold that up, neatly, so we can reuse it for another time," she said, pulling the ribbon off the table with her other hand. She then carefully wrapped it around one set of fingers as she watched Darien fold up the birthday paper and set it aside.

He shook the box, uncertain what might be in it. It was larger than a shoebox and slightly taller than one that would hold a shirt or a pair of pants. He lifted the cover off to get to the tissue paper that hid what was beneath. Again, his mother stopped him. "Read the card to see who it's from and what it says."

Darien sighed and picked up the small piece of wrapping paper that had been cut and folded to serve as a gift card. "'To Darien, with much love, Mom and Pop,'" he read aloud. "Thanks, Mom. Thanks, Pop," he added dutifully.

"Don't thank them until you see what it is!" Billie muttered, a smile on his face.

Darien ignored him and lifted the tissue paper and pulled out two pairs of dress socks. Under those he found a blue oxford dress shirt with a color-coordinated, striped rep tie tucked carefully under the collar. He lifted the tie and shirt out and found the final gift in the box, a pair of charcoal-colored wool pants.

"Wow!" he said, giving as much excitement as he could muster. "These are really nice! Thank you both!" He laid them back in the box, got up, kissed his mother, and then walked over to his father where he hesitated, deciding to shake his hand instead. "Thanks, Pop," he said, giving him as firm a handshake as he could.

Darien quickly went on with unwrapping two more gifts, adding the expected level of appreciation for a pair of sneakers and a package of Fruit of the Loom underwear—the Big Boy

Basic-style briefs, not the smaller Jockey sports briefs his brother wore and that Darien had hoped he would get.

He was down to two remaining packages, a very small nearly square box and a *very* large elongated box that could've contained a BB gun or a bow and arrow set. Darien looked at the gift cards on each. The little one was from his mother and father, the larger one from his brother. He looked around the table, squinting as he tried to decide which to open next and which to save until last.

He made his decision and pulled the paper off the smaller of the two and balled it up and tossed it into a paper bag his mother had brought to the table for that purpose. "Don't need to save a piece that small, right, Mom?" he said as he opened the box and revealed a pair of gold cuff links. "Gee, these are really nice!" he exclaimed, this time with genuine appreciation, as he got up and quickly kissed his mother and, without thinking, his father too.

Mr. Edwards stiffened slightly but said nothing, but Darien immediately realized he shouldn't have done it. "You're too old for that kind of stuff with your father!" he recalled him saying when he was not yet twelve.

Wanting to change the focus of attention—he had seen the exchange of looks that was passed around the table—he backed his chair away from the table and lifted the long, large package onto his lap. "Boy, I wonder what this could be," he said as he snuck Billie a quizzical look and started to carefully remove the gift paper, careful to avoid looking directly at the carton that clearly announced "Regal Jousting Set."

"Oh my gosh! It's a jousting set, like the one you used to have, Billie!" Darien was smiling from ear to ear, remembering how he and Billie would each take one of the long poles with a leather-wrapped sponge at one end as they each stood on a small balancing platform made of butcher block wood set up out on the front lawn and jabbed at one another, trying to knock their opponent off the platform. He may have just changed from an adolescent to a teenager, but he was still young enough to feel a stir of excitement at the prospect of knocking his brother on his ass, even if he was now eighteen.

"Don't tell me you're too old to have your little brother whip your … tail … in a jousting game after supper!" he challenged.

"Better get your football gear on to protect yourself, little man!" Billie replied as he stood to leave.

"Hold on, both of you!" Mr. Edwards said. "We haven't even eaten your mother's cake yet, so sit back down and let's finish the meal properly. After you've both helped her clear the table and wash the dishes, you can go out and kill each other."

For the next ten minutes, Darien and Billie sat quietly and ate their pieces of birthday cake. Then, seeing their parents were finished with theirs, they asked permission to begin clearing the table of the few remaining dishes. When they were done, they agreed to take over the washing and drying of the dishes and quickly finished putting them away in the cupboards after they were dried. Done with their chores, Darien went back into the dining room and moved the gifts into their room where Billie helped him remove the two jousting poles and the balancing platforms from the box and carry them through the dining room into the living room, where their mother and father were now sitting, she knitting and he reading.

"We'll be out on the front lawn," Billie announced as he opened the front door and stepped onto the large front porch.

"Yeah, and if you hear someone screaming, it'll be *him!*" Darien added over his shoulder as he followed his brother out the door. He'd picked up that kind of bravado from his brother, but saying it and believing it were two entirely different things. Inwardly, he wasn't so sure. After all, Billie was almost six inches taller and at least forty pounds heavier. But Darien reasoned he was shorter and therefore had an advantage. He could poke his brother in the stomach and possibly knock the wind out of him if he kept low and avoided any attempt on Billie's part to hit him in the head.

That thought frightened him because he recalled having been hit in the jaw by a neighborhood bully and being knocked out. That had been a jarring and scary moment that had left him feeling like a weakling because he hadn't been able to defend himself and had run away crying once he regained consciousness a few moments later. That was nearly two years ago, but he still felt the old feelings whenever he recalled it.

But Darien reminded himself that he was now a teenager and was bigger and a bit stronger. Just *maybe* he had a fighting chance to knock his brother off and to the ground. He held onto that thought as he prepared himself for battle.

Chapter Twenty-Nine

Later the Same Day: A Battle for Manhood

Darien and Billie moved into the middle of their front lawn, each carrying a round balancing board and a three-foot jousting stick with a heavily padded ending, much like a boxing glove without the thumb. They mounted their balancing boards, which were spaced about three feet apart, and steadied themselves.

Darien squinted because he was facing the setting sun and hopped off the board. "Hey, Billie, you've got an unfair advantage! I'm facing the sun and you aren't. How about evening up this match by switching spots with me? Besides, you're older and have a longer reach than me!"

"Okay, little brother … oops, I mean, now-a-teenager-not yet-a-young-man," he said and chuckled.

Darien was determined to ignore his brother's taunting. He just *knew*, without knowing how, that he was going to beat his brother. He picked up his board and walked past Billie, adding his best version of a swagger to his walk. He turned around and dropped the board to the ground. With his back now to the sun, he stepped onto the board and took the starting position, his feet slightly spread, his body in a crouched position, and his jousting stick at the ready. He was determined. "Take your best shot, big brother!"

The jousting match was on. Darien maintained his crouched balance, waiting to fend off Billie's first jab. Billie was standing up fairly straight so he had a height advantage as he raised his stick and made several short downward jabs toward Darien, missing him each time.

"Think you're clever, do ya? Just keep it up, little man. I haven't begun to show you who's boss!" Billie said, sneering, as he continued to poke at Darien.

"And you ain't seen nuthin' yet from me either!" Darien replied, shifting his body in one direction and then another, wanting to avoid being slammed in the event Billie's thrusts became longer. He used his jousting stick to keep his balance, raising it in the opposite direction of his shifting body. He could see by the look on Billie's face that his skills with the jousting equipment were impressing his older brother, who now took longer, more forceful thrusts toward Darien.

"Looks to me like you're getting winded, ol' man. All that smokin' you do when Mom and Pop aren't around," Darien added, as he managed to dodge yet another forceful jab.

"Pretty cocky little shit, aren'tcha? Well, take this!" Billie wasn't smiling any longer as he took both hands and, holding the jousting stick over his head, drove it down at Darien's chest.

Surprised by his brother's shift in attitude, Darien instinctively took on an aggressive manner. *Enough of this crap! You wanna play tough? I'll show you tough!* He managed to twist his body out of the way without falling and then realigned his weight to keep his balance on the gyrating small round board. He could see that Billie was beginning to breathe with more difficulty, his fatigue beginning to show as his breaths became shorter and faster. Now his swings with the stick were less controlled and more forceful. Darien waited, continuing to avoid being struck while conserving his own energy, waiting for the right time. Then it came.

Billie thrust wildly and forcefully, nearly making contact with Darien's shoulder, but Darien pulled back and, at the same time, lowered his body into a full crouch. Then he sprung up and thrust forward with all his might, driving the end of his jousting stick up and into Billie's stomach. The force of the blow took the breath out of his brother and propelled him off his pivot board and up against the wooden steps of the front porch.

Billie let out a garbled cry of pain as his back slammed against the steps and his head bounced off the edge of the porch. He lay sprawled out, motionless.

Darien dropped his stick, jumped off the pivot board, and leaped toward Billie's lifeless body. "Billieeeeee!" he wailed, shaking him by the shoulders. He didn't expect what happened next.

Billie opened his eyes and smiled as he grabbed Darien by the shoulders and easily lifted him up into the air and onto his back as he rolled over on top of him in one swift motion, pinning him to the ground.

"Whadya have to say now, little brother? Is that all you've got? Huh?" Billie pressed down on his shoulders a little harder, and Darien realized his brother had been faking it all along, letting him think he was getting the better of him.

Darien managed to smile sheepishly and said, "I knew you weren't really trying. But neither was I," he added, making an effort to seem serious.

Billie burst out laughing, and Darien joined him as his brother pulled him up off the grass and put a headlock on him with one arm while he tickled Darien's stomach with the other hand. Then he let go of him, swatting him on the ass as he directed him up the steps and into the house. "Go get yourself another piece of your birthday cake, Mr. In-Between. And cut me a piece while you're at it!"

Chapter Thirty

Three Years Later:
A Young Man in the Making

The cold air felt good on his cheeks, invigorating, as Darien plodded through the freshly fallen snow. It had come down most of the previous day, turning to sleet during the night. The temperature dipped into the low twenties in the early-morning hours, unseasonably cold for the middle of November. The few inches of new snow were frozen over. It crunched under foot, creating a hypnotic pattern of sound that lulled him into another world as he made his way up the slippery hill toward the high school.

At sixteen, Darien's other world was not of becoming a pilot or discovering a solution for the plight of the starving millions around the world. Or even of becoming the next Norman Rockwell or Mario Lanza, although those images both appealed to him.

Darien's fantasies were of fitting in, of being happy. He saw himself living in his own home, far away from people and surrounded by dogs and wild animals he tamed. It would be a solitary life but a happy one. He pictured himself independent and self-sufficient. A life with none of the numbing sense of disconnection that had become his everyday inner reality. A reality he carefully hid from others.

"Hey, Big Dee, wait up."

The request interrupted his fantasy, and he turned in the direction of the voice. He saw the figure of a young man running and sliding toward him as he cut across a large expanse of lawn, now completely covered by the crusty snow. It was Sandy French, a classmate and friend. Most of Darien's classmates called him Big Dee except in front of the teachers. He liked it better than Darien.

"I thought you were driving to school now that you got your license, Sandy." Darien waited for his friend to catch up with him before he resumed walking.

"I usually do," he replied, breathing heavily and trying to catch his breath as the stocky teenager reached Darien. Once his wheezing stopped, Sandy continued speaking. "But my old man wouldn't let me drive my Chevy because of the icy roads."

"Too bad."

"It doesn't bother me. The snow will be gone by tomorrow, if it warms up."

"At least he let you get your license and a car. Mine won't even let me practice driving ours."

"How come?"

"I dunno. Guess he's afraid I'll scratch it." Darien wasn't about to tell his friend the real reason, that he was afraid to try anything in front of his father. He remembered back to earlier that year, shortly after his sixteenth birthday. His father had offered to teach Darien how to drive. Darien had been so scared, his legs shook and he had trouble synchronizing his use of the clutch and the gearshift and had caused the gears to grind. His father had pulled up on the hand brake and yelled his favorite admonition, "If you can't do it right the first time, dammit, don't do it at all!"

"So?"

"So I'll wait for driver's ed class to start in the spring and learn then." Darien shifted his bookbag to the other shoulder as they rounded the corner at the top of their street.

"What about your older brother? Won't he teach you?"

"He's gone away to college, so he only comes home once in a blue moon."

The two of them continued on without conversation for several more minutes. They crossed the town's common, a large, elongated strip of land that was large enough to house all the circus tents and dozens of thrill rides, like the ferris wheel, the "octopus," the roller coaster, and, of course, the merry-go-round, that came to town every fall and attracted thousands of people from all the surrounding towns.

In the summer, this nearly mile-long piece of land was a verdant green gathering place for memorial celebrations and occasional school or American Legion band concerts. One end of it, the area closest to the commercial center of town, also served as an evening hangout and gathering spot for the local wannabe cool guys who would sit on their motorcycles, James Dean style, their girlfriends straddling their backs, pretending to be far tougher than they really were. They were all lined up, each with a pack of cigarettes tucked into a rolled-up sleeve of their white T-shirts, hoping for some action but rarely ever finding any, for it was all about image.

In the winter season, the same section of the commons would be flooded with water, which, once frozen over, became a large skating rink that was used after school and on weekends by young and old alike. It wasn't as large a surface for ice skating as those offered by the frozen ponds located on the outskirts of town farther south, but it was more convenient.

As Darien and Sandy made their way toward the high school at the far end of the commons near the center of town, Sandy broke the silence. "Has anyone asked you to the Sadie Hawkins' dance yet?"

"Nope. Not yet, anyway." The dance was an annual event where the girls asked the guys to take them to the dance, and Darien was hoping Beverly Simpson would ask him. She was a few months older than he and reminded him of Loretta Young, surely the most beautiful woman he'd ever laid eyes on. Not only was she gorgeous, but he also thought she was the kindest, most caring person he'd ever met. Well, not *met*, but seen on television. But he wasn't about to share his feelings for Beverly with Sandy, and for good reason.

Sandy's older brother, Jimmy, now a junior, had begun dating Beverly when she was not quite fourteen. They had gone steady for many months and then broke up, and Beverly had moved away for nearly a year before returning. Darien hadn't really known her then, but he had noticed her on the first day they both began freshman year and had quietly fallen head over heels in love with her.

"How 'bout you?"

"Of course! Sally asked me. Who'd you think she'd ask?"

Darien saw the playful slap at his head coming and deflected it with one arm. He bent down to scoop a handful of icy snow and lobbed it at his friend's back. Then he replied, not missing a beat, "I didn't know she was your steady girl now. I thought you just took her out once in a while."

"Well, she is." Sandy jumped to one side, grabbed a chunk of packed snow piled at the side of the road, and hurled it at him.

Darien ducked, dropped his bookbag, and scooping up a handful of snow and packing it into an icy missile, fired it back at Sandy. Within seconds, they were engaged in an all-out snow fight with chunks of snow being hurled back and forth, most hitting their mark. Sandy finally pulled up an enormous piece of packed snow with both hands and clobbered Darien over the head with it, knocking him to the ground.

"Okay! Okay! You win!" Darien laughed as he caught his breath and brushed the snow from his head and shoulders. He retrieved his bookbag, and the two of them continued across the common to school. In such tiny moments like this Darien felt redeemed, freed from the nagging inner voices that fed his self-doubts. For a few exhilarating moments, he felt normal, like he fit in, and he couldn't help but chuckle to himself.

Sandy cuffed him on the shoulder and asked, "What's so funny, Big Dee?"

"Nuthin'," he replied, but he couldn't erase the smile from his face and carried it for the remainder of their trek into the school building.

★★★★

While he hoped he'd run into Beverly Simpson that day, he only caught a glimpse of her at the far end of the school's main corridor. He broke into a fast walk down the hall to catch up with her, but she slipped into a classroom. A part of him felt relieved because he wasn't sure he'd have been able to speak even if he had caught up with her. He peered through the small square window in the door, trying to summon the courage to open it and go in, although he didn't have the foggiest idea what he'd say if he did. Within seconds, he heard the teacher call to the group of teenagers to take their seats, and he watched Beverly slide into a chair and then look directly at him, a curious smile on her face. Darien felt himself blush as he returned the smile and then headed down the corridor to his homeroom. He felt like he was floating all the way.

Later the same day, he felt someone tap him on the shoulder as he left the school building. When he turned to see who it was, instantly he felt his heart speed up. *Beverly.*

He stopped and smiled broadly at her. She returned it as she finished wrapping the scarf around her neck and fastened the row of toggles on her khaki-colored woolen car coat.

"How'd you do on the Latin test, Darien?" She touched his arm as she spoke and nonchalantly shifted her weight to one hip, causing her skirt to pull tight around her thighs and long legs. Darien noticed, although he quickly looked up to meet her steady gaze.

"Not too bad, I think. How about you?"

"Not too good, I'm afraid. I didn't study that much." She ran her hands along her skirt, pushing the material down to cover her knees.

Darien wondered if she'd seen him looking. "I'll bet you did great." She was an honor roll student who came from a family that valued education. He'd heard Billie speak of them, and he knew Beverly also had an older brother who attended college.

There was an awkward pause before either of them spoke again. He felt his cheeks flush and looked away, unable to find words to fill the silence.

"Do you have plans for the dance?" She folded her arms and tilted her head to one side, a smile forming on her face as she lifted one eyebrow.

"Ummm, not yet."

"Well, would you like to take me?" She lifted both eyebrows, making her eyes seem even larger.

She is a dead ringer for Loretta Young. He couldn't believe his luck. "Sure!" He broke into a wide smile and nodded, just in case he hadn't made it clear. And then his jaw dropped as it dawned on him. *I don't have my license! How am I gonna take her?*

He could have his parents drive him. *God, no!* That's what had happened the year before when they'd allowed him to have his first formal date for the Christmas dance. Embarrassing. No, that was out of the question. Maybe Sandy would double-date. But what if he wouldn't? One of his uncles had a car service business. Maybe he'd drive them. Darien quickly dismissed that option. Too much money. He was running out of ideas.

"My girlfriend Barbara is taking Cliff Hanifin, and he has a car. Would you mind going with them?"

He felt the tension drain from his body. Inexplicably, he experienced a sudden surge of energy vibrate throughout him and a momentary lapse in consciousness. In the next instant, he heard come out of his mouth, "Thanks, Sundeep."

"What did you just say?" She cocked her head to the side, looking puzzled.

"I said, 'Thanks run deep.' It's an ancient way of saying I'd love to … to double-date with your friend and her date." He did his best to maintain a straight face as he took credit for being fast on his feet, although he wondered what had prompted him to think of Sundeep, a name he hadn't uttered or even thought about in well over eight years.

"Then it's a date! I'll let you know the details after I speak with Barbara." Beverly waved good-bye and dashed down the walkway toward the waiting school bus.

Darien watched her board and find a window seat. As the bus pulled away, he flashed her a wide smile as she looked back and waved again. He couldn't remember ever being so happy. He thought mostly about her on his way back home, but his mention of Sundeep still confused him and the question weaved its way through his fantasy of being on a date with Beverly. By the time he arrived home, the fantasy of Beverly had regained his full attention, and he was hard.

"Not even a hello? Where are you going in such a rush, Darien?" His mother moved to one side as he rushed into the bathroom and closed the door.

"Had to go, Mom," he replied through the closed door. He pulled down his trousers and briefs and grabbed his penis and began pumping. Relief came within seconds, and he let out a shuddered sigh through clenched teeth. He hoped she hadn't heard.

Chapter Thirty-One

Later That Same Day: Oh, What Rumors Can Do!

Darien swirled the remaining peas and fried hamburger into the lumpy mashed potatoes, lost in his thoughts and unaware he was humming a familiar tune, "Vaya Con Dios."

"What've I told you about singing at the table?" His father gave him "the Edwards Eye," as his mother called it, a narrowed squint that felt icy on the receiving end.

"Sorry, Pop."

"You've been unusually chipper, Darien. Something in the way of good news you'd like to tell us about?" His mother tilted her head as she continued to pour herself a second cup of coffee.

He hesitated and stole a glance at his father as he weighed his response, wanting to sound casual. "Nothing too special."

"Oh?"

He couldn't hold back his excitement any longer. "I got asked to the Sadie Hawkins Dance, Mom." He sneaked another quick look in his father's direction, wishing he hadn't responded.

"How nice, dear! Who's the lucky girl?"

Darien felt a smile creep over his face and his skin flush.

"Beverly Simpson." His embarrassment instantly turned to apprehension as he caught the looks exchanged between his parents.

His father slammed his cup down onto the table, chipping the edge of his dinner plate. "That girl's nothing but a damned slut!"

"Stanley! I won't have that kind of talk!"

"Well, she is and you know it!" His father fingered the edge of the chipped plate and shook his head.

"Those were just rumors and, besides, it's not our place to judge her. And certainly not in front of Darien!" She stood and reached across the table to pick up the plate. "Hand me the chip. Maybe I can glue it back on."

Darien felt numb as he tried to make sense of it all. What leapt to mind first was the obvious: Beverly and his friend Sandy's older brother had gone steady for almost a year. He'd heard some of his classmates talking about going steady, and that it sometimes involves more than heavy petting, but he only knew one guy who bragged about going all the way. Beverly wouldn't have done that. Not at fourteen! Or would she? Two years earlier, Beverly had moved away for nearly a year and then came back. *Had she gone to one of those places for unwed mothers? Maybe Sandy's brother had forced her. Or maybe it never happened, and he'd made it up to spoil her reputation.* Darien certainly had never heard anyone say anything bad about her.

"I don't believe it!" He pushed his chair away from the table and started to stand up.

"Sit down! And watch your tone with me, young man."

"Please, Stanley." His mother turned toward Darien. "This isn't anything you should concern yourself with, dear. Whatever happened is in the past. We're happy you like this girl and that she's asked you out."

"Were you planning on us driving you to the dance?" His father's eyes were still narrowed, and there was no smile on his face.

"No, Pop. Her girlfriend's date is Cliff Hanifin. We're double-dating, if that's okay with you and Mom." He looked over at her, hoping for her support.

"That's Maynard Hanifin's son, Stanley. He's a very responsible young man. You know that." Virginia smiled at Darien and gently touched his arm.

"Go ahead, if your mother says it's all right. I guess with you we don't have much to worry about anyway." His father shook his head, stood, and walked out of the room.

Darien sagged in his chair as he watched his father disappear into the living room. *Rack up another strike for the Big Dee. Jesus, I wish I had the guts to tell him to fuck off!*

"Eat up, Darien. You mustn't let this upset you."

"I'm not really hungry anymore, Mom. Maybe I'll eat it later." He cleared his dishes and then stopped by his mother's chair on the way to his room. "Just call me when you're ready to wash the dishes. I'll dry."

"No dessert?"

"Uh-uh." He turned and walked out. He didn't feel like humming anymore.

Darien went to his room, closed the door, and sat down at the small maple desk that had become his when Billie left for college, flipping on the desk lamp as he did so. He grabbed an edition of Shakespeare's *Julius Caesar* from a stack of schoolbooks laying there, opened it up at a yellowed 3x5 card that marked where he'd left off the day before, and began reading.

"Act II, Scene II. Caesar's house. It is thundering and lightning as Caesar enters, in a nightgown and speaks aloud: 'Nor heaven nor earth have been at peace tonight. Thrice hath

Calpurnia in her sleep cried out, "Help, ho! They murder Caesar!" Who's within?'"

He stopped and closed the book on the marker. His father's words crowded out the words on the page, and he let out a heavy sigh. "I guess with you we don't have much to worry about." The insinuation was clear to Darien: *You're not like other young men your age. You're not man enough for us to worry about you knocking up anyone.* Once again, he didn't measure up.

He tightened both hands into fists and pounded them on the desktop. It felt good, and he did it again, this time with more force as his anger grew.

"What's going on in there?" It was his mother, calling out from the kitchen.

"I'm sorry, Mom. It's nothing. I just dropped a couple of books on the floor." He held his breath, hoping she wouldn't come into his room. "I'm working on my literature reading assignment for tomorrow. I'll be quiet, I promise."

There was no response, and he breathed in relief. Now he could try to weigh his father's remarks about Beverly Simpson against what he knew to be true.

Yes, she looked older than her years and acted older as well. But she was also very bright, even a bit of an intellectual, some might say, probably because of the glasses she wore. In direct contrast to this, she wore tight-fitting angora sweaters. Darien had wondered, on more than one occasion, if she didn't wear cone-shaped falsies he'd heard young girls sometimes wore to accentuate their breasts. She also wore skirts that clung to her shapely hips and legs and barely covered her knees. But from what he observed of her, she seemed oblivious to her sexy appearance and, for the most part, kept to herself at school.

As for the fact that she'd dated his friend's older brother for a short time, that didn't necessarily mean she was a tramp, as his father had said. And the fact that she'd moved away for the better part of a year didn't mean anything. Maybe she'd traveled to New Hampshire to spend time with her grandparents. He'd overheard Billie talking with Beverly's older brother once and had heard some talk about them having family up there. Yes, that's what must've happened! Darien felt better already. Maybe he'd figure a way to ask her about it on their upcoming date and prove his father wrong, once and for all.

Chapter Thirty-Two

Sadie Hawkin's Night:
His Fears Confirmed

Darien heard the crunch of tires on the snow-packed driveway outside and called over his shoulder to his parents, "They're here. I'm leaving. Bye."

"Remember, midnight! No later, you hear?" It was his father.

"Yes, Pop." He let the door slam shut behind him and trotted to the open passenger door of the freshly waxed Buick Road Master.

"Hi, Barbara."

"Hi, Darien. Can you squeeze in?" She leaned closer to her boyfriend and pushed the back of the bucket seat forward so he could climb into the empty rear seat.

"I appreciate your picking me up and letting Beverly and me double with you." Darien shook Cliff Hanifin's massive hand, trying his best to hide the discomfort he was feeling from the squeeze as he settled in and set the small corsage box on the seat next to him.

"No sweat. You and Bev don't live that far out of the way." Cliff adjusted the radio, tuning it up as he backed out of the driveway and headed toward Beverly's home in the south end of town.

"Vaya Con Dios" rose above the hum of the snow treads on the salted macadam road. It was the song he'd been humming around the house the evening he'd told his parents about his date. Now it brought up stuff he didn't want to think about, things about Beverly. He heard his father's words once more and silently dismissed them. *No damned way I'm gonna let him screw up my evening!* Darien eyed the couple in front of him and imagined himself driving, one hand on the wheel and the other wrapped around Beverly Simpson as she nestled next to him.

By the time they reached Beverly's house, Darien was kissing her and her hand was pressed against the back of his neck, holding him close. The sudden stop ended his fantasy, and he quickly slid out of the car and smoothed the front of his trousers, willing his erection to go down before he reached the lit porch.

The door opened even before he knocked. There she stood, smiling and looking radiant. "Hi, Darien. I thought I heard the car drive up." Beverly's gaze dropped for an instant and then returned to hold eye contact with Darien, her expression giving no hint she was upset by what she saw. She held the door open and motioned for him to enter.

"Hi, Bev. You look great!" He hesitated, jerking his head toward the parked car.

"That's okay. We'll only be a minute." She waved toward the car and then ushered him into the foyer where her father and mother stood, observant eyes on him.

He managed a tentative smile and took a step forward, extending a hand to her father while nodding courteously to the mother.

"Darien, these are my parents. Mom, Dad, this is Darien Edwards."

"Pleasure to meet you, ma'am. Mr. Simpson." Darien shook her father's hand forcefully. "You can judge a man by his handshake," his father often said, and he hoped he'd passed the test.

Mr. Simpson's expression remained flat. "Make sure you have her back here before midnight, young man. And you tell that Hanifin kid to watch his speed."

"Yes, sir." Darien nodded again politely. Her father reminded him of his own, and he wondered if all fathers were so gruff. Remembering he had the silver gift box in one hand, he offered it to her as they stepped back onto the porch.

She lifted the cover and removed the corsage. "Oh! The gardenia is beautiful, Darien! Thank you."

"You're worth every penny of it!" The response slipped out and he wished he hadn't said it. *You're never supposed to talk about what things cost!* She was grinning as he slipped it onto her wrist, and he knew she'd accepted it as a compliment. He took her hand in his and walked her to the car. His date was off to a good start.

★★★★

The evening passed much too quickly for Darien. They had danced to nearly every number, including the Lindy, although he'd avoided getting up when the music required them to dance the Charleston, a dance step he didn't feel confident about. He held her as close as he dared now while the lights flickered, signaling the final dance of the night. His attentiveness to her had worked in his favor. She nuzzled up against his neck, one arm resting around his shoulder, while he held her other hand behind her, pressing her lower back against his body.

He felt heat between them and knew he was aroused. He was sure she knew it as well, although she didn't move away. In fact, she seemed to be pressing toward him, and that excited him even more. He was feeling a bit lightheaded but confident, and he pressed her closer. He couldn't wait until later. It was only 10:30, and he didn't have to have her home until midnight. He hoped Cliff would decide to leave the dance early and drive down to the pond to park for a while.

His hopes were answered a few minutes later when Cliff and Barbara approached them and whispered that they should meet them in the parking lot. Once they were all in Cliff's car, it took only minutes for them to reach a desolate wooded area in the southern end of town just off the main road that weaved its way through a wooded stretch between Hammerville and Palmer City.

Darien was thankful he wasn't driving, for the backseat was roomy and a crescent moon above left the sky and the inside of the parked Buick in darkness. He stole a furtive glance toward the front seat but could see nothing. The rustling of crinoline and soft whispers suggested Barbara and Cliff were oblivious to whatever might be going on between him and Beverly.

Darien quickly turned his attention back to her, feeling drawn into her by the magnetic force of her large hazel eyes. He kissed her, tentatively at first, and then more forcefully when he felt her slide one hand down his side and begin to knead his hip. He opened his mouth slightly, and she obliged his tongue, allowing it to explore the ridges of her teeth and the inner gums. He felt her tongue probing his and heard her soft moaning as she pressed closer into him.

Her other hand pulled at his shirt, and he felt its warmth as she gently explored his back. He shifted his position, raising up on one knee as he slid her farther down along the seat and gently lowered the weight of his body onto hers.

They were both pushing against each other, and he thought his penis was going to explode through his trousers as the rhythm of their thrusts gained momentum. She was gasping and moaning, and he reached beneath her skirt and fumbled for her panties. Suddenly, he felt her hand shove his away and push at his chest.

"Stop! We can't do this. Not now!" She whispered, breathless.

"Why?" He kept his voice hushed. *Why now? What am I doing wrong?*

"I'm not that kind of girl! I'm not!" She was crying.

He sat up abruptly and tucked his shirt back in, avoiding eye contact with her as he worked to slow his breathing down to normal. *What is she, some kind of tease? You make out hot and heavy, get a guy going, and then say stop? Well, fuck you! See if I care. Pop was probably right anyway!* He folded his arms across his chest and stared out the side window into the cold, black darkness of the night. He ignored the gentle tug of her hand on his arm.

"Anytime you guys are ready to leave is fine with us," Darien announced to no one in particular. He wasn't whispering now, not that it mattered. The front seat duo were too deeply involved in making out to even hear Darien, and he sat back, his arms tightly crossed against his chest, as he stared out the windows, avoiding eye contact with Beverly.

The drive back to her house felt like an eternity and the silence like a shroud, hiding all the anger, awkward feelings, unasked questions, and baseless decisions. For Beverly, no second chances. *I can't trust you!* For himself, he heard declarations of his father. *"You get it right the first time or not at all!"*

Darien still couldn't look at Beverly when they pulled into the driveway. He let her get out by herself, only once stealing a quick look in her direction as she walked up the steps and closed the door behind her.

Back at home, he'd successfully fielded the questions, providing safe, satisfactory answers. "Yes, we had a great time at the dance. We stopped for sodas and ice cream. Yeah, maybe I'll ask her out again." But he knew he wouldn't. He couldn't take the risk. He'd have to explain his actions, and how could he when he didn't even understand himself? *Is this how a real man acts?* He didn't think so. *Fake it till you make it!* That would be his unspoken credo.

Chapter Thirty-Three

A Few Weeks Later:
An Attempt at Reconciliation

The passing of time didn't do much to change how Darien felt. He still believed he'd failed, big time, and he slipped into one of his solitary moods, one that lasted for several weeks. While he tried to act as if nothing had gone wrong, particularly when his classmates asked him how the evening had gone, it was difficult for him to lie. It left him feeling guilty and ashamed. But he was learning how to hide such feelings, and he wasn't doing such a bad job in the lying department either. He felt mildly relieved that he hadn't run into Beverly even once during the following days, and he suspected she had also been avoiding him as well. When their paths did finally cross, she had simply kept her head down and nodded as she passed him.

He knew he'd reacted badly when she'd stopped him from taking their making out to the next level. After all, it was their first date. What did he expect? Had he hoped maybe his father was right? That she was an easy lay? Was that why he'd tried to get her to have sex with him? What did that say about *him*? These questions repeatedly ran through his mind when he was by himself, when he felt it was safe to allow them to resurface.

Darien still had strong feelings for Beverly, but he didn't know how to approach her to even speak with her. He wondered whether he might talk to her friend Barbara, but he didn't really know her well enough to seek her alliance. And besides, she was a close friend of Beverly's. What made him think she'd help *him*?

★★★★

Fate seemed to intervene a few days later while he was walking the main corridor of the high school, his head down, deep in thought about the algebra test he had coming up later in the day. He felt the impact with someone and, startled, looked up to see books and a notebook drop to the floor. He reached out to grab the girl's arm to keep her from falling and then locked eyes with her. It was Beverly.

He felt her twist away from him, and he released his hold on her arm. "Gosh! I'm sorry! I wasn't looking where I was going," he said as he bent down to scoop up her books.

This is awkward, he thought, as he watched her rub her arm where he'd grabbed her. "I didn't mean to squeeze you so tightly. I just meant to keep you from falling."

"I'm fine, really," she said as she took the books and notebook he was extending to her. He could tell she was as embarrassed as he was by how she looked away, at her books, at the clock on the wall ... anywhere but at him.

If I am ever going to repair things with her, now is the time, he thought to himself. *Just apologize!* "About what happened after the Sadie Hawkins, Beverly—"

"You don't need to say anything more. You made yourself pretty clear that night! You don't get what you want and you dump girls, don't you? Well, that's just fine with me. I—"

"No, it's not that way!" Darien said. "You're partly right. I did get angry because you … you—"

"I *what*? What did I do that was so wrong, other than say stop? What made you think I was that kind of girl, Darien?" She was whispering now, looking around at the students passing by, obviously not wanting their conversation to be overheard. Her eyes were becoming moist with tears, and her bottom lip and chin quivered as she spoke.

"I just felt led on, Beverly. The way we were making out and all. I just thought that's what you wanted, and when you stopped me suddenly, I felt like you were being a tease. But you're right. I acted like a creep and I'm sorry. I really am!" He felt himself relax a little. He'd done it. He'd apologized, and he felt better for it.

She lifted her eyes until she was looking directly at him. Her gaze softened and an ever-so-slight smile crept over her face. He knew she was studying him, deciding whether or not he was sincerely sorry and not just trying to pick things up where they'd left off. After a few moments she said, "Okay. Apology accepted." She reached out and touched his hand, and he immediately felt an erection happening. He felt himself blush and just hoped she wasn't looking in *that* direction, although the embarrassment he was now feeling quickly caused him to go limp, for which he was grateful.

"So maybe we can go on another date?" he asked.

"That would be nice, Darien, but let's not make it one where *that's* likely to happen again anytime soon." She adjusted a few curls along the side of her face and glanced at the clock. It was almost time for the next class to begin.

Darien stood there, taking it all in, still surprised and definitely very happy with her answer. Smiling broadly now, he said, "I'll definitely call you later this week and …" He was at a loss for what to say next, so he simply said, "I'll call." He bent his head slightly, a nod of sorts, and then pushed off to his next class, leaving her shaking her head but smiling.

Chapter Thirty-Four

Two Days Later

Darien studied the face looking back at him in the mirror and then refocused his attention back down at the partially sketched face on the large pad of drawing paper he held on his lap. He studied the eye he was working on and then glanced back up into the mirror, careful to not move too much, and quickly returned to the self-portrait that was emerging on the paper. Applying quick, light little strokes, the pupil of the eye began to come to life as he shaded in the darker portions of it, still leaving a spot of white off to the right. Switching back to the eyelid, he added a few strokes of shading that allowed the flat surface of the paper to appear rounded now. He moved his pencil to the arched brow above the eye and then thought better of it and stopped sketching. The transformation taking place on the matte surface of the paper pleased him. He took in the rest of the sketch. It *did* look a bit like him! Not exact yet, but a very close resemblance. He smiled and put his number one pencil down and stretched.

He had enjoyed drawing for as long as he could remember. Well, it hadn't really started out as drawing. His first realization that he seemed to have an ability to recreate things he saw was when he was given a beginner's set of modeling clay at age seven. It had included small blocks of gray clay and wooden sculpting tools to dig the clay out as objects were formed. But Darien felt much more at home using his fingers, and he had begun by creating forms that took on life as he rolled pieces of clay between his two hands to make the trunk of a body. When it looked how he thought it should look, he would use his fingers to cinch the clay into a waistline. He would twirl bits of clay into little arms and legs, using the tips of his fingers to shape them. Even tiny hands and feet he would form in this manner and stick them onto the arms and legs. He'd do the same thing to make a little head and neck. When he was through, he would twist and bend the figures into different positions.

He was a Michelangelo in the making, or so his mother had thought when she first discovered some of his clay figures secreted away in his bureau drawer.

"These are beautiful, Darien! Why haven't you ever shown me what a wonderful artist you are?" she asked, showing him one of the clay creations she'd found.

Darien had scrunched his shoulders, remaining silent and feeling very embarrassed. And just a tiny bit proud, as he allowed a smile to form on his face.

After that incident, it hadn't taken long for Virginia to make a visit to a five-and-dime in Holyoke and bring home some drawing pads and pencils and charcoal sticks. Soon Darien began copying pictures that he thought he could draw. Over the next several years, he continued to develop his skills, and even spent one summer attending art trips to a neighboring town where an artist held farm trips for young artists, allowing them to draw and paint scenes and objects around the farm.

Over the past nine years, Darien's artistic ability had grown as he continued to draw and paint. He'd even gone out and bought himself a set of oil paints and brushes, complete with an artist's wooden palette. But pencil and charcoals were his favorite mediums. It almost felt like the drawing was coming out of his fingers. He could spend hours at a time copying a famous painting or a photograph of a face he was drawn to.

Now, as he gathered up his art supplies, he gave the sketch a final look before putting it under his bed. *Not bad*, he decided as he moved out into the dining room and sat down at the desk where they kept the telephone. It was time for him to call Beverly and make a date.

Chapter Thirty-Five

Two Days Later:
Score One for Big Dee

It had been the perfect answer to Darien's dilemma: where to take Beverly for this important date. With the late-fall temperatures suddenly dropping into the low forties, the idea had come to him when he saw the ad in the local newspaper the day after his run-in with Beverly:

> Saturday Night Hayride—Leaves the town center at 6:30 p.m. and ends at 10:30 p.m. $5.00 per couple, cider and homemade donuts included. Chaperoned by Coach Amberly and his wife, Emily.

Darien had let out a cheer. It was just the right setting for a great date. A romantic countryside hayride, and it would be chaperoned, which would reassure Beverly if she had any worries about him trying to take advantage of her.

And so he called her. She'd said she was available, after she'd asked a lot of questions, and thought the hayride would be "nifty." He had also been especially relieved when he found out his father would be out of town that weekend attending a special gathering of Masonic grand masters. He knew his mother would give him permission to go on the hayride with Beverly, and he had been right.

Bundled up in a white turtleneck and a fleece-lined woolen jacket, Darien craned his neck as he looked around for Beverly in the gathering of couples that waited in the town center's parking lot for the horse-drawn wagons. He checked his watch, a gift he'd received from his parents the previous Christmas. It was 6:05 p.m. Beverly had said she'd be there by 6:00 p.m. so they could get a good spot on one of the wagons, but she wasn't there, and neither were the wagons.

He cupped his hands around his mouth and blew into them, his chilled breath creating a rush of mist as he tried to warm his hands. The temperature was now dipping into the low forties again and likely to drop even further as the evening went on. He wished he'd brought along some gloves, if not for himself, then maybe for Beverly. A gesture of chivalry, he thought. He stuffed his hands into the pockets of his dungarees and walked around a group of older teenagers, some of whom he recognized but didn't really know, and scanned the other side of the parking lot and the street beyond facing the package store and Olsen's meat market.

A newer model Hudson caught his eye as it pulled into an empty space in front of the Lion's Club meeting hall, which was sandwiched between the package store and the meat market. The rear door on the passenger side opened, and Darien spotted Beverly as she stepped out.

"Hey, Beverly, over here!" he called as he picked up his stride and met her in the middle of the street.

She was wearing an emerald green velvet jacket and black slacks, slightly overdressed for a hayride, but she looked gorgeous, with her auburn hair framing her face with curls and flowing down onto her shoulders. Darien was tongue-tied. She smiled back at him as he awkwardly patted her on both arms, wanting to hug and kiss her but afraid to start this date out on the wrong foot.

She turned around to see if the car had pulled away, and when she saw it had, she turned to face Darien again, leaned in, and kissed him lightly on the lips. "Sorry I'm a little late. My brother had trouble starting the engine. Don't know why. It's only two years old. Must have been because of the sudden drop in temperature this week. He … My gosh! I'm rambling on here, aren't I?"

"No, you're not. I like hearing you talk," he replied, taking her hand and guiding her back to the parking lot where four horse-drawn wagons, each tethered to a pair of draft horses, were now lined up in a row. The wagon beds were covered with hay and two rows of tightly packed hay bales stacked down the center, providing enough room for couples to sit on them around the three sides, with plenty of room for couples to also sit on the wagon bed and hang their feet over the edge.

They walked back around the gathering of older teenagers and one or two adult couples—clearly at least their parents' age, Darien thought—and took up a spot near the back of the wagons where he figured they would board. Maybe the adults were the chaperones, he reasoned, since with four wagons there had to be more chaperones than Coach Amberly and his wife.

Darien and Beverly remained quiet, only exchanging occasional quick glances at each other, but their entwined hands were communicating, an exchange of subtle squeezes that aroused him. He wondered if she was feeling any similar sensations as he allowed a shy smile to creep across his face.

She tossed her hair to one side as she returned the look, her eyes locked with his. He couldn't wait to get on one of the wagons and sit close to her, but the mere thought was turning him on even more, so he quickly dropped her hand and feigned the need to stretch, bringing both arms around his shoulders and twisting to one side and then the other, all an elaborate attempt to alter his mental fixation on sex and think about something else. Then a loud voice echoed out of a bullhorn held by one of the male chaperones.

"Okay, everybody! Please listen up."

The low-level buzz of chatter faded into silence as the crowd focused its attention on the announcer.

"First of all, welcome one and all! We've got a fine turnout this evening, and I can assure you there'll be more than enough room for everyone on the wagons once we are all set to get on."

The crowd began to move toward the wagons, and the heavyset man in overalls barked, "Now just hold your horses! We're not quite ready for you to get on board. We've got cups of cider and some donuts to pass out before you get on. So if you'll just move over to the area where the ladies will serve you … slowly now … you can all get something to drink and a couple of donuts. Home-made, mind you! And just so you know, the chaperones will bring along jugs of cider and more donuts if any of you are still hungry after you board and we get going."

Couples started for the serving area before he'd even finished. Darien took a step to where the others were moving and then stopped when he spotted a face he recognized and knew all too well—Jimmy French, Sandy's older brother, who had dated Beverly a couple of years earlier and who had also knocked him out a few years prior to that after Darien and Sandy had taken one of Jimmy's girlie magazines and scribbled mustaches and goatees on the faces of the women. A sensation traveled up his spine as he glanced over at Beverly. She'd seen him as well and dropped her eyes to the ground.

"What's the matter, Beverly?" He already suspected that he knew but didn't let on.

"Nothing," she responded a little too quickly. "Why would you think there was something the matter?" She gave him her best attempt at a look of confusion as she wrapped her arm around his and began walking to the back of the refreshment line, pulling him along with her.

Darien glanced back in the direction of where he'd seen Jimmy French, but he had evidently moved because now Darien couldn't spot him. "I don't know … I guess I just thought you had a look on your face, is all." He decided to let it go. Maybe she *hadn't* seen her old boyfriend. Maybe it was just his imagination and his … what? Jealousy? The idea of her possibly having had sex with Jimmy *did* bother him, but he'd get over it, he told himself.

"You're just too sensitive," she said as she leaned her head on his shoulder and gave him a crinkle-nosed smile, adding, "But I think that's sweet." They arrived at the front of the line and were now being handed tall cups of apple cider and a small napkin topped with two freshly deep-fried donuts.

"Oooh! The donuts smell so good!" she said as she maneuvered a bite from one of them.

"You're right. They taste a lot like the ones Mom makes for us at home," Darien replied with genuine enthusiasm as he took a large bite of one. His mom made some of the best desserts he'd ever tasted. "You should try hers some time. They're super crunchy on the outside and just right on the inside."

"I'd really like to!" she said, giving him a look that said, "Why don't you invite me?"

Darien was already thinking ahead to their next date and how he could arrange to have her over for dinner or an afternoon picnic or something … and make sure his mother baked a batch of her special donuts. He was sure this date was heading just where he wanted it to, as the two of them, cider and donuts in hand, left the food area and headed to one of the wagons that now had a few couples already on it, sitting on the inside row of hay bales.

Darien set his napkin with the one remaining donut and the cup of cider down on the edge of the wagon and hoisted himself up with the help of one of the chaperones who extended a hand to him from above. Once on the wagon, he reached down to Beverly and brought her up in one easy pull, grabbing her around the waist to steady her once she was on the wagon bed. She felt light as a feather and moved in against him, setting off another mini-explosion of hormones. He quickly backed away and guided her to sit on one of the bales of hay in an area that was still empty.

When the last of the stragglers were settled in, the heavyset man with the bullhorn got everyone's attention with a final orientation about the hayride.

"We're going to move out of the parking lot and down onto South Main and then travel to the outskirts of town, where we'll get off the main road and take Oak Ridge Road into the area known as Oak View Hills. For those of you who haven't been there before, Oak Ridge Road makes a complete circle through that entire area and loops back around onto itself. The whole ride covers about eight miles of gravel road and should take us around two and a half to three hours to get back onto South Main. From there, figure another twenty minutes or so to get back to this parking lot. All in all, about three to three-and-a-half hours of taking in the night sounds and the full moon that's already beginning to light up the sky above," he said, pointing to the night sky. "And for some of you guys who get lucky, maybe a bit of spoonin' time as well! Just keep things proper, and you know what I'm talkin' about!"

A few guffaws and a titter or two broke out from different spots on the wagons as the drivers, one after another, picked up the reins, tightened the tension on them a bit, tapped their whip lightly on the haunches of their horses, and moved out onto the street that circled the commons and headed for South Main in single file.

Chatter and laughter broke out among the couples as the convoy of wagons headed south past the library and the old Victorian homes that lined South Main Street, the horses' hooves mixing in with the cacophony of voices that filled the air.

Darien put one arm around Beverly's shoulders and laid his hand on her arm, giving her a little squeeze. She responded with a smile and snuggled up closer to him. Settled in now, he looked around the wagon to see who else was on it. He spotted one of his classmates, Jerry Farley, who upon seeing Darien and Beverly, shouted, "Score one for Big Dee!"

Darien felt himself blush but simply smiled and waved in return. Inwardly, he was happy he'd been noticed out on a date with Beverly. His manhood was validated by the remark. But it was about to be tested in a way he hadn't planned.

Chapter Thirty-Six

A Few Hours Later:
A Matter of Pride and Honor

As the horse-drawn wagons made their way back onto the macadam of South Main, their shoed hooves clattered and then smoothed out into a regular pattern of sound. The teenagers were now mostly quiet, dreamy-eyed couplings that were either soaking up the exciting feelings, the security of one's first love, or were nodding in sleep.

For Darien, the hayride and his date with Beverly had turned out better than he had hoped. He'd gotten to first base—second base, actually. She hadn't resisted kissing him and had even allowed him to rest his hand over the breast area of her soft emerald green jacket. That was plenty enough action for him to feel that she liked him and to show him that he might expect their date to progress into more frequent dating, maybe even going steady, a thought that appealed to him very much. He pulled her closer and kissed the top of her head as she rested it against his neck and continued to knead his other hand with both of hers. He was content, and it appeared she was as well. He closed his eyes and savored the feelings for several minutes until he sensed someone standing over them.

The tall, broad-shouldered, older teenager stood very close, his legs spread slightly and his hips thrust forward, nearly in Beverly's face. Jimmy French was staring at her, ignoring Darien as if he weren't even there.

"Hi, Bev. Long time no see. How are ya these days?" There was a slight grin on his face, one that, along with the continual eye contact, conveyed strong sexual energy. Apparently even Beverly felt it because she opened her eyes suddenly, stirred out of a light sleep. And now she looked scared. Or was it embarrassed or something else Darien couldn't figure out? Darien removed his arms from around her and stood up, forcing Jimmy French to take a step back to maintain his balance.

"Hey, Jimmy. What's on your mind?" Darien said, mustering up as much bravado as he could yet still trying to remain calm and casual.

"I think I was talking to Beverly, *Big Dee*. Or maybe I should say *Little* Dee!" Jimmy broke into laughter and turned to wink at another older teenager sitting a couple of hay bales away. "That's what I hear, anyway. Ya know what I mean?"

More laughter.

Darien felt a rush of anger flood through his body as he tightened his fists. A memory flashed through his mind, followed by a second or two of fear. But the rage he felt pushed the feelings away, and it didn't take but a few seconds more for him to react.

Bringing his left arm behind him, he drove it as hard and as fast as he could into Jimmy's mouth and nose, catching him off balance and unable to ward off the blow. It brought blood and caused Jimmy to grab onto Beverly to keep his balance.

She screamed as she grasped the straw bale she was sitting on. Jimmy quickly recovered his balance and repositioned his stance, lowering his center of weight as he hauled back his massive right arm and connected with Darien's midsection, knocking him onto the wagon bed and nearly off onto the roadway.

"Stop it, Jimmy!" Beverly yelled, now grabbing hold of Darien's jacket to keep him from tumbling off the wagon.

"Hey, you two!" shouted one of the chaperones, who rushed from another part of the wagon to break up the fight. "Stop that right now!"

Jimmy was over six feet tall, burly, and a good twenty years younger than the older man, who was also a good thirty pounds lighter and obviously not used to fighting. Jimmy pushed him out of the way without any real effort and then pulled Darien back onto his feet and punched him with his other fist, landing an upper cut to Darien's jaw, sending him off the wagon to the macadam road.

Darien let out a guttural sound as he catapulted through the air and hit the pavement on his shoulder, trying to roll as he'd seen guys do on television and in the Western movies. The damage was done. He heard the cracking of something and the immediate rush of heat to that part of his body. His head also slammed against the hard surface of the road, and he fell silent.

Screams broke out on the wagon as the driver pulled the horses to a stop and both the driver and the chaperone dropped down onto the pavement and knelt over Darien. Beverly began crying and rushed over to the wife of the chaperone and buried her head on her shoulder as the woman tried to comfort her and calm her down.

Jimmy French straightened up and swaggered back over to his date and his friend and his girlfriend. "Fuckin' serves him right!" he said as he sat back down and shook his head defiantly. Those around him quieted, avoiding eye contact with him.

"Darien. *Darien*! Can you hear me?" the chaperone Dennis Sullivan asked, lightly tapping Darien's chest. Darien laid there, his eyes vacantly staring up at the night sky. Dennis frowned and turned toward the wagon driver, shaking his head. "Jesus, God Almighty! This doesn't look good, Earl. We need to flag down the next car that goes by … get him to a doctor or the nearest hospital." He felt Darien's wrist for a pulse.

"He's still alive, but it's not a very strong pulse."

Earl Riley ran back past the two remaining wagons stopped behind them, shouting as he went by, "The kid's hurt pretty badly! We need to flag down the next car that passes." Pointing to the wagon driver at the rear, he said, "Can you get all your people off the wagon bed and maneuver around us? Get those horses going as fast as you can toward town, and stop at the first house you see with lights on and a car or truck in the front yard. Ask whoever lives there if they'll bring their car back down here so we can get this poor kid to the hospital. We think he may be in a coma. And if you haven't found anyone by the time you reach Dr Willard's, bang on his door and wake him up if you need to! This kid's gotta get medical attention—soon!"

As Earl made his way back to the scene of the accident, he waved some of the teenagers who had begun to dismount from the wagon behind the one from which Darien had been shoved. "Please, everyone! Stay where you are. We need to keep the area in front of you clear so we can get to the young man who's been hurt."

"Who's been hurt?" "How did it happen?" "Did he fall off?" the concerned teenagers and chaperones shouted.

"Please, everyone, stay calm. We've got everything under control. There was a little fight between the young man who's hurt and some other kid. He fell off, and we don't have any more information than that right now. Just stay in your places on the wagon … and maybe say a prayer. He looks like he could use some."

Chapter Thirty-Seven

Same Evening:
A Place in Between

Darien felt weightless as he gazed down at all the activity below him. He could barely see two figures ... men, kneeling over a lifeless body. Beyond them were several horse-drawn wagons, both in front and behind, filled with more figures huddled in pairs, all seeming to be in prayer, their heads bowed with hands clasped in front of them. He heard little beyond a low murmur of whispered voices, some reciting the rosary, others in quiet conversation ... or so it seemed to Darien. Others, farther beyond the line of wagons and horses, milled around at the side of the road.

He felt surprisingly calm and unafraid. The last memory he had was of feeling a blow to his jaw and another impact as he landed on his back. A violent slam on the back of his head followed and then nothing. He was feeling no pain whatsoever ... just a kind of tranquillity. That he was now floating above this scene, viewing what he intuitively knew included him in the middle of it, did not seem strange though he certainly knew it should at some level. No, this reminded him of other times he couldn't clearly recall, times when he'd experience flying through the sky with lots of others flying with him and around him. He searched his memory for a better sense of when, but it all seemed timeless and blurred together.

He looked at the space around him and saw nothing, no other people floating up there with him, although he had the distinct impression he wasn't really alone up there some twenty to thirty feet above the scene below. His hearing seemed to be much sharper than it had ever been before, not so much for hearing what was being said down there by all those people, but other whispers from around him up wherever he was.

He looked up, sensing that was where he would find the source for the faint voices he heard. And then he felt himself being sucked up into a spiral of brilliant white light. He was suddenly surrounded by an energy storm of dazzling colors— vivid blues, deep purples, and iridescent shades of gold and yellow and that singularly pure, white light at the center of it all. He was a part of it; his body dissolving into gloriously beautiful sparkles of those same colors. He saw other similar entities that had no discernable physical shape. Yet he knew instinctively they were people he had known.

There was his birth mother, looking so very different from that time he'd seen her in the hospital, and a brother he had never seen in life and yet recognized. One of the first couples that had ever taken him in, as a very young infant, was there. And he sensed a grade school friend who had been killed by a hit-and-run driver when he was barely nine years old. All of this was unexplainable to Darien, and he felt fear for the first time during this extraordinary experience. Was he dead? Had he just "passed over" as he'd heard his mother call it when people died?

And then he heard himself pleading, over and over, "Sundeep, be with me now. Sundeep, be with me now!"

"Pax vobis ego sum nolite timere (Peace be to you. It is I. Fear not.)." And the faint voice grew nearer and said again, this time as if whispering right into his ear, "Pax vobis ego sum nolite timere."

And that was the last Darien remembered of that evening.

Chapter Thirty-Eight

Palmer Hospital:
Four Days Later

Virginia Edwards took in the swollen, barely recognizable face that was Darien Edwards. Closed, puffy eyelids covered any sign of life. His head was bathed in white bandages, lightly stained with spots of pink, yet she maintained her stoic smile and focused on the lifeless body in the hospital bed, determined he would be greeted with an assuring "everything's going to be okay" countenance when he awoke from the coma-like state he was in.

"Is he going to be okay, Mom?" asked Billie, who stood to one side of her. A look of deep concern spread across his face as he shook his head, unaware of the movement that outwardly expressed what he couldn't bring himself to say.

"Of course he is, Billie. He's going to be just fine." She looked up at him, continuing to smile, encouragingly. "Yes, he is," she added, almost as if to herself. "Aren't you, my son?" she continued, now looking back down at Darien. She took one of his hands in hers and gently rubbed it.

"But he looks so awful, Mom. How long did the doctor say he might be this way before he wakes up? It's been four days." Billie took in the back brace that kept Darien from moving too much and the shoulder and arm cast that enveloped Darien's upper left side from his neck down to his waist. He moved to the other side of the bed and laid one hand on Darien's good shoulder and shook it lightly.

"Come on, Big Dee, wake up. We need to have you back here with us." Billie continued to stare at Darien, shaking him every few seconds. No response. "Listen to me, Big Dee! This is Billie, and I'm telling you—no, insisting! Wake up!" he said louder, shaking him more roughly. "Dammit! Wake up, for Chrissake!"

"William, watch your language!" Virginia hissed, trying to be quiet but still letting him know that she was his mother and he'd better listen, even if he was nearly twenty-one. She broke into a coughing spell and leaned away from the bed as she took a handkerchief from her sleeve and coughed into it, sputtering to catch her breath. She was having one of her wheezing spells and stood holding onto the bed as she made her way toward the door to the outer hallway to get more air.

"Mom, wait! Look! Look at Darien! His eyes are fluttering. I think he's waking up!" Billie shouted.

She stopped dead in her tracks and spun around to see. Yes, Darien *was* trying to open his eyes! "Nurse! Quick! Someone!" she cried out. "He's opening his eyes!" She motioned toward the door to Billie. "Go find your father, Billie! I think he's in the visitor's area down the hall."

Billie hesitated and then raced out the door and down the hall. Within seconds, he and his father reappeared at the door and hurried in. Stanley Edwards squinted as he took in the scene of his younger son lying in the bed. "Has he said anything?" he asked, looking at his wife and then at the nurse, showing no hint of what he might be thinking or feeling over his son's condition. But his wife understood him and didn't react.

"Not yet," Virginia replied.

Darien strained to see through the blurred image of something or someone standing over him. Now a second and a third object appeared, and he felt someone pat both sides of his face.

"Can you hear me, young man?" the nurse asked, now checking his pulse.

He struggled to speak but couldn't get his mouth to move the way he wanted it to. "Uhhh huhhh," he finally managed to say.

Seeing the concern on the faces of Darien's mother and brother, she turned to them and said, "He can't speak too clearly right now because of the jaw fracture. But the fact that he's able to respond is a very good sign indeed." She turned back to Darien and asked, "Can you raise your left hand?"

He struggled to raise a finger. It moved ever so slightly.

"How 'bout the other one, young man? Can you wiggle your fingers?"

Darien lifted the tips of his fingers and then let them drop. Exhausted, he dropped back into a deep sleep.

"What's happening to him? Is he okay?" Billie asked, fear replacing the look of relief he'd just shown a minute ago. He reached behind the nurse to shake Darien again, but Virginia, who had come up close to Darien when he awoke, thrust her arm toward Billie and said, "Don't try to wake him up, dear. He needs to rest."

Having gone through nearly two years of training at Bellevue Hospital in New York City, a hospital that offered one of the finest nurses training programs in the country, Virginia had some understanding and experience with trauma patients.

She knew Darien needed rest, and the nurse confirmed it when she said, "Your mother's right. He needs to sleep." The petite nurse tucked some errant strands of hair back beneath her nurse's cap and added, reassuringly, "He's going to be all right. He's going to be all right."

"Did you hear that, Stanley? He's going to be okay!" Virginia reached to her husband and grabbed his arm as she wiped away a tear.

Stanley put his arm around his wife's waist and said, "Good. That's good, dear. And when he's able to talk, I want to find out just what happened on that hayride because Dennis and Earl have avoided telling me exactly what went on. I'm going to find out, come hell or high water!"

Chapter Thirty-Nine

Three Days Later: Making Sense of It All

Darien opened his eyes as the sound of the squeaky food cart and rattle of dishes stirred him from an early morning half-sleep. He was able to see more clearly now with the swelling of his face beginning to lessen. The day before, the doctor had instructed the day nurse to remove all the bandages from his head and to replace them with a more localized set of gauze and adhesive bandages. That had allowed Darien's face to begin looking more like it did before the altercation with Jimmy French. And he was now able to speak a little more clearly, although it still hurt for him to pronounce certain syllables.

"A tasty breakfast today, Darien," announced the sprightly nurse in a clearly British accent as she removed a covered tray from the stainless steel cart and placed it on his side table. "French toast with bacon and real New England maple syrup," she added.

"Looksh almosh ash good ash what Mom makesh," he replied, struggling not only with his speech but also with getting in a more upright position to eat.

"Let me help you with that," she said, grabbing hold of his hospital gown and pulling him forward as she adjusted the pillows behind him. She rolled the side table over closer to the bed and positioned the attached metal tray in front of him so he could reach his meal. She moved the covered breakfast plate onto the tray and handed him a napkin and fork and knife. Finally, she placed a plastic container of milk, a straw, and a small cup of orange slices onto the tray and backed away. "There, that should do you for a while. I'll leave you to eat in peace. You don't need a bloody Brit to spoon-feed you now, do you?" It was not so much a question as a statement, delivered with a hearty smile.

"Thanks, Mishes Fallon," he said as he watched her leave the room.

Darien had taken to her bubbly personality the moment he first became aware of her the day after he came out of the coma. She was the only one of the nurses and attendants he felt really comfortable with. She was a bit like what he thought a kindly mother might be like.

Not that his own mother wasn't wonderful to him, but she just wasn't … what was the word he was searching for? Joyful? Happy? Yes, and light about things. As much as he cared for his mother, she always seemed so serious about life. He wondered sometimes if that was because she came from such a large, fairly poor family—eleven brothers and sisters, although three of them died before Darien was adopted. One had succumbed to diphtheria and two from cholera, diseases very common in the early 1900s.

He'd heard his mother and father speak about their lives growing up during the Depression. Those had been really tough times the way they spoke about them, anyway. He remembered how they'd talk about living on a quarter a day. Having to eat lots of potatoes. How they'd make a pound of ground beef last for an entire week. When he heard those kinds of stories, he felt pretty fortunate to be living as well as they did, for they really never wanted for anything they needed. *Maybe not what I've wanted,* he thought, *but all I've needed.*

Darien returned his thoughts to the food in front of him and lifted the aluminum cover off his plate of pancakes, poured some syrup over them, and managed to cut into one with his fork. He lifted the fork and slowly opened his mouth and pulled the piece of gooey pancake off the fork with his teeth. It was difficult to chew, but it tasted good, and he stabbed at another portion, following that with a piece of bacon. He was in heaven.

As he continued eating, his thoughts wandered back to that night. He hadn't heard anything from Beverly, and he wondered why. Had she called and his father had answered and simply hadn't told him? But of course Darien realized there hadn't been any opportunity for his father to speak to him about anything since he hadn't made the trip in to visit him in the hospital since the day Darien awoke from his coma-like condition. And that was good actually. He felt much more able to talk to his mom than to *him.*

Maybe Beverly hadn't called at all. That thought wasn't very encouraging, and he tried to push it into the back of his mind, but it wouldn't leave. He wondered about Jimmy French and why he'd done what he'd done, approaching Beverly the way he had that night on the hayride. He had a girlfriend with him. What would be the reason he'd decide to get up and start talking to Beverly that way ... sort of cocky and flirty? Jimmy was known to be a bit of a lady's man, talking about how he always scored with any girl he dated. He'd heard that from his friend, Sandy, Jimmy's younger brother.

Darien found himself remembering the conversation that night at the supper table when he'd first told his parents of

Beverly inviting him to the Sadie Hawkins dance. How his father had referred to her as a tramp. The fact that Beverly had gone away for almost a year, not too long after she'd been Jimmy's steady girlfriend. Was it true she'd been knocked up by Jimmy and went away to have the baby in secret? And had given the baby up for adoption? He didn't want to believe that. No, Jimmy was just being a prick and a bully, just like when he'd knocked Darien out cold a few years before that and for no apparent reason. At least not one Darien could understand.

He felt good about his having stood up to the bastard, a word Darien frequently used in his thoughts but never allowed to slip off his tongue, for fear he'd do it in front of his mother or father. Then there'd be hell to pay!

Yes, even if Jimmy had knocked him off the wagon and all this had happened as a result, he still knew he'd acted like a man. He smiled to himself as he went over the fight. He'd connected real good when he'd landed that first punch to Jimmy's nose. Got him good, blood and all! No, he didn't have anything to be ashamed about. He'd stood up for his girlfriend. There! He'd said it. She was his girlfriend now. And that made him feel good.

He finished eating his breakfast and settled back in the bed for a little nap until his mother came for her daily visit later that morning. Thoughts of himself, mounted on a steed and dressed in shiny armor and holding a lance, surfaced. In the vision Beverly was seated close behind him, her arms around his waist. These images filled his mind as he drifted into sleep, defending her from the evil arch enemy, Jimmy French.

Chapter Forty

Later That Morning:
Their Little Secret

Darien opened his eyes and smiled when he heard her voice and glanced up at the round clock on the wall of his hospital room. "Hi, Mom. Right on time!"

"Hi, Darien. How're you feeling this morning? Better and better in every way every day?" This was a saying his mother often used. For all her stoic ways, she quietly led her life believing in mind over matter. Actually, not so quietly because that was also a statement she frequently made whenever he or anyone else was complaining about or facing a cold or some aches and pains.

Darien had once found some pamphlets and reading material from some group called Science of Mind, material his mother had picked up on one of her evenings out. It wasn't too often she would go anywhere with their car in the evening, particularly by herself, unless it was to one of her Eastern Star meetings in the center of the town. But he recalled there were a few times when she drove into Springfield alone, and that had been one of those times. He'd looked through the little booklet she'd left on the desk when she arrived home that evening, but he didn't really understand what he was able to read and, besides, religion had never seemed very important to him, nor did he really understand why people went to church every Sunday. He certainly didn't get much from the sermons, other than sometimes feeling guilty because he thought things he shouldn't and even did things that were against the Ten Commandments. That thought always caused Darien to feel clammy and uncomfortable, so he quickly shoved it out of his mind.

Darien reached out, as best he could, to offer her a hug. She bent in toward him and accepted it and planted a kiss on his cheek before she pulled up a chair and sat down next to him.

"I'm feeling better and better, Mom." She always liked it when he repeated one of her pet sayings. He looked at her for a moment and then asked, "Has Beverly called for me?"

"Actually, she did, the morning after your ... accident. I was the one who picked up the phone. Your father was still out of town and didn't arrive home until later in the day." Virginia paused, studied her son, and then went on. "She was quite worried about you, as were we all! She apologized several times, as if she thought it were her fault. Of course, at the time, I didn't know anything except that you'd fallen off the wagon. I knew you were with her, but that was all. And then when I pressed her for more information, she told me. It was very difficult for her to talk about it.

"She said Jimmy French had come up to the two of you and started acting in a way that made her uncomfortable, that you'd stood up to him in her defense, and that he had said some unkind things about you and that you punched him." She shook her head and then laid a hand on Darien's chest and took a deep breath as she flipped her head back. "I'm very proud of you, young man! You know I don't condone fighting, but you stood up for her and for yourself. You shouldn't feel bad about your own actions or the fact that …" Her voice trailed off for a second. "That he … that you were knocked off the wagon. He was bigger and older than you and should be ashamed of himself!"

Darien felt tears well up in his eyes, not from sadness but from gratitude that he'd made his mother proud of him. He cleared his throat and asked, "Does Pop know about any of this? That I was on a date with Beverly and how it happened that I got knocked off the wagon?"

"No, dear, I didn't think it was necessary for him to know any of that. At least not about Beverly being involved. Now about the fight between you and Jimmy French, I think he may have to know of that. He's bound to find out when he pushes Dennis Sullivan and Earl Riley for more details."

"Can't you tell him it was just an accident, that I stumbled and fell off? That way he won't start asking me all kinds of questions about why we started fighting or even that Jimmy got the better of me." That was the crux of the matter for Darien. He didn't want his father to find out he'd been beaten by another kid, even if the kid was two years older than he. "Tell him you already talked to Mr. Sullivan and Mr. Riley. Then he won't need to call or talk to them."

"Honey, I can't lie—no, I *won't* lie to your father. He may not be very happy to hear about you having another date with Beverly, but he still needs to know everything about what happened. And I'll be sure to let him know you asked for permission to go. I'll tell him it came up at the last minute, after he'd left for his Masonic affair in Boston. How's that?"

"Will you be sure and mention that I stood up for her and landed a pretty good punch before I … lost my balance and fell off the wagon?" That was not really lying, just explaining it in a different way, he reasoned, hoping she'd agree.

She waited a few seconds before she answering. "I don't think that version of the events strays that far from the truth, do you?" she asked, smiling in a conspiratorial manner. "I just won't mention anything about 'what caused you to lose your balance and fall off.'"

Darien breathed a sigh of relief. He could live with his father not liking his dating Beverly as long as he didn't hear that another kid had the last punch.

Virginia sat back in her chair and fell into what looked to Darien like deep thought, although she continued to gaze over at him.

"What, Mom?" he asked, sensing she wanted to ask him something.

"Mr. Sullivan said you mumbled something while you were on the ground after you fell. Do you remember saying anything?"

"No. What did he think I said?"

"He wasn't sure, but he thought you said 'so deep,' or something like that. Does that ring any bells for you?"

"Not that I ..." Darien paused as a thought came to mind. *Why would I have mentioned that name, Sundeep?* It had been several years since he had even thought about that magical friend he'd clung to during his early years. But hearing the name in his head set off another very vague, and much more recent, memory. *Why am I having a memory of being somewhere else right after my fall? The incredibly beautiful balls of light ... and the sense that I somehow recognized them as people from my past?*

He realized he was frowning and that he hadn't answered his mother's question. "Not that I can think of, Mom. It was probably just something I might've said as a result of hitting my head on the roadway. You know, my brain was scrambled or whatever." He gave her a kooky grin and pointed at his head, making a circular motion of his index finger.

She shrugged and said nothing further.

Changing the subject, he said, "Mom, has the doctor told you yet when I will be able to go home?" He was already thinking about getting back to his regular routine. And of seeing Beverly again.

"We'll be seeing him during his late-morning rounds, I would imagine, and we can ask him. But judging from how much better you look and are talking, I wouldn't be a bit surprised if he didn't release you later today or tomorrow."

Darien perked up and added, proudly, "You know I'm now able to walk pretty well, even without any help. Last night after you left, I walked down to the waiting room and back."

"Then I'm sure they'll tell us you can leave real soon."

Encouraged by his mother's comment, Darien sat up, pulled the sheet off, and dangled his legs over the side of the bed. He carefully stood and walked over to the other chair in the room and sat down.

"What are you doing? Did they say it was okay for you to move around like this?" She asked, a concerned look spreading across her face.

"Mom, if they let me walk down the hallway, I can certainly sit in a chair!" he said.

"But you need to be careful with your shoulder, dear. It needs time to heal properly."

"I am being careful, Mom. See? I'm not leaning back against the chair, and I'm being real careful with how I move my right arm."

She nodded and then said, "I meant to tell you. Your homeroom teacher, Mrs. Cleary, called earlier this week to say how sorry she was to hear of your accident and to check on how you were doing. Of course at that time you were still in a coma, so that's all I could tell her. But I did call her yesterday and told her you were doing much better and might even be coming home within a couple of days. She said she was arranging for your teachers to get her a list of what's been assigned so far and also when any tests are scheduled. She said she'd have them all and I could pick them up any time it's convenient for us."

Darien hadn't given any thought of school or of the fact that he was missing classes and probably had a ton of homework to face when he got home. The thought brought him down from the temporary excitement he was feeling about getting out of the hospital and being back at home. He sighed audibly.

"Honey, don't worry about your catching up with your schoolwork. You're a very good student. You know that. You'll be on top of it in no time." She leaned toward him and said, "Oh! And one of your classmates, Jerry … Jerry …"

"Jerry Farley?" he asked.

"Yes, that's who. He called and said he'd be happy to help you work through your Latin class assignments and also with algebra, if you need him to, although those are classes you're doing quite well in, aren't you?"

"Yeah, but I could use the support once I catch up on reading the chapters I've missed." His mind was now racing ahead, trying to review where they were in his Latin class. Fortunately, it was still the first half of the year for both courses, and he'd only missed four days of school, so it wouldn't be that difficult for him to get up to speed. He relaxed back in his chair a bit. But the mention of his Latin course jogged yet another memory from the night of his fall. *"Pax vobis ego sum nolite timere."* Darien saw the Latin words clearly but was having difficulty translating some of it. Something about peace and fear or no fear. *That's weird*, he thought. Maybe more nonsense caused by the whack on the back of his head. Yes, that must be why. He was recalling some portion of a recent reading assignment from his Latin I textbook. But try as he might, his explanation still didn't sit quite right.

Virginia studied her son. Darien sensed she was about to ask another question, so he quickly shifted her attention back to his discharge from the hospital. "So will you ask the doctor when he makes his rounds to see me in a little while? Will you ask him if I can go home?"

"Sure, dear, as soon as he comes by."

Chapter Forty-One

That Same Evening: Home at Last

Darien entered the living room and sat down on the faded burgundy couch, setting one of his schoolbooks down beside him as he eyed his father sitting in one of the overstuffed armchairs that faced the small Zenith television set across the room. It felt good to be home again, and he took in the room as if sitting there for the first time, not wanting to start his homework yet.

His father lowered the newspaper he was reading and looked over at Darien, a brief hint of a smile crossing his face before he spoke.

"So how does it feel to be back home and out of the hospital?" He kept a steady eye on Darien as if he weren't yet finished with his questions, but he waited for Darien to answer.

"Great, Pop. I'm glad to be out of that hospital gown and back in my own clothes. I still have to get used to having just one arm in the sleeves of my shirts, though." He pointed to the injured shoulder and arm that was firmly bandaged and taped to his side, covered by the shirt, the sleeve hanging empty at one side. "I just hope it won't be too many more days before I can get the bandaging off and use my arm again."

Stanley chewed at his bottom lip and continued. "That was some fall you took! That *was* what happened, right? You *fell* off the wagon. Is that how it happened?" He still had not broken eye contact with Darien, not blinking once. Darien felt himself begin to perspire.

"Pretty much. It all happened so fast I'm not sure I remember exactly. I guess I must've stood up too quickly and lost my balance." Darien glanced down at his hands and saw they were trembling. He brought them together in his lap in an effort to keep them from shaking. When he looked back up at his father, he saw that he also had noticed this.

"Huh. I heard today some talk about—"

"Stanley, could I see you for a minute?" Virginia had come into the dining room and had caught the last part of their conversation.

Darien's father jerked his head in the direction of the dining room and frowned at his wife. "Can't it wait, Virginia? Darien and I were just talking about—"

"I know, dear, but I really do need to speak with you in the kitchen. Right now, if you don't mind too much?" she said firmly but with a sweet smile on her face.

Darien listened to the exchange in silence and watched as his father stood and followed her into the kitchen. He leaned forward trying to listen, but none of their conversation was audible. He sat back for a few moments and then opened his history book and began to read, making an effort to focus on the words on the page. His mother's promise to him when he was in the hospital crowded out his concentration, and he worried now how she would keep it. His father generally ruled the roost, although Darien had witnessed his mother smooth things over on more than one occasion, and that gave him cause for hope. *Maybe she'll convince him whatever he heard was just gossip,* he thought.

He looked up when his parents came back into the living room. He tensed but then relaxed as his father returned to his chair and resumed reading the newspaper. *He'd forgotten what he was about to ask before being interrupted? Or had she managed to dissuade him from pursuing it further?*

His mother approached Darien, her back to his father, and gave him a wink as she reached over to the small side table next to the couch. She picked a piece of unfinished needlepoint off the bottom shelf and retreated back into the dining room where she turned on the overhead chandelier and sat down at the table where the light was better for such up-close work.

Darien scooped his schoolbook off the couch and walked to his bedroom where there'd be no further distractions or the possibility of more questions from his father. Once in his room with the door shut, he allowed himself a few more thoughts about the whole hayride affair, ones that would put it behind him, he hoped.

He was still pleased with himself for having stood up to Jimmy French and for having connected with a good punch to the prick's face, even if he had been knocked off the wagon and nearly killed. Beverly had seen it all and must have felt good that he stood up for her. He reviewed the conversation he planned to have with her the next day once his parents were both out of the house to do their Saturday morning errands in town. He just knew she'd be happy to hear from him and to know he'd be back at school the following Monday. He closed his eyes for a moment and visualized her, *all* of her, and it brought a smile to his face before he settled into his schoolwork. *I am one lucky son of a bitch!*

Chapter Forty-Two

The Next Monday:
A Big Hand for the Big Dee

When Darien swung open the front door to the school building, he was startled by what greeted him: a group of fellow freshman classmates that broke into a loud cheer and clapping of hands. And there were even a few upper-class students, ones who had been on the hayride or had by now heard about the fight and the accident that resulted from it. Among them all was Beverly. She stood off to one side and near the back of the collection of fifteen or so students, but Darien quickly honed in on the fact that she was among them, and he was pleased. And at the very center of the crowd was his homeroom teacher, Clarissa Cleary, an attractive woman who looked to be in her late thirties. She smoothed out imaginary wrinkles from her gray skirt, pulled down the bottom of her pale pink sweater, and stepped forward, motioning the students to quiet down as she spoke.

"We're happy to see you up and walking, Darien. You'll have plenty of time to catch everyone up on your last few days, but I'd like to see you for a few minutes before your first class begins, if you'd come with me to Mr. Higgins' office." She waved him around the students toward the principal's office, leaving the buzz of whispered conversations as the students dispersed and headed off to their classes.

As soon as Darien and his teacher entered the office, she pointed him to a chair and took the one next to him, opposite George Higgins, who was sitting behind the large chestnut desk, his elbows resting on it as his hands played with a lacquered baseball covered with faded signatures. Darien couldn't quite make them out, not that he would've recognized any of them unless they were those of Babe Ruth or Ted Williams, both names he'd heard his father talk about when he was younger.

George Higgins placed the ball back in the clear glass cup where he kept it on his desk and pushed his hands though his full head of graying hair before he spoke. "Darien, first Mrs. Cleary and I want to tell you how relieved we both were to find out your injuries weren't any worse than they were. Not to minimize what happened to you last week on that hayride." He shot a quick glance at Clarissa Cleary, signaling her to join in.

She straightened up and adjusted her position to look more directly at Darien as she spoke. "Yes, we realize that must've been a frightening experience for you … being knocked off the wagon that way and then suffering such a shoulder injury and the concussion on top of that."

"And I want you to know," Principal Higgins added, "that Mr. French has been placed on suspension for two weeks. You needn't worry about running into him any time soon. At least not here at the school."

Darien stiffened upon hearing this last comment but remained silent. He was waiting to see where the conversation was heading.

Clarissa nodded and said, "His parents have been made aware of what happened and will be contacting your parents to address any hospital and other medical expenses this has caused them."

"While the school bears no legal responsibility for any of what happened," the principal said, picking up control of the meeting and passing a look at Mrs. Cleary that caused her to shrink back into her seat, "we do share concern for anything like this that happens and involves any of our students. So we are doing everything we can to make sure this incident goes no further. At least not on school grounds."

Is he saying I need to look out for something happening off school grounds? Like on the way home from school or while I'm in the woods by myself? These thoughts Darien kept to himself.

"And to that end, we'd like to hear from you why you think this … this skirmish happened between you two. Just exactly what happened as you recall things, and what might have led up to it happening in the first place? Was there some kind of ongoing ill will between you and Mr. French?"

Darien squirmed in his seat and licked his lips. *How much should I tell them?* he thought. *I certainly can't mention the real reason Jimmy punched me out a few years ago. And I don't want to bring Beverly into this and maybe stir up any old gossip about her and Jimmy.* He would simply act as if he didn't have any idea about what prompted the fight. And if they questioned why he landed the first punch, he'd say he thought Jimmy was making a play for his girlfriend. Yes, that would be his answer. But it wasn't necessary.

When he replied that he didn't have any idea, Principal Higgins and Mrs. Cleary simply exchanged glances. Then Principal Higgins stood and said, "Well, if anything comes to mind, feel free to share it with either Mrs. Cleary or me." He waited for them both to stand then added, "Mrs. Cleary, perhaps you can stop by again during one of your breaks between classes?"

"Certainly, Principal Higgins." The formality was, of course, part of keeping up the appearances of a business relationship, showing deference to a position of authority. But Darien knew otherwise, having overheard the rumors about his homeroom teacher and the principal from upper-class students.

Darien followed his teacher out of the office and down the hallway back to his homeroom. When they passed the restrooms, Darien pointed and nodded as he escaped into the boy's room to take a moment and think in private.

This saga wasn't over for him. Not by a long shot. The parents of Jimmy French were involved now, and that meant they'd be talking to his parents about this. Jimmy and Darien's friend Sandy, Jimmy's younger brother, would be dragged into the middle of this. *Blood is thicker than water,* he reminded himself. It would all be out there and he'd have to live with it. He shook his head, unaware of the young man, a fellow classmate, who'd just entered.

"What's up, Big Dee?" He slapped him on the shoulder and added, "Glad to see you back!" as he disappeared into one of the stalls.

"Yeah, great to be back." Darien muttered without conviction as he exited and headed back to his homeroom. It was going to be a long day.

Chapter Forty-Three

That Evening:
A Time of Reckoning

Darien toyed with dessert, a vanilla custard his mother had made, one he would normally finish quickly and then ask for seconds. But tonight he was delaying the inevitable, a serious sit-down talk with both his mother and father. It would be about the call Darien had overheard his father have with Conrad French, Jimmy's father and close friend of his parents.

The Frenches had lived up the street for as long as Darien could remember. Conrad and Phyllis French were frequently invited to parties his parents held almost monthly. These parties of four or five other couples would start out with quiet conversation that led to raucous laughter, the telling of off-color jokes, and outbursts of singing as the bottle of rye or bourbon whiskey was emptied over the course of the evening, which ended long after Darien went to sleep. Not that any of them were alcoholic; they just liked to "have a good time," as his father told him one morning when Darien asked about the boisterous noise from the night before that had awakened him during the early hours of the morning.

Darien was puzzled by this other side of the man he had grown to be wary of and to be careful about what he said and how he said it when he was around for fear of a stern warning if he said something his father didn't like. At these parties, he heard his father and mother laugh, sometimes working themselves into nonstop, rolling laughter that would cause his mother to leave the room in search of a handkerchief to wipe the tears from her eyes. He wondered if all the laughter had something to do with the whiskey they drank … highballs, he heard his mother call them. Darien had considered sneaking a bit from one of the open bottles when they weren't around but didn't dare. He'd been too afraid of their finding out, so he hadn't ever tried any. Not yet, anyway. Maybe when he was just a little older, like in a couple of years when he got to go on his senior class trip to New York City.

He felt his father's stare and quickly scooped up the remaining spoonful of custard and wiped his mouth with his napkin. He knew he couldn't stall any longer.

"Ready, Pop? Mom? I know you said you both needed to talk to me about something before I get to my studies." He added this final bit in hopes they'd keep it short.

His father's eyes narrowed as he kept them trained on Darien. "You'll have plenty of time to work on your studies," he said as he stood and walked into the living room and took command center in his chair, the one no one even thought of using unless he wasn't home.

Virginia picked up the remaining dishes and took them into the kitchen. A few seconds later, she reappeared in the living room and sat down on the other end of the couch where Darien was now seated, trying to act casual and making an effort to look like he had no idea what they wanted to talk about. But the perspiration that was breaking out on his forehead likely was telling them quite the opposite, he suspected. He quickly ran his hand over his brow to wipe the sweat away. It was his father who spoke first.

"I got a call from Jimmy French's father earlier today. He tells me you had a fight with Jimmy last week at the hayride, and that's the reason you ended up in a coma with your shoulder fractured. Care to tell us more about that?"

Darien hesitated, shifting in his seat as he frantically tried to assemble an answer. He hadn't felt quite this nervous around his father in a long, long time. Usually his mother would step in and say something that would result in his father backing down his rhetoric or softening his attitude a bit. But this wasn't going to be one of those times, he decided after a furtive sideward glance at her was met with her furrowed brow and eyes that avoided his.

What seemed like an ancient memory to Darien suddenly flooded his mind. He was in the woods, near his favorite rock, and a sparkling blur he could hardly see or make out filled the space in front of him. Only now it seemed like it was right there in the living room, but he quickly dismissed that notion. With the memory came a sense of calm that surprised him. He felt at peace and somehow knew that whatever he said, if he spoke the truth from his heart, would be the right words. He would be okay when this was all said and done. He relaxed and met his father's stare with an open, nondefensive gaze.

"I'm waiting."

"That's true, Pop. I was in a fight with Jimmy French. I was sitting with my date, minding my own business, when he came up and made my date very uncomfortable. He stood over her and very close, so close she had to back away to avoid his crotch. It was a disgusting show of …" Darien searched for words to best describe what Jimmy French had done. "He simply wasn't respecting her, and someone had to stop it. So I did. I stood up and asked him what his problem was, and he responded by making fun of me … of my manhood, and I hauled off and punched him in the face. And then he grabbed at her and evidently landed a good punch to my stomach. The next thing I knew, I was flying off the wagon. I don't remember much of anything after that until I came to in the hospital." Darien took in a deep breath and exhaled as he sat back against the couch. He still felt calm and ready to accept whatever else his father might say or do.

His father's stare softened as he seemed to consider what Darien had just said. He looked over at Darien's mother and then back at Darien before he spoke. "I'm proud of you, Dari." In his kinder moments, he called his son Dari, and this was apparently one of those times. "You did what any red-blooded young man should do, given the situation."

Darien's jaw dropped, and he felt his heart lift in his chest as he broke into a smile while he quickly wiped away a tear welling up in one eye.

"But," his father went on, "I suspect I could teach you a few things about fighting so the next time you have reason to hit someone, you'll know how to avoid the sucker punch he gave you."

"Sure, Pop, if you think it might help, although I bet I could get Billie to show me some stuff. He told me he's been entering some amateur boxing tournaments up near his college. Not that I'm planning on getting into any fights with anyone anytime soon!" he said, pulling up his T-shirt and rubbing his bruised belly that was still a bit sore. Figuring the talk was over, Darien stood, intending to go to his room to finish his homework.

His father nodded and motioned him to sit back down.

"Just who was this date with? I don't recall you telling us anything about going on the hayride or asking permission to go out on a date with anyone. Those are the rules as long as you live under our roof. You know that!"

Darien dropped back into his seat and gave his mother a pleading look to say something.

Virginia sat forward and cleared her throat. "Hon, Darien *did* ask me, and I gave him permission. It was a spur of the moment thing that came up. You had already left for your weekend trip for the Master Masons conference in Boston, remember?"

"Oh." The room was quiet as Stanley considered his wife's explanation for a few moments. "Who was your date?"

Darien slouched down into the sofa as if all his energy had left him. He had hoped this conversation could be avoided, but it was happening whether he liked it or not. He looked over at his mother and caught an almost imperceptible nod. *No support this time. I'm on my own,* he thought. He took a deep breath and mentally crossed himself. *And I'm not even Catholic!*

"I know you heard rumors about her that went around, but—"

"Rumors? You talking about that Simpson girl? They weren't just—"

"Stanley, please don't continue that thought! You don't really know the girl, and if Darien likes her—"

"Mom, I appreciate your standing up for me, but I need to speak for myself, even if I say something Pop doesn't agree with." He took another breath as he leveled his attention on his father, looking him directly in the eyes.

"I've heard those rumors too, Pop. And I don't really know if they're true or not, but this I do know. She's not like that, not the Beverly I know. She's sweet, she's smart as a whip, and I think she's pretty … darned pretty! And I really, really like her, Pop." There! He'd said it, and he felt good about it, although a part of him was cringing inside, waiting for his father to explode.

Instead, all he got was the Edwards Eye. Darien stood his ground, though, continuing to maintain eye contact without appearing disrespectful. Stanley shifted his stare over to his wife, and then it softened and the creases around his eyes and on his brow relaxed. He looked back at Darien and said, with measured words, "Well, if you think that much of her, I expect you'll arrange to invite her over for supper or a Sunday dinner one of these days. Just make sure you get your mother's permission before you invite her." He then picked up the latest issue of *The Saturday Evening Post*, his way of letting them both know the conversation was over.

Chapter Forty-Four

Five Months Later: A Matter of Trust

The Thanksgiving and Christmas/New Year's holidays came and went, and by early the following spring, Darien and Beverly were going steady. They were a couple, as far as Darien was concerned. Even his father had begun to warm up to the idea of him dating her, although she had confided in Darien that she hadn't felt very comfortable around his father shortly after the first time she had dinner with Darien and his parents.

Around the same time, Darien had taken the school driver's education course and had passed his driving test with flying colors. It was then that his father grudgingly agreed he could buy his very own car, an old 1941 Plymouth coupe. He'd even agreed to kick in half the cost of it, provided Darien took responsibility for tags and insurance and would be responsible for maintaining it. This seemed to be a turning point for Darien. He began to feel like he was his own person and that his father wasn't such a bad guy after all.

Now as Darien made his way up the street toward the high school, every now and then leaping across puddles that had collected on the sidewalks after the spring rains, he recalled how he and Beverly had agreed to meet at the skating rink in the center of town the day following that dinner during Christmas break.

It had been while they were circling the man-made pond, its four inches of water now frozen solid after two months of below freezing temperatures, that she told him.

"Darien," she never called him Big Dee like most of the others at school did, and he liked that, "I really enjoyed my time with you and your folks last evening. The meal was wonderful! Your mom is such a good cook. And she's so easy to talk with. I felt like she actually liked me."

They slowed down as they glided around the perimeter of the pond, steering clear of several other skaters who were wobbling along on their skates. Darien took her extended hand and guided her to a stop near a set of benches along one section of the rink. They sat down, and Darien waited to see if she had more to say. She remained silent as she looked away and then back at him.

"And my father?" He paused before going on. "Not so much, huh?"

She studied his face for a moment before responding. "I'm sure he's a very nice man, Darien, but I just felt like … like he didn't like me. I dunno …" She hesitated again. "I felt like he was … judging me." She shifted her position on the bench and looked away.

"That's just the way he is, Bev. He's like that with me too. I don't know why, but you shouldn't take it personally," he said, although he thought otherwise.

"Really?"

"Yes, really!" Darien reached over with both hands and gently turned her face back toward him and kissed her softly and then more deeply as her lips parted and she did that thing with her tongue that aroused him and left him feeling dizzy.

He let go of her and dropped his hands into his lap, feeling flushed and awkward. But he saw she was also red in the face and breathing heavily. He felt pretty certain she was feeling the same, and that brought a crooked smile to his face.

"What?" she asked, her cheeks now growing an even deeper shade of red before she bent her head, trying to hide her own smile.

Darien cleared his throat, regaining his composure before he spoke. "Time to get back onto the ice and take a few more laps around the rink before we call it an afternoon." He picked up his pace, leaving her several yards behind him. He worked his way into a couple of spins and then reversed his direction and began skating backward to her, stopping suddenly just before he reached her with a big smile on his face.

"Show off!" she said, laughingly. "Think you're the only one who knows how to do that fancy stuff?" She pushed off into a long-speed run. She then leaped into the air and managed to complete a rather impressive axel jump, moving right into a glide on one skate, her other leg extended behind her as she made a large, graceful circle back to within a few feet of Darien and stopped.

"Wow!" was all he could say, and that was enough. She curtsied and then took his hand and they skated quietly for another half hour, each lost in their own thoughts.

Darien couldn't remember feeling as happy as he had that afternoon. She was his steady girl, and he felt complete.

Suddenly, he was startled out of his thoughts.

A horn blared as a car slid to a stop, causing him to look up to see he had nearly walked into the path of an oncoming automobile as he had begun to mindlessly cross the main street, which intersected with the end of his street at the top of the hill. He gave the driver one of his sheepish grins as he stepped back to allow the car to continue and for his stomach to settle back where it belonged.

A few minutes later, as he neared the high school building at the southern end of the town center, he heard his name called and turned in the direction of the voice.

"Hey, Big Dee, wait up!" It was one of his classmates and close friends, Frankie Allen, who came into view as he stepped out of Calligan's Drug Store and Confectionery Shop, a family operated business that sold just about anything you could imagine, from magazines, greeting cards, and stationery and school supplies, to cameras and film and even prophylactics, usually purchased by men and teenagers who would motion the owner or an employee they trusted to the back of the store and whisper their requests out of hearing distance from any other customers who might be in the store at the time.

Darien saw Frankie stuff something small into his back pocket as he jogged to catch up with Darien.

"What'd you buy, Frankie, as if I didn't know?" he asked, giving his friend a knowing wink.

"That's for me to know and you to find out," Frankie said, settling into Darien's pace, which was now more leisurely as they approached the main walkway leading up to the set of large oak doors that served as the main entrance to both the school and the small town's offices of the town treasurer, town clerk, and tax collector that took up space at the front of the building.

His friend held the door open for Darien and then put a hand on his shoulder and stopped once they were inside the large vestibule. "So how are things with you and Beverly? All right?" The way Frankie asked the question was unsettling for Darien.

"What do you mean? Why wouldn't things be all right?" He was feeling defensive and wasn't sure why.

"Oh, I dunno. Just wondering, is all."

"Is there a reason why I should think otherwise, Frankie? I mean, do you know something I don't?" Darien backed up, almost like he was distancing himself from the answer he was about to hear.

"Look, Big Dee, you know I'm not about gossip, but—"

"But what?" Darien realized he had raised his voice and tried to shake out the tightness he was now feeling in his shoulders and neck.

"It's probably nothing … but I did hear that someone saw that big guy that transferred here from Palmer, the one that's such a great addition to the senior varsity basketball team. His name is Steve Olsen. Everybody's talking about him."

"Yeah, what about him? And what's he got to do with Beverly? Huh?" Darien was almost shouting now, and other students turned to look at them as they walked by. Darien lowered his voice and asked again. "What's his connection with my girl, huh?"

Frankie hesitated and then continued. "I overheard someone say they saw him slipping a note to Beverly between classes yesterday."

Darien fell silent and just stood there.

"It could've been nothing, good buddy. Just a … a note asking about a homework assignment or something." The way Frankie looked away, Darien could tell he didn't believe what he was saying.

"He's not even in our class, for Chrissakes! So don't try to feed me any BS, Frankie!" With that, Darien turned and quickly walked away. After a few feet, he stopped, turned around, and said, "But thanks for at least being honest with me … about what you heard, that is. Catch up with you later." Then he hurried to his homeroom.

His heart was racing as his mind conjured up his worst fears. *It was true. All of it!* And with that thought, Darien felt the all-too-familiar feeling in the pit of his stomach. He wanted to run. To hide. And the last thing he was prepared for was to see Beverly. But there she was, standing near the open door to their homeroom, with an innocent, open smile on her face.

"Hi, hon!" she whispered as he approached her. She laid a hand on his arm, but he flinched at her touch and pulled away from her without a word as he headed straight to his desk on the far side of the room. He dropped his books on the desk and sat down before glancing up and giving her his best piercing "if looks could kill" stare. And then he sat back and folded his arms across his chest as he silently fumed.

She shook her head with a confused look on her face, but Darien continued to send her his best version of the Edwards Eye. He'd seen it enough growing up under the often-disapproving evaluation of his father. Beverly sank into her seat near the front of the room and continued to shake her head, as if trying to understand this sudden change in Darien. She briefly turned to face him, her look now turning from one of confusion to what Darien could only interpret as irritation. "Fuck you!" he mouthed, causing her to immediately turn away and bury her head in a book.

Chapter Forty-Five

The Truth Comes Out

"Why are you so glum these days, Darien?" Virginia asked as she gathered the breakfast dishes from the table and walked them over to the sink. She rinsed them under running water before placing them on the rubber mat where the dishes would sit until Darien was ready to wash them in a large pan of soapy, hot water before he left for school. She waited for a response, but there was none. So she walked back over to the table, sat down and sipped at her coffee, keeping her gaze on Darien. "Something going on that you want to talk about?"

"Nothing, Mom. Really," he replied, his head down as he played with the last bit of scrambled eggs on his plate. He scooped up a final mouthful and laid the fork down, pushing himself farther away from the table as if he was planning to get up.

"Don't be in such a rush to get away. You've got plenty of time to finish the dishes and get to school before 8:30 now that you have your own car to get you there. Now please tell me what's going on. And don't give me the 'nothin', Mom' stuff." She took a final gulp of the remaining coffee, set the empty mug down, and folded her arms across her chest.

Darien looked up and studied his mother's face for a moment as he formulated his response. "I'm a bit upset, is all." He fingered the end of his fork.

"Go on. About what?"

This was tough for Darien. Speaking aloud the truth of what he'd found out was like adding an engraved headstone to a burial spot—it gave permanence to the reality. Someone had died. No way around that. The name was there with the date of death chiseled into the stone for all to see. Beverly had been secretly involved with this older student, this probably stupid jock with a big schlong who was pumping her for all it was worth. And putting voice to it now meant it was out in the open for him, no longer just a painful thought he kept to himself.

Tiny drops of perspiration formed on his forehead. He felt them trickle to his eyebrows and reached up and wiped them away with the back of his hand. *Go ahead. Tell her. She's probably already figured out what's bothering me, anyway.* "I found out Beverly's been sneaking around behind my back and messing with some senior jock, that's all!" he said, his hurt and anger broadcast in his voice.

A pained expression traveled across his mother's face as she reached across the table and laid a hand on Darien's arm. "Are you absolutely certain?"

"Of course I am!" he said, his irritation rising to the surface.

She looked away, shook her head, and then looked back at Darien and sighed. "I'm so sorry, Darien. I know you liked her a lot. But better you should find this out now than later. You've heard that old saying, right? 'There's other fish in the sea!' And you're still young, honey. Why, you'll probably fall in and out of love several more times before you meet the girl of your dreams—that girl who's just perfect for you and you'll be perfect for her." She smiled broadly. But he didn't seem to want to be cajoled into having a lighter heart, so she added, "You deserve better, Darien! And I'm sure you'll feel more your old self in a few days. And when you start smiling again, some really pretty classmate or one of the freshman or sophmore girls will bat her eyes at you and you'll quickly forget about Beverly."

Darien blushed at the thought, and a small smile tried to make its way onto his face, but he wasn't about to let the things he was feeling go. *She doesn't understand!* Flashes of him and Beverly skating, of the two of them making out in the backseat of his car, both of them wanting to strip down naked and go all the way but both too afraid to do that, surfaced. And then an image of Beverly and the jock forced its way into his mind, an image of them actually doing it. Darien felt the gray void sweep over him, and he stood up.

Putting on his best "I'm really okay, Mom" look, he ventured a second-long smile and, checking his watch, said, "Hey, it's getting late." Without waiting for a response from his mother, he collected the remaining dishes from the table, walked over to the sink, and set them in the basin. He ran hot water into it and poured some dishwashing powder into it, stirring it with his other hand. When he finished washing his dishes, Darien set them on the rack to dry and emptied the basin into the sink, his mind still ruminating over Beverly and Steve Olsen. *That's what I wish I could do with you—flush both of you out of existence!* he thought as he watched the soapy water disappear down the drain.

Chapter Forty-Six

Reckoning Time

For the the next several weeks, Darien was on high alert when he was at school, careful to avoid running into Beverly face to face. Since they shared one class, English history, the best he could do was make sure he sat far away from her. He would try waiting until the last minute before entering the classroom and then checking to see where she was seated. There were two entry doors into the room, one on each side of the teacher's desk, which was positioned between the two doors. Darien would then choose the entry that allowed him to find a seat farthest away from Beverly. He would keep his gaze downward to avoid any eye contact with her as he made his way to a seat. It was awkward, to say the least, but at least he was able to stay focused on his schoolwork, though little else.

The day came, however, when he could no longer avoid a confrontation. He had been scanning one end of the hallway as he headed to the side exit door of the school building at the end of the school day. His back had been to the door as he turned to take one last scan of the stream of students exiting classrooms into the hallway. He pushed the door open and backed directly into Beverly as she was standing on the outside steps, beyond the door. Their backs collided and books flew out of her grasp and onto the steps below.

"Watch where you're going!" She yelled, shaken by the unexpected shove from behind. She whipped her head around. When she realized who it was that had backed into her, her expression changed from annoyance to shock to guarded surprise. "Oh …" she managed to get out.

"Sorry. I shoulda been looking where I was going," Darien said, immediately bending down to scoop up her books and papers and handing them back to her, still avoiding eye contact with her.

She gave him a steady, direct stare as she seemed to be evaluating whether to respond or simply take the books and loose papers and turn and walk quickly away. But she remained standing, the two of them now far enough away from the exit door to allow other students to exit around them. Her eyes remained on him through several furtive glances on his part as he gathered up the courage to at last meet her gaze and maintain the connection. Then she spoke.

"Are you going to keep on avoiding me, or are you going to explain why you're so angry and giving me the cold shoulder all these weeks?" She stood taller as she adjusted her books, bringing them up to her chest and folding her arms around them, creating a defensive shield, like a breastplate of armor.

"You don't know why? Come on, I wasn't born yesterday! I know what's going on with you and that jock. Everybody does!" He shook his head as the image of her with the other young man flashed through his mind. He didn't know whether he could sustain the angry feelings that were just barely blocking out the sadness and the flood of tears that were already beginning to well up. He fingered his glasses as he flicked a finger across the bottom edge of one eye to wipe away the tear that was about to move down onto his cheek, hoping she wouldn't notice.

If she did notice, she didn't let on, but she was clearly shaken by the accusation as a shocked and embarassed look came across her face. Within seconds, tears flowed down her cheeks, and she made no attempt to hide them as she quietly sobbed. In spite of the tears, she continued to stare back at Darien with a look of total disbelief.

"I can't believe you would even think that of me!" she said, a little too loudly, as one or two students within hearing distance stopped and glanced their way.

"Look, Beverly, people *saw* you and him passing notes! So don't give me that innocent look as if you don't know what I am talking about." As he began to give voice to his pent-up feelings, the anger surged and took over. Now he was shouting. "My dad tried to tell me you were a tramp, but I was too stupid to believe the rumors."

"My God! What are you—"

"You know exactly what I'm talking about! You and Jimmy! You let him screw you and you got pregnant and had to go away to a place for girls like you! You tried to hide it by leaving town, but people knew!" He was so mad that he was shaking.

One of Beverly's girlfriends had just come through the door and saw Beverly crying and caught the last part of Darien's verbal attack. Without any hesitation, she shoved Darien, catching him off guard and knocking him off balance. She moved in between them and wrapped one arm around Beverly's waist as she turned toward Darien and said in a quietly threatening manner, "You shut your dirty mouth, you creep! If I weren't a lady, I'd kick you in the balls, not that you have any! Come on, Bev. Let's get away from this asshole!"

Darien was stunned into silence as he stood and watched the two girls hurry away from him and out into the school parking lot where the bus was waiting for other students to board. Neither of the girls looked back at him as they climbed onto the bus and disappeared from view.

He let out a heavy sigh as his shoulders sagged, mirroring his feelings. He felt deflated and sick to his stomach as he replayed in his mind what he'd just said to Beverly. *You are a self-centered bastard! Why did you have to lash out like that, for chrissakes! Why?* He looked around and became aware of a few students who had witnessed the exchange. When Darien looked their way, they averted their eyes and shook their heads as they walked away. Not one made any attempt to talk to him, not even Kenneth, someone he considered a casual friend. *See? Nobody really likes you. They may act like they do, but it's just that, an act! And you know why? Cuz there's something wrong with you!* And with that thought, all the thoughts he didn't want to think about, the ones that had kept coming up all through his early childhood days came up. And with them, all the stuffed emotions bubbled to the surface. He broke into a trot that morphed into a sprint to his car in the back parking lot. Safely in the car, he slumped over the steering wheel and allowed all the sadness and self-loathing out as his sobbing turned into a wail of despair.

Nearly an hour passed. The other students were gone, and only the cars of the janitor and the principal remained. Darien wiped away his tears with a shirt sleeve. An old, old thought surfaced as he recalled an instance when he was barely six. He had been particularly upset with his mother over something he couldn't even remember. But he did recall, vividly, how he'd decided he would run away from home ... for good! His words echoed in his mind as he pictured himself with a pouty but determined look on his face as he announced to his mother with a hastily packed overnight suitcase in one hand, "I'm leaving, and I'm never coming back!"

His mother had calmly reached out, straightened his jacket, and replied, "That's a pretty long walk and to have to carry that suitcase too. Would you like me to drive you to the bus stop?" She never cracked a smile. Of course he didn't get very far, perhaps one hundred yards, before he turned around and went back home, sheepishly sneaking in the side door. No one ever said a word about the incident. It was as if it had never happened. But Darien wasn't a little kid anymore. He was determined to get away. Only this time there was only one way out. And he was never coming back.

★★★★

That thought remained with Darien through the next few weeks as the end of the school year grew nearer. A plan began to form in his mind, and he became calmer and felt more at peace. He no longer made any effort to avoid Beverly or any of the other students. He simply moved through each day, doing what was necessary for that day. He took notes during classes and studied his homework assignments in the afternoon and in the evening when he needed to in order to be prepared for any quizzes or to write papers that needed to be handed in.

During each school day, he generally ate lunch by himself, savoring the egg salad or Spam sandwich his mother nearly always prepared for him, neatly wrapped in wax paper and placed in brown paper lunch bags she saved from her grocery shopping. When finished with his meal, which he usually ate out on the small grassy area behind the school or on one of the wrought-iron benches on the commons across the street from the high school, he would carefully fold the bag so his mother could reuse it for his next day's lunch, stuff it in his back pocket, and toss the wrapper in one of the receptacle barrels located in several spots along the east side of the commons as he headed back to school for his afternoon classes.

In another few days, the school year would be over and he'd be free for the summer. Only this summer would be his last in this little town of Hammerville. While that thought both saddened him and frightened him, he was resolute in his determination to carry out his plan.

Chapter Forty-Seven

Summer Vacation:
Time to Slip Away into the Night

Darien pondered over the articles he had spread out on his bed. There was the securely banded group of First Day of Issue stamped envelopes, each with its colorful image of the stamp affixed to it, his name carefully written on the face of the envelope in perfect cursive penmanship by his maternal grandfather, the person who had first piqued Darien's interest in collecting stamps and old coins. Seeing that Darien was genuinely appreciative of seeing the collection his grandfather had amassed over his seventy-odd years, the old man had begun sending Darien posted commemorative day issues of new US postal stamps back when Darien was barely twelve. Their arrival every few months had always been an exciting moment for Darien.

Now Darien carefully set them aside from the rest of the items on his bed and, taking a small notepad and pencil, scribbled the name of one of his closest friends on a page of the pad: **Sandy**. He tore the sheet from the pad and slipped it under the rubber band holding all the envelopes together before moving on to the next item on the bed.

It was a small leather-bound box intricately tooled with a leaf pattern. He opened the brass clasp and lifted the lid to reveal the contents of the box: over seventy-five aged coins, some silver, some copper, a bronzed piece, and one or two made of gold. These were mostly US coins Darien had collected over the past few years. Some he'd run across in change he'd receive from stores, and some he'd bought at a flea market. He fingered them, unaware of the sad look on his face as he spotted several old Roman coins that were extremely worn almost to the point where he couldn't really see much in the way of detail. Any serious coin collector would realize these were in extremely poor condition, probably not worth more than a few dollars, but for Darien they were priceless. So were the Indian head pennies, of which he had many, and the silver dollars from the mid-1850s.

He closed the lid, fastened the clasp, and wrote the name **Billie** on another sheet of paper and laid it on the leather box. He set the box next to the packet of commerative day covers and heaved a sigh.

For the next half hour, Darien poured over the remaining items: his art supplies, the Brownie Hawkeye camera he had received two Christmases ago, the air rifle he'd been allowed to buy with some of his summer job savings, and a set of gold-plated cufflinks with an inlay of black onyx stone. He carefully attached to each a piece of note paper bearing a name. When he had finished, he arranged all the items in the bottom drawer of his bureau and closed it. Satisfied that he had done what he wanted to do, he moved over to the single padded armchair in the room and sat down, closing his eyes to block out any distractions and pondered his next step.

Billie was away most days attending summer classes at his college. And when he wasn't at school, he spent the bulk of his time with his girlfriend. That meant Darien didn't have to concern himself with Billie being around and making it difficult for him to carry out his plans. His father, of course, was now at work during the week, as was his mother. That gave him plenty of time to do what he needed to do. And when they did get home, he knew there would be explanations thrown out by all three of them, but Billie's offering would be closest to what he had planned. And even *his* explanation of where Darien might be would be off by a half mile or more. By the time real concern had set in, replacing parental anger, Darien knew it would be dark and hardly the time anyone was going to start traipsing through the woods, looking for him. And by the time they did start searching for him, perhaps even calling friends and the local constables to help in the search, he'd be long gone.

Having such an active imagination, it was difficult for Darien to not begin to think about how his family and friends would react, how *Beverly* would feel, when this was all over, but he hoped people would feel bad and responsible for the actions he was about to take. Yeah, they should feel bad! His visions seemed to help justify his plan, and that gave him impetus to do it, though a part of him really didn't want to. He saw that part of himself as weak. A chickenshit! Well, he *wasn't,* and the only way to prove that was to get up and do what he had to do.

Darien remembered the earlier time, when he had been barely six, that he'd hastily packed his little suitcase and headed out the door crying after an upsetting exchange with his mother. He had failed to carry out his threat. But not *this* time!

Darien went to the closet again and pulled out a spare pillow and two blankets Virginia had stored there for the cold winter months. He carried them over to the bed and pulled back the spread. He took the two blankets, rolled them together, and slipped them onto the middle of the bed. He folded the pillow into a ball and placed it between the rolled blanket and the pillow that he normally slept on and pulled the spread back over the makeshift body. A few more adjustments to the arrangement and he was satisfied. If she should open the door to look in on him, she wouldn't know the difference unless she turned the light on, and he didn't think she'd do that.

He stood and walked out of the bedroom and into the kitchen, heading to the stairs that led to the lower level and the storage basement. He nearly jumped out of his skin when the telephone rang. It was a jolt of fear, for he hadn't expected anyone to be calling, and the jarring ring tone, two short bursts, had interrupted his focus. *Should I answer it? Yes!* If it was his mother or father, he or she might wonder where he was or what he was doing if he didn't answer, and he didn't want to arouse any suspicion or questions that would prompt them to possibly call his aunt and uncle who lived across the street and ask them to check on him. He took a couple of deep breaths as the phone rang for the third time and then picked up.

"Hello?"

"Darien, I just called to tell you your father is picking me up from work and taking me to see your Aunt Celia. She's in the hospital. Nothing too serious, but she's alone, and I want to check in on her and make sure she doesn't need anything."

Darien felt a load drop from his shoulders, no longer needing to worry about either of his parents coming home unexpectedly that day. He managed to get out an "Oh."

"We won't be home till at least eight o'clock tonight. You can have some of that shepherd's pie that's in the icebox. All right?"

"Sure, Mom," he said with more conviction, not that he'd be there to eat any of it. "Don't rush home on my account.

I'll be fine. Say hello for me, and … I'll see you later tonight, although I might be in bed by the time you get home. I'm pretty tired."

"When have you *ever* gotten into bed *that* early! Eight o'clock? What's the matter?"

"Nothing, Mom. I just didn't sleep all that well last night, that's all. I'm fine. Really! But if I should happen to go to sleep early, I'll have my bedroom door closed and would really appreciate it if you didn't try to wake me when you do get home."

"Are you sure nothing's wrong? You don't normally go to bed *that* early unless you're not feeling well. Are you feeling feverish or grippy? Maybe you should take your tempera—"

"I'm not sick, Mom! I'm … I'm just a bit tired." Darien waited, hoping she wouldn't ask any more questions.

"Well, I still would like you to take your temperature to make sure you're not coming down with anything, all right? And if you do have a fever, take two aspirins. Okay?"

"Okay! I gotta go now, Mom. Nature's calling, you know what I mean?"

She laughed. "Okay, dear. We'll talk tomorrow when you get up. Bye."

"Bye, Mom." He hesitated, for he wanted to say something more, but thought better of it and hung up the phone. It was time.

For the next hour, he methodically went about collecting what he would need. First, he pulled his gym bag out of the closet and brought it downstairs where he knew the items were stored. One by one he located them and placed them in the bag. When he'd found everything, he zipped up the bag and went back upstairs and into the kitchen. Rumaging through the drawer of utencils, he found two of the last three things he needed and slipped them into the gym bag. But before he zipped it back up, he opened the refrigerator and took the final item out and carefully placed it in the bag and then closed it up. He was as ready as he was ever going to be.

And then he remembered something he'd almost forgotten. He ran back into his room and straight to the small dresser drawer where he kept a stack of photographs. Quickly scanning through them, he found the two he was looking for and stuffed them into his shirt pocket. He returned the rest back to the spot where he kept them, underneath his handkerchiefs and socks, closed the drawer, and left the room. He stopped in the dining room and slowly took one final look around. Taking a deep breath, he picked up the gym bag and headed out the door.

Chapter Forty-Eight

Later That Afternoon: A Silent Good-bye

Darien was breathing heavily now as he came to a complete stop and dropped the gym bag he had been carrying and settled onto his haunches, leaning his back against a large elm tree that stood in the midst of a cluster of smaller ones. The sun was dropping behind the trees in the western sky. It would be dark in another half hour or so.

He had walked some distance from home, perhaps as much as a three miles, and quite deep into the woods that bordered Collier Way, a dirt road that connected their street with the southwestern section of the town where another aunt and uncle lived. He reached over and unzipped his gym bag and pulled out a quart-sized, amber-colored bottle of Hampden Ale. He fished around in the bag for the bottle opener he'd taken from a kitchen drawer before he left and pulled off the beer cap. He knew both his parents would wonder where the ice-cold bottle in the icebox had gone and would probably suspect Billie, who would fiercely deny it. And rightfully so. And they'd likely be even more upset when they found the bottle in the woods. But then it would be too late.

He tilted the bottle back and took a swig. He'd only tasted beer on one other occasion, and he had had the same reaction. It tasted awful. But he also knew that he'd adjust to the malt flavor, and after several more mouthfuls, it would be okay, as the strange, lightheaded feeling took over and he felt that floating sensation.

He reached into his shirt pocket and removed two photographs. One was of Beverly and himself perched on the fender of his parents' car. They both looked happy, and she looked gorgeous, he thought as he looked at it and recalled how it was to have his arms around her waist. He felt the same warm sensation in his groin and the arousal reaction, but it disappeared just as quickly as his thoughts turned to less-happy moments, like finding out she was cheating on him.

He covered the photo with the second picture he'd taken from home, one of Billie and him when he was much younger. Billie wore a mischievous smile as he stood with one arm draped over Darien's shoulder and a hand nestled inside his shirt. A loving pose to the eye of anyone who looked at it. What only Darien knew was that Billie had been pinching his nipple underneath the shirt, which explained the somewhat forced smile that was really a hidden grimace because it had hurt. Darien placed the pictures back in his pocket and took another drink.

Was he *really* prepared to do this? Yes, he told himself. This thing with Beverly was the final straw. He now knew for certain he could never trust any girl—any *woman,* actually. Not to love him, anyway. His mother hadn't. His *real* mother. Nor had his adoptive mother. He'd been convinced early on that she'd only taken him in because she felt sorry for him. And that wasn't love. That was pity, and he didn't want anyone's pity, though, the truth be told, he'd played the pity card on more than one occasion to get attention and for a brief moment to feel like someone cared, that someone felt sorry for him. And Billie had more than once inferred that Darien had been adopted because their mother couldn't bear any more children. From that fact, Darien concluded that she had settled, that she didn't have a choice. And he knew from the very first moment his adoptive father had laid eyes on him that he as sure as in hell didn't care much for him.

The truth of the matter was he didn't *feel* loved. By anyone. He didn't really know what being loved felt like, but he was pretty sure how he felt wasn't it. And it wasn't something one could talk about with anyone else. *That* would've meant he was a sissy, and he wasn't about to let anyone think that about him. As these thoughts swirled around in his head, Darien realized that too many people already thought that of him. His father. Billie. Some of the guys at school, particularly the ones who were good at sports. And older kids like Jimmy. Who was he kidding? Not any of them. Just himself. Yeah, the bitter truth he'd been hiding from was just that: he was a friggin' *sissy*!

Well, maybe he *had* been, but he would show them. He took several more swigs of the ale and felt his courage rise. Yeah, he was ready to do this. He reached into his gym bag and pulled out the nearly six yards of clothesline he had found in the basement before he left his home for the last time. He stood and looked up at the large elm. Just within his reach was a large lower branch about three inches in diameter. Darien tossed one end of the rope over it and pulled on it, bringing it down near eye level. Letting go of the rope, he reached up with both hands, locked them together above the branch, and then allowed the weight of his body to pull him down until his arms were stretched to the point of discomfort. He raised his knees, tucked his legs and feet under him, and hung, suspended nearly two feet off the ground. He held that position for several seconds, making sure the branch would support his weight without snapping.

Satisfied, he extended his legs and stood again. Grabbing hold of the shorter end of the rope, he pulled it down in front of him, and laying it in the palm of his other hand, he created a loop and then allowed the end of the rope to extend in the opposite direction until he had a second loop that looked like an infinity sign with yet another six or seven inches of unused rope. Taking that piece of the rope, he began to wrap it around the makeshift infinity sign and a hangman's noose began to materialize. After making four loops around itself, he carefully tucked the end through the top loop, and holding onto the remaining two inches of rope, he tightened the knot until the knot was firm. Then he pulled on the loop and drew the length of rope through the knot until the loop was large enough for him to place it over his head and around his neck. Placing the loop over his head, he guided it down to around his neck and slowly slid the noose down, taking up the slack until he could feel the noose cutting into his Adam's apple. Satisfied it was working properly, he slid the knot away from his neck and slipped out of the noose.

He drank several more gulps of the ale and set the bottle aside. Next, he took hold of the other end of the rope and brought it over to the trunk of the tree and continued to pull on it until the noose was now hanging at chest level. He briefly studied its placement. When he was sure it was dangling at the right distance from the ground, he wrapped it around the diameter twice and knotted it. He pulled on the noose until the rope held firmly against a smaller branch and then checked the distance from the ground again. It was a bit lower, but he was certain it would still work as planned.

He checked his watch. It was after 7:30. He picked up the bottle of ale and lifted it to the fading light. There was only an inch of ale left. He raised it to his mouth and leaned back as he allowed the remaining liquid to slide down his throat. He was beginning to feel a bit tipsy and grabbed at the tree to steady himself. It was time.

Darien stood in front of the noose, slipped it over his head, and slowly bent his knees as he allowed his body to slide toward the ground. The noose was now cutting into his throat, and for a second, he felt panic set in. He grabbed for the rope line above the noose and stopped the process as he steeled his courage to let go.

He was crying now and closed his eyes, as if that would somehow undo the fact that a part of him was frightened beyond any other time in his life. He wasn't just frightened. He was terrified because he was continuing to slip lower, the noose ever tighter, and he was losing strength to resist and was losing consciousness. He could now feel his hands relax but could do nothing as they limply fell to his sides. For just a fraction of a second, he struggled against the tightening noose. And then everything went black, and he felt nothing. Although he had opened his eyes just an instant before, he did not see the nearly formless figure that hovered over him. Had he, he might have cried out, "Sundeep!"

Chapter Forty-Nine

Earlier the Same Evening: An Empty House

What Darien couldn't have anticipated was that Virginia and Stanley had arrived back home earlier than they'd planned. It was nearing dusk when they unlocked the door and she called out Darien's name as she turned on the overhead light in the dining room.

"Darien?" She looked into the darkened living room. He wasn't there. She noticed the bedroom door was closed and thought that was really quite strange. It was barely 7:00. She turned to her husband and said, "Do you really think he's gone to sleep already?"

"Only one way to find out," Stanley replied, walking to the closed bedroom door. He rapped his knuckles on the paneled door, giving it several quick knocks. No response. With that, he turned the knob and pushed open the door. Seeing what he thought, at a quick glance into the darkened room, was Darien asleep, he closed the door and turned back to his wife. "Guess he *was* tired. No sense waking him up."

Stanley followed his wife to the kitchen and then turned upon hearing a car door slam. A moment later, the side door opened and Billie lumbered through, dripping wet with sweat.

"What the hell have you been doing to work up such a sweat?" Stanley asked.

"We had a great game of scrimmage at the college." Billie lifted the towel from around his neck and wiped his face as he headed to the room he now shared with Darien whenever he was home from school, which was infrequent.

As Billie laid his hand on the door knob, his father said, "Darien's sleeping in there, so we thought we'd—"

But not quickly enough. Billie pushed the door open wide, letting light from the dining room partially illuminate the room, which was enough that Billie saw what his father had not been able to. He did a double-take, stepping back from the room with a confused look on his face. "What the heck?" He reentered the room, walked over to the bed, and pulled the spread away, revealing the rolled-up blanket and pillow.

Curious now, Stanley followed his son into the room and squinted at the bed. His look of curiosity turned to concern and he called out to Virginia. "Hon, do you know what this is about? You spoke to him this afternoon. Did he say anything to explain this?" Not waiting for an answer, he laid one hand on Billie's shoulder and asked in a raised voice, "You have any idea what this is about or where he might be?"

By now, Virginia had squeezed into the room, a look of fear on her face as she saw the empty bed. "Oh my God! Why in heaven's name would he lie to me and then go to this extreme to make us think he was here sleeping? Billie, do you have any idea where he could've gone? Any at all?"

"No, Mom. Not that I can think of. You know I don't see that much of him since I started living at the college. And when I do see him, he doesn't say much." But Billie wasn't entirely truthful. He *did* have some idea about where he might be, where he might've gone, but he didn't want to worry his parents unnecessarily.

"I'm going to check his closet." Virginia hurried over and opened the door and pulled on the chain that lit the bulb hanging from the ceiling inside. "Looks like everything's here except for whatever was on those two hangers. Probably what he wore when he left. She moved over to the large dresser and went straight to Darien's private bottom drawer and pulled it open. Immediately, she noticed the carefully arranged and labeled possesions. Ones she knew were important to Darien.

"Oh, dear God, Stanley!" She brought both hands to her face, a panicked look on it.

"What!?" her husband yelled, now showing concern, though he didn't yet know why. He peered over her shoulder at the open bureau drawer and saw the articles and was able to read the name **Billie** on a small piece of paper. He moved his wife aside and grabbed at the leather box underneath and opened it. Seeing the coins, he gave his wife a puzzled look. She was clearly fighting to hold back tears.

Billie let out a gasp.

"What do you know about this, Billie? I can tell you know something! What is it?" Virginia asked in a pleading voice.

"I … I'm not sure, but I think I know where he might be. He had a couple of places in the woods where he used to go. He took me to them once to point out some wildflowers he'd found at one of them."

"But why would he go into the woods and stay there after dark?" Virginia leaned back over the open dresser drawer and scanned the other groupings and the slips of paper attached to each, shaking her head as she became more distressed at the implications of this. She'd had enough exposure to psychiatric patients and doctors during her nurses' training to know about certain signs of extreme depression and distress and the actions that often followed. She knew they needed to take action, but what? "Let me call Conrad and Phyllis French! Their son Sandy is Darien's closest friend. Maybe he knows what's going on or where he might be." She hurried to the phone, but Billie extended an arm and signaled her to stop.

"I really think I know where he might be, and I don't think we should be wasting time making phone calls. Come on! Let's jump in my car before it gets any darker!" he urged as he reached into his pocket for his car keys and headed to the door. Virginia and Stanley both quickly followed him outside, not even bothering to lock the door.

Within minutes on the familiar dirt road, Billie pulled to a stop and shut off the ignition.

"Why are you stopping here?" Virginia asked, visibly shaken and frightened.

"I told you! This is one of the places where he used to go and spend time. He took me here once, and I remember it's here because of that rusty piece of iron gate. Right there! See it?" He pointed at a partially bent iron structure at the side of the road. "The spot is not too far from here, straight out into that wooded area over there." He directed their attention to an area dense with trees and underbrush.

"Do you have a flashlight in your car?" Stanley asked his son.

"Yeah, in the trunk, I think." Billie jumped out of the car and ran to the trunk and opened it, fishing around the sports gear and several cardboard boxes until he found it. He turned it on. The beam was dim but still gave off enough light to see five or six feet ahead. Not waiting for his parents, he headed off into the woods, now running as fast as he could through the underbrush to the spot where he hoped he'd find Darien.

What he'd never told their parents was what Darien had once said to him, almost as a threat, after he had teased Darien to a point where he had begun screaming and crying. He could hear his words now as he raced deeper into the woods, feeling panic in his chest as the threat echoed in his mind: *"You'll be sorry!! Someday you'll be sorry about what you made me do! All of you will! And then it'll be too late cuz I'll be dead, and it'll all be your fault!"* At the time, Billie had dismissed it as an idle threat, simply another temper tantrum put on to make him feel sorry for Darien. Now Billie was really worried. He should have said something to his parents when it happened, maybe not mentioning what had percipitated the threat, but at least telling his mother what Darien had said. She might have insisted that Darien be seen by a psychiatrist, although she'd have had to do that without letting their father know about it. He was dead set against those kinds of doctors. They were for people who were "weak-minded and looking for sympathy," as he liked to say.

Billie heard his parents yelling behind him, but he ignored them and kept up his pace, now scanning the area of the woods in front of him, looking for signs of Darien. He stopped for a second and tried to recall what he'd seen when Darien had taken him to the place Darien liked so much. Strange. He felt almost as if he was being nudged to change direction. He shifted the beam of the flashlight to his left and moved the beam in an arc.

Off in the distance, he caught sight of something, but he couldn't make out what it was. He focused the beam of light on the spot that had gotten his attention. It was something hanging low to the ground. Off a tree branch.

"Oh, God Almighty! Oh, Jesus, no! Darien!!!" he screamed as he sprinted toward the object. He covered the distance in under five seconds, and dropping the flashlight to the ground, he wrapped his arms around Darie's waist and hoisted him up, screaming over his shoulder, "Pop, help! Quick! I need some help here!" And then he added, almost to himself, "Oh, Darien, why did you do this? Oh, God, don't let him die!" Now Billie was sobbing, trying to stifle his fear and not let his father see him cry.

A minute later, he felt his father behind him, reaching toward the noose and pulling it loose. "Hold 'em up, Billie! I'm going to slip the noose over his head."

When Billie was sure the noose was off, he lowered Darien's body to the ground. He picked up the flashlight and turned the beam onto Darien's face. Even in the dim light, he could see the blue pallor of his skin and his eyes were closed. Billie realized he didn't know what to do. He tried shaking him gently, then harder. No apparent response. Billie looked up as he felt someone pulling on his arm. It was his mother.

"Billie, let me get to him!"

He backed away as she moved in next to Darien and opened one of his eyes with two fingers and examined the pupil. She could see a slight change as the pupil dialated. She moved her fingers to his neck and felt for a pulse. "He's got a pulse!" she shouted. "We have to get him to the doctor! Stanley, can you and Billie lift him up and carry him back to the car? He needs to see a doctor. As soon as possible!"

"Who are we going to reach at this time of day? It's after 7:30!" Stanley said as he and Billie carried Darien back to the car.

"We can take him to the state hospital! They've got at least one doctor on call at all times," Virginia said as she hurried along just behind them, trying to catch up.

Within a few minutes, they reached Billie's car. Virginia opened one of the rear doors and stepped aside so Billie and his father could slide Darien onto the backseat. While they maneuvered him into place, Virginia ran to the other rear door and slid in, placing Darien's head in her lap as her husband and son closed both rear doors and jumped into the front seats. Billie started the car and shifted into first gear, made a U-turn, and shifted into second and then third gear as he gunned the engine and headed back onto their street and down the hill toward the hospital.

In the backseat, Virginia undid the top two buttons of Darien's shirt and ran the fingers of one hand across his chest as she had when he was sick as a child. He loved being touched, although that rarely happened, except when he was sick. With her other hand, she pressed her fingertips against his neck and checked for his pulse. It was there but faint. She bent her head and uttered a prayer that was barely audible, and as she did, the hair on her arms stood up and she looked up quickly and glanced around.

Stanley was leaning over the front passenger seat, observing his wife as she held Darien, and saw the startled look on her face. "What?" he asked. "Did he stop breathing? Why are you looking that way?"

"No, he still has a pulse and he's breathing. But I just felt a … I know this sounds silly, but I felt a presence. Like someone or something was here in the car with us." She shook her head, still confused by the feeling. And then she heard Darien take a breath. A short little sound, like he had inhaled or caught his breath. She raised his head with her arm that was cradling him and he stirred.

"He's responding, Stanley! He's responding! Oh, blessed Jesus, thank you, oh, thank you! Can you hear me, Darien? Can you hear me, dear?" She thought she saw a slight flicker of his eyes but still no response. Or did he just try to move his lips? She wasn't sure, but she was hopeful.

"He's gonna be okay, Mom? Really?" It was Billie. "We're almost at the hospital, Mom. Should I still take him to the front entrance?"

"Yes, Billie. A doctor needs to check him over thoroughly to make sure he's not suffered any kind of brain damage." Her words conveyed a mixture of excitement and concern. They wouldn't know for certain until the doctor had run some tests. At this point, all she could do was pray.

Chapter Fifty

7:45 the Same Evening: Sitting on the Edge

Darien wasn't at all sure just what he'd feel after he was dead. He wasn't even sure if he *was* dead. He was still seeing images around him, though he couldn't make out what they were. He had no frame of reference, and perhaps that was why. It was all new to him. But he did have a sense of direction, like he was floating upward in some kind of channel that contained a transparent substance. *An energy source* was the term that came to mind. And what was *that?* he found himself wondering. They weren't even words he would've put together so easily. And what was this? He had thoughts! But he was dead, wasn't he? Now he was even more confused. He was somewhere he couldn't really define and felt like he was being moved along … to where? And for what purpose? He had always thought being dead was the end of it. *Ashes to ashes and dust to dust. So why am I seeing things?* he thought.

What was that pinpoint of blinding light way, way in the distance? Was he moving toward it? Yes, but as he felt himself being drawn or pushed nearer to it—he wasn't sure which—he sensed some kind of resistant barrier. It, whatever it was, was slowing his ascent and, now, even reversing it. If he'd had a body, he would've held his stomach, for he was feeling dizzy and nauseated. But he didn't have one, a body, that is.

Suddenly, Darien felt himself being squeezed through some kind of amorphous material he couldn't see but could feel. In an instant, he felt himself hurtling back into a familiar atmosphere. He was breathing and able to make out forms around him. The constriction he had felt for just an instant was no more. He felt himself, his actual body, being lifted and then carried through what vaguely looked like woods. Familiar woods. He sensed some aspect of himself separate from the body he'd just experienced, and now he was viewing his own body and his mother, brother, and father.

His mother was praying, and at that point, he felt a powerful vibration as he once more became connected to his body. And hovering above him, just above the branch he had used to hang himself, a vaguely familiar image appeared. It was Sundeep. A moment later, he was gone, and everything went dark again.

★★★★

"Can you hear me, Darien? Open your eyes, dear. You're okay. We're here, all three of us. Let us know you hear me. Please!"

He heard his mother's words, spoken haltingly, her voice filled with uncertainty and fear. Darien opened his eyes, grateful the light in the room was dim, allowing him to adjust to the realization that he was not dead. He was alive, and for some reason, he felt relieved. Maybe another chance to find what he was searching for? And what was that? He really didn't know. He just had a … a feeling, a feeling there was more for him to discover. He didn't know what or how, but he somehow knew this was true. He was glad he had been unsuccessful in his attempt to take his own life.

Did it mean he was a failure? That he was a coward that just didn't have the guts to carry it out? That was what one voice in his head was saying, but another one said, *"No! You are just sad things didn't work out like you wanted with Beverly. And you were angry with yourself for allowing her to fool you into thinking she felt the same about you as you did for her."* But at some level, Darien knew that was a smokescreen, that his trying to kill himself was about something far deeper and more painful to even think about. That thought caused him to look to where Billie was standing. Seeing his older brother studying his face and wearing a look of concern, he wanted to cry. Darien fought back the tears and finally nodded in response to his mother's question as he slowly raised one hand and brought it to his face, wiping away a tear with the back of his hand, all the while hoping his father hadn't noticed.

"Can you talk, dear? If it hurts too much, don't try," she said. She gently rubbed his other arm that rested alongside him on top of the bedcovers. She leaned in closer to his ear. "Can you, Darien?" she asked softly.

He tried to speak but couldn't form the words. All that came out were several unintelligable sounds. Even to his own ear it was clear that what came out wasn't what he'd tried to say, and seeing the change of her expression—the raising of her eyebrows, which lifted her upper eyelids, revealing more of the whites of her eyes than normal—he knew his utterance had made no sense to her either. Afraid now, he tried again. What came out was more of the same. The kind of sounds one might make if they had no tongue. And at that thought, he lifted his hand to his mouth as he opened it at the same time and laid two fingers into the opening. It was there! He could feel it. Relieved, he let his hand drop back onto the bed and closed his eyes. He would sleep, he reasoned, and when he awoke, everything would be fine. And if he didn't? The last line in a familiar prayer floated across his mind as he drifted into sleep: "And if I die before I wake, I ask the Lord my soul to take."

Chapter Fifty-One

Two Days Later:
Let's Put This Behind Us

Darien felt better now as he rested by himself in one of the Adirondak chairs in the backyard as an unseasonably cool morning breeze rustled the leaves of the ash trees that swayed at the edge of the lawn. The scent of peonies drifted by him and he inhaled, reveling in the aroma. He studied the stretch of lawn in front of him, noticing the growth that had taken place over the past week, realizing it hadn't been mowed in over nine days. That was *his* job, and he silently scolded himself for not having done it. The fact that he'd tried to hang himself and had almost succeeded was no excuse. "Self-absorbed and too much focused on that damned girl," he could imagine his father saying. He took in the four-inch high grass and shook his head.

He still wasn't ready to resume his summer job at the local dairy bar and restaurant at the northern edge of town. His parents had called the manager and made up a plausible excuse for why he wasn't able to work that week. Maybe next week. Since he was still going to be around for a while longer, he would need the money if he was going to have any fun at all over the rest of the summer. If he were to be asked what that fun would look like, he'd have been hard-pressed to say since all he could think of were the planned dates he'd hoped he would have had with Beverly.

And now that was out of the question, out of the picture. Maybe he could drive to the lake or take in an afternoon picture show in one of the nearby towns large enough to have a movie theater. And there was always the free Monday night movie at the state institution where his mother worked. He could sit in the balcony, where invited "outsiders"—the family of employees, usually—could sit and watch a five- or ten-year-old black-and-white film shown to the patients and wards of the state who lived there. Occasionally, they would even show a film in glorius Technicolor. Those were rare and almost always starred Esther Williams or Roy Rogers. But it was a cheap night out. Sometimes he would invite Sandy or another friend to come along and he'd manage to sneak them in by distracting the attention of the person monitoring the side door he used to gain entrance.

His thoughts returned to his failed attempt at suicide and, with it, a squeamish feeling in the pit of his stomach—fear that it would get out and he'd have to deal with those looks from people. "Poor Darien. Didja hear? He tried to off himself! Yeah, his ol' man 'n ol' lady found him swinging from a tree in the woods! I always thought he was a little weird."

Of course none of that was at all likely. Stanley and Virginia had decided it would be best to keep what happened a secret and had gotten Billie to make an oath on the family Bible that he wouldn't utter a word about it to anyone. Not even to other members of the family. No one was to know.

But Darien knew. And now this was just one more secret he had to keep. He raised his hand to his neck and ran his fingers along the bruising the rope had caused. It was pretty apparent to anyone who saw him that *something* had happened to him. How would he explain it? The idea of claiming it was a hicky came to him and he laughed to himself. Yeah, right! With who? Not with Beverly, that was for sure! He could wear a lightweight jersey turtleneck, but it was summer, and that would just prompt more questions. He thought for a few minutes about how such bruises might be caused, and after several ideas surfaced but failed to hold up after further thought, he came up with one that passed the reasonability test. He had been tree climbing in the woods, or maybe in the monstrous old spruce tree that towered over his uncle and aunt's home across the road, and had lost his balance, fallen, and become wedged at the point of a large branch and the trunk of the tree. In the process of falling, he had scraped his neck on the rough bark of the tree, and the circular bruising resulted from the impact and rubbing of his neck against the trunk and the branch. Why, he was lucky he hadn't broken his neck! Yes, that explanation would hold water, he thought.

Then an afterthought occurred. His mother had told the restaurant manager that he had come down with an intestinal grip, so how would he explain his having been well enough to be out climbing but not back at work? "Well, I actually was tree climbing earlier in the week, and it was from the fall that I think I must've also hit my stomach. My mom called it a stomach grip because the symptoms were sort of the same: my stomach and intestines hurt; I probably bruised them as well." Having fabricated this answer aloud, it sounded reasonable to his ear, enough for him to decide to use it, if necessary. He was beginning to feel a little better already.

Chapter Fifty-Two

One Day Later: A Bad News Day

Darien straightened up and surveyed his handiwork as he brushed the rich, dark soil from his hands. He'd been asked by his father to develop some plant beds around several of the larger maple trees in the backyard, and he'd spent most of the morning working at it.

Having marked out an eighteen-inch radius around each tree trunk and dug away the grass, he proceeded to fill in each circle with shovels full of fresh soil he'd retrieved from an area of his uncle's property that bordered their backyard. He had been careful to cover the area on his uncle's property with dried leaves so no one would notice.

Next, he lined the mounds of soil with eight- to ten-inch pieces of shale rock that had been gathered from their own property several years ago when the once-wooded lot was converted into lawn. He had carefully pressed the flat sides of the rock against the soil, forming a circular barrier between the lawn and the plant bed. Then he had transplanted into the beds a variety of irises from a cluster that were beginning to crowd out other perennials in a bed near the house. He'd done the same thing with some phlox that he had dug out from two other plant beds on the upper level of their property, effectively thinning out the older beds and making room for new growth the following season.

Darien was satisfied with his efforts and was pretty sure his parents would approve. He was just picking up the gardening tools and cleaning them off when he looked up to see Billie arrive in his '49 Chevy. He stopped, puzzled, as he watched him get out of the car and lope slowly down the driveway to the lower level.

"What brings you here in the middle of the day, Billie?"

Billie seemed hesitant to answer. He had a look of concern on his face that Darien had seen before, when he'd had to break the news to Darien that their grandmother had died.

When another few seconds had passed and still Billie hadn't said anything, Darien pressed him with another question. "What? Tell me, Billie. What's happened that should bring you home to see me in the middle of the day?"

Billie stepped closer until he was within reaching distance and placed his hands on Darien's shoulders as he bent down so they were nearly eye to eye. "It's about Beverly, Darien."

"What? Has she got herself knocked up again?" Darien let out a sound of disgust. "Is that what you've come to tell me? Like I should care?"

"I think you should sit down, Darien, cuz it's nothing like that."

Darien's heart began to race. "What? Just tell me, for chrissakes!"

"She's dead, Darien. I just heard about it from Aunt Eileen. She heard about it from one of the volunteer firemen she knows."

"What?" Darien felt dizzy now.

"She ran off the road near Middle Pond and went over an embankment down into the ravine near McHenry Road."

"She's ... she's dead? Honestly? You're not just playing a sick joke on me, are ya?"

"I'm serious. She's dead. She drove off the road, and the car evidently rolled over several times before it landed at the bottom of the ravine, upside down."

Darien slumped to the ground and stared blankly into the distance, his mind reeling with all kinds of thoughts that blurred together. Tears ran down his face, and he brushed them off with one hand, surprised by the tears, since all he felt was numb.

It was several minutes before Darien broke the silence. "Do they know if she suffered at all?"

"From what Aunt Eileen told me, she broke her neck and probably died instantly. Least that's what the fireman told her."

"Fireman?" That fact just registered in Darien's mind. "Why would firemen have been there? Isn't it the constables and maybe an emergency ambulance that handle an accident?"

"The car burst into flames when it hit the bottom of the embankment, according to someone who was driving behind her. He stopped to try to help when he saw her go over, and that's when he saw the explosion and the fire. He drove to someone's house just a ways down the road, and they called the fire department."

"When did this happen? Today?"

"Early this morning."

"Was she by herself?"

"Yeah, she was."

Darien shook his head. For just an instant, he had hoped that *other* guy had been with her. It would have seemed like justice, but Darien knew that wasn't right ... to wish anyone dead just because they had stepped in and taken his girl away from him. Now he wondered, had she *ever* been *his* girlfriend or had he just fooled himself into believing they had once been an item?

He looked up at Billie and then touched him on the arm. "Thanks, Billie. I appreciate your coming down to tell me. I really do." He turned and then added, "I think I'll go inside and take a little nap. All this yardwork has tired me out." He slowly walked back toward the house without looking back, his mind unable to think about anything but Beverly. *Dead* Beverly.

Chapter Fifty-Three

Four Days Later: A Mourning Revelation

Darien stood at the edge of the gathering of mourners who had assembled in front of Saint Francis church, waiting for a signal from one of the funeral directors to open the large carved white doors and step aside for them to enter.

The mid-morning sun shined down on the church steeple, reflecting off the gilt trimmings of the giant cross that topped it, serving as a reminder to all how prosperous the Catholic community in Hammerville was.

He caught sight of a hand waving at him from a distance, a fellow classmate he hadn't seen since the end of the school year earlier that summer. Darien tensed, not wanting to talk with anyone if he could avoid it, but his classmate, Ernie, was already heading toward him, an urgency in his gait.

"Hi, Big Dee. How you doin'?" He reached out and touched Darien on the arm and continued to speak. "Really sad, the way she ended her life, don't you think?"

Darien let the words sink in. He felt his knees weaken and straightened up, forcing his weight to align over his legs to keep them from buckling beneath him. *The way she ended her life?* Was Ernie saying what he thought he was? That Beverly's accident was no accident? But why would she have? Or was Ernie simply telling Darien, indirectly, that he'd heard about *his* attempt to take his own life?

Sensing Darien's confusion, Ernie said, "Oh, you didn't hear! It wasn't an accident. She drove off the road on purpose. She committed suicide!"

Darien's jaw dropped open as he stood there in shock. *How could they know that?* "How could they know that?" he asked, repeating his thought aloud to Ernie.

"I heard from her cousin that she left a note ... in her bedroom, he said. Her parents found it the next day when they went into her room. Awful, huh? I mean, I know you two had broken up, but still, it must feel weird, knowing she did this so soon afterward. Know what I mean?"

Darien ignored Ernie's last remark, more focused on the revelation that Beverly had left a note. "Did they say what was in the note?" he asked, knowing it was most unlikely that her parents or anyone else in the immediate family would ever let *that* kind of personal information slip out and become common knowledge.

"No, but I wouldn't be a bit surprised if it had something to do with that run-in you had with her just before school ended this year. I wasn't there to see what happened, but I was told what you said to her was pretty brutal. I mean, I'm not blamin' you or anything like that. I'd probably have said the same thing if I was in your shoes."

Darien felt a chill run through his body. The thought he might be indirectly responsible for her death felt like ... like *awful! Why would she have deliberately killed herself if it wasn't all the truth? No, she did it because she felt guilty! That's why.*

But what if she wasn't? What if every bit of what he'd heard, about her and Jimmy French and her and Steve Olsen, was just gossip and none of it was true? He shook his head.

"What, Big Dee?" Ernie asked.

"Nuthin', Ernie. I was just thinking about something else." Darien looked around. He needed to get away from this conversation. He heard the church bells ring and saw the crowd now entering the church. "I think I'm going to go on in and get a seat. I'll catch you later." He set off in a hurried trot, up the concrete steps, and into the narthex of the building, leaving Ernie with a puzzled look on his face.

Once inside, Darien noticed there were stairs at both sides of the narthex and signs above them that read "Gallery Seating." He hurried to the one to his left, stopping only long enough to accept a memorial card from an usher before rushing up the stairs. He arrived at the balcony level and saw there were few people up there. He began to relax as he took a front-row seat, farthest away from the three others sitting at the other end of the same row. He glanced in their direction. He didn't know them, and that meant they didn't know him. He settled against the back of the pew and looked down at his feet, feeling something in the way. He'd never been in a Catholic church before, so he was unfamiliar with the knee rests that could be folded out of the way when not in use. But not knowing that, he frowned and spread his feet apart, leaving the wooden foot rest in between them.

He studied the memorial card. Her full name, Beverly Maria Simpson, and the date of her birth and of her death appeared beneath a striking picture of her. It had obviously been taken by a professional photographer, most likely in one of the many *Olson Portrait Studios* that could be found in every city and town in New England, even in a town as small as

Hammerville. In Hammerville, however, it operated out of the private home of one of the town's local residents, Emily Jackson, a young mother with three children of her own. She'd began taking pictures of children and families for Christmas photo cards and had been fortunate enough to land a contract with the schools in town to take all the class pictures each year. And now she was also producing funeral memorial cards.

The photograph of Beverly looked so angelic, so beautiful, and in sharp contrast to how he supposed she looked when they finally extricated her from the fiery crash. Darien felt his eyes water, and he quickly brushed them with the back of his hand. Underneath the dates that marked her too-short life was a brief statement, printed in calligraphy style: **"She had a beautiful heart that stopped beating much too soon."** He sighed and turned the card over. On the reverse side was the traditional "Psalm of David." He slowly read through it until he reached the line that read: "Thou preparest a table before me in the presence of mine enemies …" He choked, unable to even silently speak the words. *Had he been the enemy that brought her to take her own life?*

Darien peered over the low balcony railing down at the gathering of family and mourners below and the closed casket that was nearly hidden by the blanket of white chrysanthemums and clusters of deep red roses. He scanned the number of pews on either side of the aisle and did a visual count of the heads in each pew, mentally calculating the number in attendance. Seventy-three, if his count was correct. He was impressed and wondered if even half that number would've been at *his* funeral had he been successful at his attempt to commit suicide. He shook his head and closed his eyes. His stomach felt queasy, and he straightened up, hoping that would take the pressure off his abdomen and ease the discomfort. As he did so, he heard the heavy footsteps of someone making their way up to the balcony. He turned slightly and caught sight of a tall young man coming into view. He felt himself get lightheaded as he recognized the person as the one pointed out to him during the final week of school before the summer break when he'd asked another friend what Steve Olsen looked like.

He looked away but not soon enough. Their eyes met for a fleeting second, long enough for Darien to realize that Steve Olsen also recognized him. He walked slowly but directly toward Darien and sat down next to him.

Darien had never had more than a brief look at the young man when he was pointed out to him the first time. Now, as he had an opportunity to watch him approach and take a seat beside him, Darien realized that he was definitely built for football, with wide shoulders and muscular arms that filled out the short-sleeved dress shirt he was wearing. He was taller than Darien as well. But Darien also thought he looked kindly—a strange word for Darien, but that was what came to mind. *He looks like a gentle person,* he thought. Not what he'd conjured up in his mind when he first heard about the passing of a note between him and Beverly. He felt himself choke up. Again their eyes locked.

"I think you probably know who I am," the young man said in a deep voice. "Steve. But I'm afraid I'm not so good with names. You're … Daniel? Or is it Darrell?"

"Close, but no cigar." Darien was surprised at his own level of comfort with this relative stranger, someone who had stolen his girl. He pushed that thought away and added, "Darien. It's Darien." And for some reason, he extended his hand, which was met with a warm handshake in exchange.

"Beverly was the one who pointed you out to me shortly after I moved here this past spring."

"How long have you … I mean, how long *had* you known Beverly, Steve?"

"Oh, not very long at all. And I didn't really *know* her all that well, although she told me *you* thought something was going on between her and me." Steve's face bore a look Darien couldn't quite interpret, perhaps sad judgment coupled with disdain.

Darien was surprised by Steve's directness and decided to be just as direct. "And why wouldn't I think that? People saw you passing a note to her. You think it wouldn't get back to me?" he asked in a hushed voice. Darien felt the chords in his neck stiffen, but he was determined to remain in control of himself.

"You should've asked her what the note was about instead of assuming the worst of her" was the young man's response. He wasn't smiling any longer.

Darien was uncomfortable now and felt perspiration form on his upper lip and the back of his neck. But he wasn't going to back down. "So I'm supposed to believe it was all innocent, that nothing was going on between you and ber?"

"Yes, Darien, that's what I'm telling you," Steve responded, now with an edge to his voice. "Her older brother and I both served as youth counselors last year at a camp in North Adams, and I was simply passing her a note to give to her brother Jason because I was thinking of applying for another summer job and had lost the contact information I needed."

Darien slumped against the pew as his whole body seemed to lose muscle control. His arms fell to his sides, the fingers of his hand opening, and the memorial card dropped to the floor. Stunned by the revelation, he was at a loss for words.

Steve stood and started to turn in the direction of the far end of the pew, but turned back and bent down so he was eye to eye with Darien. He studied Darien's face for a moment and then said, in a deliberate manner, "Maybe if you'd asked, she might still be here." Then he turned and walked away, leaving Darien weeping.

Chapter Fifty-Four

Later the Same Day

Darien felt his mother's gaze as he picked at his supper, head down and eyes averted. He didn't want to talk about the funeral or about what Ernie had told him outside the church earlier that day. He didn't want to talk about his exchange with Steve Olsen either, and he sure as shit didn't want to tell her how he was feeling. He pushed the now cold and limp broccoli spears around his plate, avoiding having to eat the remains of one of his least favorite vegetables, particularly the way his mother made them—cooked until they turned a gray-green and the florets near mush. He moved his fork over to the small pile of equally cold mashed potatoes and lifted a bit of them, closing his mouth over the fork and scraping the food off its prongs with his teeth. He was stalling and he knew she knew it as well. He kept his head lowered over his food but raised his line of vision until there was eye contact. He swallowed what was in his mouth and chewed on his lower lip, unconsciously shaking his head, ever so slightly, from side to side.

Virginia continued to study his face for a few seconds longer and then broke the silence. "Darien, I know all this is very troubling for you … the funeral, the accident …"

Darien gave her his version of the Edwards Eye, causing her to pause in mid-sentence. *Accident? Let's call it what it was! Suicide! She took her own life! Had bigger balls than I did. Or was smarter cuz she was successful at it,* he thought.

"I know you were very smitten with her, and you probably feel even worse because of your falling out with her before school let out for the summer. You never had a chance to patch things up with her." She reached over the table, laid her hand on his arm, and gently caressed it. He didn't move his arm away.

"I wish you'd talk to me about what really happened between you two and what's going on for you ... inside." Her hand moved down his arm and closed around his.

Darien felt the warmth of her hand and sensed it move up through his arm and then throughout his whole body. He felt his own heart open up, and all at once, his tightly held feelings released along with a flow of tears he could not stop.

Virginia slid her chair closer to him, pulled him to her chest, and wrapped her arms around him as his body convulsed in grief and he sobbed uncontrollably for several minutes.

Emotionally spent, Darien looked up at her. Even through the blur of his own tears, he saw her love and somehow knew he'd be okay. He'd get through this and would move on with his life. He had no idea what that life would look like now, but he knew he would be able to put all this into the past and get on with it. "One day at a time," as his mother sometimes said.

Darien kissed her on the cheek, cleared his throat, and reached for a paper napkin from the dispenser on the table. He blew his nose and balled up the napkin, leaned toward the wastebasket across the room, and made a perfect shot. He smiled, and so did Virginia.

"Thanks, Mom, for letting me get that out. I feel much better already. And maybe sometime I'll feel like talking about what happened with Beverly and me. But for now, can we just let it go? Okay?"

"That's fine, dear. I wasn't trying to pry. Just wanted to help if I could."

"You did, Mom. You really did." He gave her another peck on the cheek before excusing himself from the table and walking out of the room. Tomorrow would be another day.

Chapter Fifty-Five

Early December 1955

Darien nodded to the owner, Jeffrey Shields, offering him a half-hearted smile without stopping as he hurried through the restaurant's front doors, taking off his heavy winter jacket and scarf as he did so. Darien glanced up at the clock on the wall of the large and airy restaurant: one minute to clock in. He headed toward the swinging doors that led to the kitchen and back rooms where the waiters, waitresses and busboys kept their work uniforms—kahki-colored jackets for the teenage boys and similarly colored above-the-knee aprons for the female staff.

"Just under the wire, Big Dee! What happened? Your Blue Blaze stall out on ya?" It was the owner's youngest son, Buck, who spoke, referring to Darien's robin's-egg blue 1941 Plymouth. Buck was a year older than Darien but had been held back when he was in fifth grade after contracting a serious liver condition that left him bedridden for nearly four months. Darien liked him because he was a good-natured class clown and had always been friendly to him.

Darien gave him an index finger and a smile as he shook his head and continued through the kitchen into the back room. Once inside, he stopped at a small table-top file cabinet, opened the top drawer, and thumbed through the alphbetized files until he spotted his name. He pulled out his time card and made an entry as to the date and time he was beginning his work shift. Today was from four o'clock in the afternoon until nine in the evening, a five-hour shift he worked on Tuesdays and Thursdays. He also worked every other Saturday from eleven in the morning until seven at night. He actually enjoyed the full-day Saturday shift since he only had to work it every other week. This left him with the rest of the evening to have a date or make plans with friends if someone was having a party, not that there were that many parties going on in a high school that had less than one hundred and fifty students, all four grades combined.

He slipped his coat and scarf over a wooden hanger and hung it on one the wooden coat hooks lined up on the off-white wall next to the table. He steppped a few feet farther into the room where several kahki-colored jackets and aprons hung along the same wall. He checked the label in several of them until he found his and then slipped it over the light-blue shirt he was wearing, a mandatory part of the uniform at the restaurant. "It makes the waitstaff all look like college-prep students, and people like that look when they're being waited on" was what the owner had said the first day he started the part-time job two months earlier. Darien headed back to the kitchen and stopped for a moment as he glanced in a mirror to one side of the door. Satisfied by what he saw, he pushed open the swinging door and looked over at the owner who was now standing next to his son.

"What station am I working tonight, Mr. Shields?" he inquired.

Jeffrey Shields pulled a small notepad from his back pocket and flipped through a few pages, hesitating at each one as he studied the station entries he'd made on each. "It's a little slow right now, but I expect it'll pick up in another half hour or so. Why don't you take the counter area, Darien? You haven't worked that since last week. Buck here is taking care of the front tables, and Cynthia will cover the booths in the rear when she gets here at five."

Darien tried to hide his disappointment—no, irritation. The customers who sat at the counter were generally lousy tippers. Even more irritating to Darien was the fact that at the earlier hours of suppertime, it was mothers with their young children who came to the counter, ordered takeout, and then sat there, taking up space, while they waited for the meal to be prepared and boxed up in the kitchen. Darien had to take the order, deliver it to the kitchen, and then come back to cover the counter in case new customers came in and sat in his station. Then when he heard the bell ring, he would hustle back into the kitchen to see if the order was ready or not.

Plus, he had to contend with whiny three-year-olds who would sometimes crawl up onto the counter or grab at the napkin holders and salt and pepper shakers. And if their mother had given them a candy bar (to pacify them and stop their crying when halfheartedly scolded for acting unruly), they would smear their sticky fingers all over the surface of the counter and Darien would have to clean up after they left. And they rarely left any tip because it was takeout. Like he wasn't waiting on them? Good grief!

"Okay," he said, managing a strained smile. *"Be grateful you even have a job!"* he heard his father say in his head. Darien strode back into the main area of the restaurant, buttoning his jacket as he did so. Once on the floor, he turned his attention to the counter and gave it a sweeping glance. Two teenaged girls had slipped in while he was in the kitchen. They sat there with their heads together, both looking at him as they smiled and whispered to each other. Darien picked up two menus on the counter and wasted no time getting over to where they sat. He recognized one of them as a sophmore, the red-haired one with the freckles. He knew her last name, Westwell, but he wasn't sure what her first name was. The brunette didn't look familiar, although he was surprised that he didn't know her. He was sure he wouldn't forget the name of anyone that attractive, so he assumed she was either new in town or visiting. He gave them a big smile, making every effort to form it like he thought James Dean would. He apparently failed, presenting them with more of a grimace than a smile, which prompted confused expressions on the faces of both young girls.

"Here are menus for you lovely ladies," he said, hoping to restore his chances as he handed one to each of them with a bit of flourish. "Or do you already know what you want?" he added, all part of a canned inquiry to customers.

They raised their menus and tittered behind them. Composed, they handed the menus back to Darien and smiled. "Hi, Darien. This is my cousin, Rachael. And I'm Sally. Sally Westwell, but I think you know that, right?" She didn't wait for an answer before she added, "I'll have a root beer float, and Rachael'll have a brown cow. That's a coke with chocolate ice cream." More titters from Rachael as she gave Darien the eye.

Darien felt his face redden and quickly replied, "I *know* what a brown cow is!" He jotted down the order on the pad of preprinted forms and ripped it off as he turned to make his way over to the fountain section where the soda dispensers and five-gallon containers of ice cream were located. "I'll be right back with your orders."

He made up both sodas, placed them on a small round serving tray, and positioned the tray on the fingertips of his other hand, mimicking the manner in which he'd seen waiters bring out meals at the Italian restaurant his parents used to, on very rare occasions, take him and Billie when they were younger. Raising the tray to eye level, he quickly headed back to the counter where the two girls were seated. "One root beer float for you, Sally, and a brown cow for you, Rachael."

More titters.

Darien hesitated and then made eye contact with Rachael and maintained it as he added, "Will that be all?"

"Yes," Sally replied, both girls breaking into more girlish laughter.

Darien felt his gonads shrivel. Somehow he didn't feel six feet tall anymore. He broke into a profuse sweat as he lowered his head and finished totaling the check amount. He timidly placed it on the counter in front of them and hurried back to the kitchen for no particular reason other than to escape from sight and the dreaded feeling of embarassment.

Why were they laughing? Was it about me or are they just silly girls? Whatever the reason, he was pretty sure it had something to do with him. Maybe the way he walked or how he'd brought the tray of sodas to their table? Or had the circumstances of Beverly's death and his rumored indirect involvement managed to spread to the lower-class students at the high school?

Buck was standing off to one side of the kitchen door, keeping an eye on a table of three elderly women who were about to settle their checks, when Darien reached out to push open the door. He glanced at Darien and put his hand out to stop him.

"What's up, Big Dee? You look upset. What'd you try to do? Make a date with the hot one with Sally and get turned down?"

Darien hesitated as he made an effort to push his thoughts to the back of his mind. Time to put on his face of confidence. After all, he was his senior class vice president, he reasoned. And that meant something! He sneered, Elvis Presley-style, and laughed. "She's jailbait, Buck. Wouldn't touch her with a ten-foot pole, know what I mean?"

Buck smiled and returned a knowing look. "Yeah, but I betcha she'd put out if you gave her half a chance."

Darien smiled. Really wide. That only happened when he felt connected. And he felt connected when he didn't feel like he had to measure up to anyone's expectations. Like now. Buck saw him as a regular guy, and that somehow translated in Darien's brain as "I'm one of the guys! I'm okay." Then he said, "I think I'll steer clear of getting involved with *anyone,* at least until I finish this final year of high school. And then I wanna get as far away from here as I can!"

"How's that? You got plans to move somewhere after you graduate?"

"Yeah, I do. It's a long shot, but I'm hoping to go to an art school and study to become a portrait painter or a magazine illustrator ... like that guy John Falter, who does *The Saturday Evening Post* covers." Darien hadn't shared that dream with many people. He hadn't even told his parents or his brother. He'd heard his mother say once, "If you have a dream, something you really want to have happen in your life, don't tell a soul. Just plant the idea in your mind, pray about it to God, and then turn it over to Him. Just like you do when you plant corn." But he felt okay about telling Buck because Buck wasn't likely to tell anyone else. In fact, it looked like he'd already let it go in one ear and out the other, judging by the way he had already begun to walk to the table the three older women had just vacated after having waved to Buck that he could keep the change as they exited the restaurant.

Darien turned to see the empty counter space where Sally and her cousin had been sitting. He walked over and scooped up the check and the money they'd left on top of it. He eyed it: three one-dollar bills and some change—two quarters, a dime, a nickel, and four pennies. The check amount was three dollars and forty-four cents. A lousy quarter for a tip! He couldn't wait for the evening to be over. Or the summer, for that matter.

Chapter Fifty-Six

Spring, the Following Year: Setting the Stage for the Future

"Mom! I've been accepted!" Darien rushed into the house and handed the letter to his mother. "Look!"

"What's this?" She put her needlework down and glanced up at him, a sparkle in her eyes, as she took the letter and adjusted her glasses.

"Read it! It's from the Museum School of Fine Arts, Mom! They've accepted my application for admission!" He pointed at the second paragraph. "See?"

"Darien, that's wonderful! I'm so proud of you!"

He watched her as she read it over a second time and then saw her expression change as she carefully placed the letter on the couch next to her.

"What, Mom?" He studied her look of concern and realized its source. "You don't think Pop's going to be so happy about this, right?"

"Well, honey—"

"Is it because of the money?"

"I don't think that's so much the issue, Darien."

"I can apply for a scholarship, Mom! I can work too!" He sat down on the couch next to her and picked up the letter, rereading the portion that said, "We are pleased to inform you our enrollment committee has reviewed your application and sample artwork and find your renderings show great promise. We have therefore accepted you for admission, beginning this September, 1956." Darien had never felt as proud of himself as he did right now.

"It's not just the money. Your father and I want you to attend the university and get a teaching degree, dear. Something you can rely on."

"But, Mom!" He knew he sounded whiny. It just wasn't fair! He sank back onto the sofa, dejected, and crumpled the letter in one hand as he stared off into space. *I hate that bastard sometimes!*

"I'll talk with your father, dear. Maybe he'll have a change of heart." She leaned over and kissed him lightly on the forehead and then resumed her needlepoint.

★★★★

As they sat at the kitchen table finishing dinner that evening, Darien tossed glances at his mother, trying to get her attention and have her bring up the letter. She winked at him and cleared her throat before looking directly at his father.

"Honey, Darien has gotten some wonderful news … from one of the schools where he applied for admission." She dabbed at her lips with her paper napkin and waited.

"Oh? Which one?" His father stopped eating and raised his eyebrows.

Darien remained silent.

"A school in Boston, dear."

"Boston University?"

"No, dear, not BU." There was a momentary pause. "Boston's Museum School of Fine Arts." She looked down and took a deep breath, her shoulders rising as she did.

Darien saw the expression on his father's face, and his heart sank.

"I'll be damned if we're going to spend money sending you through some goddamned art school! Christ!" He threw his napkin onto his plate and glared, first at Darien and then at his mother.

"Stanley—"

"That's the place where Marjorie Fields studied, and you know what she turned out to be. Nuthin' but a damned Bohemian! They're all queers, if you ask me!"

Virginia opened her mouth to interrupt him, but didn't have a chance. Darien merely sat there, speechless. The skin on his entire body was flushed and he felt slightly faint. There was that word again: *queer.* It both angered and hurt him, and he felt his self-confidence drain away.

"I don't want to hear any more about this art school, do you understand?" His father was looking directly at him now. "Young man, if you want to study art, you pay for it yourself— *after* you get a four-year degree that'll put some damned food on the table! You need to be able to earn a decent living. Be able to support yourself and a family. Well, you sure as hell can't do that painting pictures! I mean, you've got some talent, but you sure aren't Norman Rockwell!" He picked up his empty coffee cup, motioning to Virginia, who reached toward the stove without getting up and grabbed the percolator. She filled his cup and then topped off her own in silence.

Darien watched his father retreat into the living room with his coffee and newspaper. He had spoken.

Darien shook his head and grimaced as he pounded his knees with his fists in a slow cadence, fueled by a seething anger he couldn't express any other way.

"We just want you to have the education we never had, dear. Trying to make a living as an artist is very difficult, Darien."

"But I have talent, Mom. They said so! And so did Mr. Gable, my art teacher from grade school, remember?" He relaxed his hands and let them rest on his lap.

"Your ability isn't being questioned, Darien. We just want you to have a real profession, like being a teacher, to fall back on."

"This isn't about me. It's about him! He's ashamed of being a grease monkey, and because he is, I've gotta go to college and get a degree doing something I don't even want to do. It isn't fair, Mom!" He shot a nervous glance toward the front of the house, afraid his father might have heard him from the living room.

"Lower your voice!" she whispered. "Don't you *ever* refer to your father that way!"

"He calls himself that, Mom! I was just—"

"I don't care. You don't have a right to talk that way about the man who has worked so hard to make sure you and your brother have everything you need!" Virginia raised her head and inhaled deeply, folding her arms across her chest.

Darien sighed, knowing there was no use talking more about it. *Be grateful they're going to send you to college at all!* He'd heard that said before and guessed there was some truth to it, although he felt little satisfaction in it now. He wondered how he'd ever be able to become a teacher. He didn't have the faintest idea what he would teach. He would just have to wait and see.

Chapter Fifty-Seven

Fall 1956:
When the Rubber Hits the Road

By the time graduation rolled around, Darien had been accepted at the local state university. That seemed to satisfy his father. Darien had convinced his mother, and she his father, to let him live on campus. The school was only twenty miles away, an easy commute, but if he had to go there, he was at least going to get out from under their watchful eyes and live life the way he wanted.

Of course, Darien had no idea what room and board would cost his parents or what strain that would put on their finances. He didn't even give it a thought. Why would he? They had never shared any of the details as to how they lived as they did, how much income they had, how much it cost them to raise two boys. He only knew that both his mother and father worked hard at their jobs and that "money didn't grow on trees." The college Billie had graduated from the year before was a well-known school in the area, and Darien had heard often enough from their father that the education Billie received "hadn't come cheap."

But Darien assumed the two scholarships he had received would cover most of the basic costs for his attending a state university. And he knew for sure it would cost them less than it had to put Billie through the top-rated college he'd attended. Darien reasoned that going to the university was their idea so he'd just have to go along with it until he was old enough to live on his own. He also wasn't ready to find a job doing manual labor if getting a college degree meant he could make more money and live a better life.

Sometimes he looked forward to moving away, but at other times, he felt nervous and uncertain. *What will it be like? Will I fit in? How will I measure up?*

The two scholarships he'd been awarded gave him some confidence. They were not large ones, however, and he knew his parents would be paying extra for his room and board and he felt conflicted about even attending college. *Am I smart enough to make the grade?* He wasn't so sure.

When admissions weekend came, Darien drove the twenty miles to Lesterton in his robin's-egg blue 1941 Plymouth packed with his two suitcases, a desk lamp, and a shopping bag filled with pens, paper, and school supplies. His parents followed behind him in their Buick, and he was glad they wanted to be there with him until he completed registration and found Warner Hall and his dormitory room.

Except for Boy Scout camp and his senior class trip to New York City, he'd never been away from them. Now, as they prepared to leave, he felt an old, familiar feeling well up inside. *It's stupid to feel like crying! I'm no baby!*

Registration took nearly two hours as he went from one line to another, signing up for each of the five academic courses he'd be taking during his first semester. Then he had to register for the sports activity of his choice. He chose freshman cross-country track, not because he was great at running but because he knew he wasn't good at team sports. He preferred an activity that allowed him to participate without fear of getting pummeled by some jock who was way bigger than he was. And he enjoyed the solitude that came with running cross-country. He'd often run by himself up through the hilly orchards his grandfather owned. He only had to do his best and try to improve each time.

Darien's final line was to obtain his dormitory and room assignment and get his room key. Now he had it in his hand, and as he walked back outside and down to the parking lot where his parents were waiting, he realized this was it. He was on his own.

"You call us next weekend and let us know how you are, okay?" His mother reached out and hugged him quickly and stepped back.

"I will."

"And make sure you spend enough time studying, you hear me?" His father extended his hand, and Darien shook it firmly.

"Yes, Pop." He wished his father had hugged him, but that had stopped when he was barely eight. *"Men aren't supposed to hug other men!"*

And that was it. He watched them drive away. When their car disappeared in the distance, he turned and headed back to his dormitory.

Darien thought about this new chapter of his life that was about to begin. He was on his own with no rule keepers around and few limits. He'd said he wanted to set his own rules, but that had been when he was in the midst of order, his father's order. *No more Mom to soften things and make me feel better. No Sundeep.* That childhood memory seemed to want to surface again, but he pushed it away as he climbed the steps to Warner Hall, the place he'd be calling home for at least the next year.

Darien unlocked the door to his room and peered in before entering. No roommate yet. He closed the door and threw himself onto the single bed he'd chosen. He stared up at the white ceiling and began to count the tiles as old memories flashed above him. The long bus rides to Hammerville, the stout little lady who had cared for him for a while, and that final ride, all by himself. It had been a frightening journey, although in the scheme of things, it had been a pretty good thing. The Edwardses had taken him in as if he were their real son, although he wasn't. He couldn't and wouldn't ever be as smart or as good at sports as Billie, their pride and joy, as he'd heard his father say of Billie more than once or twice. *Had he ever said anything like that about me? Nope. Didn't measure up. Never would.*

Images of him and Billie's friend Frankie … those he'd been trying to forget. Also, the ones that made him feel ashamed and angry. The looks he saw on his father's face whenever he didn't measure up to his expectations.

But there were many happy and carefree memories that also sufaced as he lay there on the bed. His absolute delight and wonder when he discovered his own singing voice. The thrill and ecstasy of experiencing, for the first time, the brilliance and range of his voice as he sang along with Mario Lanza. The freedom he felt as his voice soared, effortlessly. The high he felt as he grew into his teens and was able to become a church soloist. Those had been joyful moments, scattered here and there amongst the more pervading feelings of not being good enough, of being damaged goods.

Also, those months when he was certain he'd found the love of his life, Beverly. The times they had spent together only to be led to believe she was involved with an upperclassman. His own spiral into a deep depression and attempt at suicide. And then her death and the subsequent revelation that she had *not* been involved with anyone else and that his verbal attack upon her may well have been the reason she took her own life.

Darien's thoughts went further back in time to when he was much, much younger. His special place in the woods. Sundeep. That memory again. *Where is Sundeep when I need him?* The thought surprised him, and he considered chanting the prayer, but he couldn't remember it and a familiar rebuke quickly replaced the thought: "Don't be childish!"

He turned on his side and curled his legs up, wrapping one arm over his face to hide from the late-afternoon light coming through the window. Darien did not want to deal with the feeling of dread that crept over him and sleep offered a temporary retreat from that and whatever else lay ahead. But it also prevented him from seeing the pulsating energy that was taking physical form at the foot of his bed.

Unable to see or even sense what was ever present in his life, Darien slipped into a fitful sleep, his last waking thought being *I think this day marks the end of life as I've known it and the beginning of one I don't even want to imagine.* But the truth was, he had already imagined and seen glimpses of it in past moments of self-doubt and fear, and now it was about to unfold.

Printed in the United States
By Bookmasters